Sea of Lentils

Antonio Benítez-Rojo

Sea of Lentils

TRANSLATED BY

James Maraniss

INTRODUCTION BY

Sydney Lea

THE UNIVERSITY OF
MASSACHUSETTS PRESS
AMHERST

Originally published as *El mar de las lentejas*
1985 Plaza y Janés

Translation and Introduction
to the English edition,
Copyright © 1990 by
The University of Massachusetts Press
All rights reserved
Printed in the United States of America
LC 90–31381
ISBN 0–87023–723–3
Designed by Edith Kearney
Set in Linotron New Baskerville by Keystone Typesetting, Inc.
Printed and bound by Thomson-Shore, Inc.

Library of Congress Cataloging-in-Publication Data

Benítez-Rojo, Antonio, 1931–
[Mar de las lentejas. English]
Sea of lentils / Antonio Benítez-Rojo ; translated by James
Maraniss ; introduction by Sydney Lea.
p. cm.
Translation of: El mar de las lentejas.
ISBN 0–87023–723–3 (alk. paper)
I. Title.
PQ7390.B42M313   1990
863–dc20   90–31381
                                                   CIP

British Library Cataloguing in Publication data are available.

Introduction

HAVING LATELY RESIGNED, after thirteen years, from *New England Review and Bread Loaf Quarterly*, I am frequently asked what occasion marked the pinnacle of my career there. Given the volume of manuscripts I laid hands on, I naturally vacillate. The high point? Well, it may have been my personal discovery of Antonio Benítez Rojo through the publication of "Buried Statues." Or was it the journal's opportunity to present his astonishing "Heaven and Earth," or his "Death of an Absolutist"? But the Caribbean number of the magazine, assembled at Sr. Benítez's instance and containing "The Repeating Island," one of his originative essays—that, too, felt climactic. At all events, the point is that I unfailingly imagine the author of *Sea of Lentils* as the most exciting one I ever dealt with as an editor.

Now, unexpectedly privileged to extend so gratifying a relation, I find myself daunted. I am no scholar of Antillean culture. Indeed, it was precisely our sad ignorance that impelled me and my collaborators to mount that Caribbean issue of *NER/BLQ* five years back, and we subsequently felt the sting of truth in Benítez's essay:

> The main obstacles to any global study of the Caribbean's societies, insular or continental, are exactly those things that scholars usually adduce to define the area: its fragmentation; its instability; its reciprocal isolation; its uprootedness; its cultural heterogeneity; its lack of historiography and historical continuity; its contigency and impermanence; its syncretism, etc. This unexpected mix of obstacles and properties is not, of course, mere happenstance. . . . post-industrial society—to use a new-fangled

term—navigates the Caribbean with judgments and intentions which are like those of Columbus; that is, it lands scientists, investors and technologists (the new discoverers), who come to apply the dogmas and methods that have served them well where they came from, and who can't see that these refer only to realities back home. ("The Repeating Island," *New England Review and Bread Loaf Quarterly* 7, no. 4 [1985])

The sting grew more painful as we sought to assemble contributions in our usual manner, for our categories of genre, of mode, and even of value increasingly showed their poverty. "Category" itself seemed an irrelevant term in light of the work—Francophone, Anglophone, Hispanophone—that kept arriving. The experience, however, was educational if alarming (or educational *because* alarming), I hope not only for us but also for the outsized majority of North Americans who share in our innocence. May *Sea of Lentils* continue that instructive process.

Consider, for instance, the notion of "narrative." It is at best a volatile thing in Sr. Benítez's extraordinary work, and this is not simply a matter of the novel's multiple points of view. Yes, there *are* five discrete perspectives in *Sea of Lentils*, but even so simple an assertion is misleading, since in each tale the very presumption of discreteness is a sham, since any narrow perspective seems to "kill" its progenitor, just as Antón Babtista's natural son, Miguel, at length murders his father. It is less accurate to say that singular point of view is shattered than that it is washed away. More even than the blood that flows on so many of its pages, *Sea of Lentils* is liquid.

Thus, for further example, those of us trained in European modes of judgment and observation may be prepared to call *Sea of Lentils* a historical novel. But how can we accurately understand "history" here by means of our traditional premises? Benítez's fiction does consider, say, the struggle between an essentially medieval Spanish feudalism and an emergent mercantile caste; all its main figures are European; and yet the novel is written in that fluid manner I just suggested. It is a Third World work, the emblem of an Antillean author, and thus it persistently erodes the linear narrative of our historiography, which extends even to the popular realm ("In fourteen hundred and ninety-two / Columbus sailed the ocean blue"): A, then B, then C through X. . . .

Futility will also attend any effort to marshal the equally symmetrical *aesthetic* ordinations of canonical Anglo-European literature, the so-called unities of time or space or character. If, as Benítez has suggested, part of his scholarly and artistic mission is to correct misprisions of an archipelagic Caribbean world, it's a tautology that he cannot do so by means of counters from terra firma.

Yet in these respects, mightn't we consider Antonio Benítez Rojo, Third World author or not, as simply in tune with a larger, transnational current in contemporary cultural criticism? In a 1988 interview, the writer himself would seem to indicate as much, stressing that *Sea of Lentils* contains "no center"; that in it "nothing is stable, nothing is fixed"; that the book is "a deconstructionist novel, no question." Yet somehow I sense Benítez— perhaps unlike some North American literati—has arrived at his deconstructionist vision by way not of trendiness but of personal experience.

Benítez is no stranger to the world of statistics and charts. As a young man, the author studied economics in the United States. After the triumph of revolution in 1959, he served the Cuban government in various capacities. His first post was in the Ministry of Labor, but he left it after several years, partly in disillusion but primarily in order to write, a pursuit that—given the subtlety of his art—afforded Benítez a kind of freedom that had up till then been inhibited, perhaps not by government alone. To earn his bread, he did research for Casa de las Americas, Castro's national institution of arts and culture, though by the early seventies, having incurred official disfavor, he was given increasingly humdrum assignments. Ironically, the regime's suspicion would lend him access to materials that are now his stock in trade. In his solitary labors, the writer scrutinized Caribbean culture—economic, political, and literary—from the time of the conquests, ultimately becoming, unarguably, a world authority on the region.

Sr. Benítez was at length elevated to a job worthy of such a polymath. In 1979 he became director of Cuba's Center for Caribbean Studies. As in *Sea of Lentils,* his encyclopedic knowledge came soon to be reflected as well in his own fiction, which began to earn him acclaim outside the island of his birth. In 1980, having flown to Paris to participate in a learned conference, he defected, settling in the United States. He now teaches at Amherst College, where he has for some time enjoyed the collaboration of his brilliant translator, Professor James Maraniss.

One surmises that Benítez's voracious reading at Casa de las Americas did incline him along what he calls his "deconstructionist" path, for in his studies he found no scholarship adequate to the cultural produce of his native zone. The author, however, also emphasizes an extraliterary juncture in his career: in "The Repeating Island," he speaks of two old black women in Havana, who passed him by "in a certain kind of way" during the Cuban missile affair of 1962. This was, he contends, "the moment at which I reached the age of reason":

> I cannot describe this "certain kind of way"; I will say only that there was a kind of ancient and golden powder between their gnarled legs, a scent of basil and mint in their dress, a domestic wisdom, almost culinary, in their gesture and their gay chatter. I knew then at once that there would be no apocalypse. The swords and the archangels and the beasts and the trumpets and the breaking of the last seal were not going to come, for the simple reason that the Caribbean is not an apocalyptic world; it is not a phallic world in pursuit of the vertical desires of ejaculation and castration. The notion of the apocalypse does not exist within the culture of the Caribbean. The notions of crime and punishment, of your money or your life, of *patria* or *muerte,* have nothing to do with Caribbean culture; these are western notions . . . which the Caribbean adopts only in terms of declamation, or rather, in terms of a first reading. The so-called "October crisis" or "missile crisis" was not won by J.F.K. or N.K. or much less by F.C. (men of State always wind up abbreviated in these great events); it was won by the Carribean, together with that loss that any win implies. If this had happened, let's say, in Berlin, children there would now be

discovering hand tools and learning to make fire with sticks. The plantation of rockets sown in Cuba was a Russian machine; but neither the sea nor the rivers were.

It's of course presumptuous to call a writer's own terms into question, and yet it seems apt (in spite or *because* of the phrase's vagueness) to figure *Sea of Lentils* as having been written in this "certain kind of way" rather than to label it as "deconstructionist." After all, construction and deconstruction suggest dialectic, binary opposition, the likelihood of crisis—the very sort of notion that the two women dispatched merely by walking past. Again, Benítez's text is too liquid, and too charged among other things with disparate and vital *sensory* matter, to accommodate dry, theoretical descriptives. The author explains in the same essay that

> the culture of archipelagoes is not terrestrial, as are almost all cultures; it is fluvial and marine. We're dealing here with a culture of bearings, not of routes; of approximations, not of exactitudes. Here the world of straight lines and angles (the wedge, the inclined plane, the intersection) does not dominate; here rules the fluid world of the curving line. The culture of meta-archipelagoes is an eternal return, a detour without destination or milepost, a roundabout that leads nowhere but back home; it is a feed-back machine, as is the sea, the wind, the Milky Way, the novel. . . .

Despite the so-called conquests, then, we cannot rightly impose an orderly grid—of cosmology, teleology, epistemology, not to mention criticism—on Benítez's watery world. We must in short avoid the error of our old-fashioned history primers, since it's not that "once upon a time" a certain cultural scheme arrived in the Indies to uproot and supplant another. In the Antilles, as in this strange fiction, there was and is no sure beginning; no single crux; no palpable end. *Sea of Lentils* is not a specific continuous form in that sense: its continuity (or continuities) consists, paradoxically, in the very polyrhythms of interruption, divagation, reconsideration, extenuation. At the moment, for instance, when the narrative of King Philip's death seemingly begins to "frame" Benítez's tale, that narrative will be truncated, will thus show itself as perhaps no more exclusively "significant," say, than the narrative of the fly that buzzes over the king's putrefying body on page one . . . and settles on his eye, open and gelid in death, twenty-six chapters later.

Similarly, one may falsely begin to sense a determinative *style* in this novel—perhaps the one that, as in all great visionary writing, achieves an almost catastrophic particularity:

> With his greenish-white eyes, frozen like icicles, the dying man scrutinizes the frightened faces of those around him; he perceives in the distance the basilica's main altar, whose twinkling halo reaches him, through the door left open in the bedroom wall, like an ordered constellation of sparks; knowing the set ritual that each new hour carries, he feels the officious stepping of boots and sandals behind the walls, and this quiet scraping rubs his soul in a subtly irritating and unsettling way, as though he were trapped in the upper cone of an hourglass. The ras ras ras of the footsteps sends him over, trembling, into another corner of time, not of childhood games or the knights' entrance into Avila the Noble; nor into a dreamlike self-contemplation; rather he is now within his own skin and surrounded by hostile footsteps, and in a colicky, shuddering sweat. At last he dares to lift his head, and from the platform of the great hall of the Brussels Palace he looks out nervously at the pudgy faces of Flemish lords, at their scandalous dress, at their enormous pink hands that stick out from their lace cuffs like baby pig snouts; he looks askance toward where the burghers are assembled all reddened with wine and pride to contemplate him impudently with their little albino-lashed eyes as if he were a pope or a madman or a carnival king.

Is there anything more persuasive in Brueghel? Or:

> Antón saw, up above the treetops, a spurt of fireflies all in line; the insects flew over the settlement like an unexpected river of stars, and instead of flying straight they drew a wide arc above the camp and turned toward the palm roofs, over which they dispersed in spirals and ogives that held for an instant and then dissolved in a stream of green sparks. Antón, in open-mouthed surprise, stood looking at the mysterious dance of the fireflies when a gibble-gabble of plaints and cries made him stand up in alarm and run to his father-in-law's lodge to seek an explanation; he found the old

man in the middle of the enclosure, bathed in the fireflies' gleam as they threw a murmurous crown of light around his head; he was seated at his beautiful bench, immobile, very erect, his face painted black, his pupils fixed on a clay vessel broken in two, spilling out shark's teeth, shells of wasps, spiraled seashells, and human bones. Antón learned quickly that the chief was no longer alive. . . .

It is perhaps coincidental that both of these death scenes— so removed in space and time from one another—contain sparks. Effulgent images are manifold in Antonio Benítez Rojo's prose . . . but, especially when the locale is Antillean, they are shown, as here, to extinguish themselves almost instantaneously, as if to contravene the "lyrical" style's hold on our imagination, to dramatize its transience.

Style may then yield to a willfully prosaic mode, as in Chapter 18, which begins, "Who was Pedro de Ponte?" The author rapidly proceeds to "a small chronology," a list of facts and events that is itself perpetually interrupted by questions that seem equally prosey ("What does Pedro de Ponte hope to get from the young Hawkins?" or "How would the cargo get to the Caribbean?")—until we discover that they're unanswerable, or that any answer is as worthy or worthless as the next ("And what's the point of all this?"). "In the memory," for instance, "of the old, dying king [Philip]," or so we recall from a much earlier chapter, ". . . Pedro de Ponte, once recalled, begins to vaporize . . . and vanishes in the dust."

That final phrase might serve a phenomenological critic as the *cogito* of Benítez's novel: everywhere in *Sea of Lentils,* one can almost feel along the senses the instantaneous pulverization of certainty. And yet dust seems, again, an insufficiently liquid metaphor. *Sea of Lentils* shows forth the "marine" character that its author ascribes to archipelagic cultures, not only because so many of its actions take place on or near water but also because fixity and definition are so persistently dissolved, as a sandcastle by wave or tide.

One may think of another great mariner, whose famous narrator is doomed—cursed *and* blessed—to a kind of ceaseless feedback, an eternal return. Ishmael must recount his experience over and over, in the impossible attempt to make metaphysical "sense" of it. Yet Benítez goes Melville a step further (though my admiration for the Cuban is immense, I here speak heuristically and not evaluatively): there is no supervening "I" in *Sea of Lentils,* as if its author recognized the fictiveness even of *that* construct. We search vainly through his remarkable pages for a single protagonist whose effort to make coherent observation can, for all its vanity, be applauded as heroic. The open-endedness of Benítez's meta-archipelago defeats such narrative bravado a priori.

Lest this appreciation and introduction appear *too* daunted, let it finally appeal once again to "The Repeating Island," in which our novelist asserts that the Caribbean, "although it includes the first American lands to be explored, conquered and colonized by Europe, . . . is still, especially in the discourse of the social sciences, one of the least known regions of the modern world."

The barb at the social scientists must pierce the flesh, too, of literary critics, be we naive, commonsensical, belletristic, or theoretical; for none of us has yet discovered a language adequate to a novel like this one or to the culture it so splendidly reflects. To arrive at a suitable discourse about an unknown region, we may have to pass through the vertiginous, exciting, and frightful sea of unknowing itself. We must jettison our false maps in order to navigate that fluid domain. No author could encourage us to do so more readily than Antonio Benítez Rojo.

Sydney Lea
Orford, N.H.

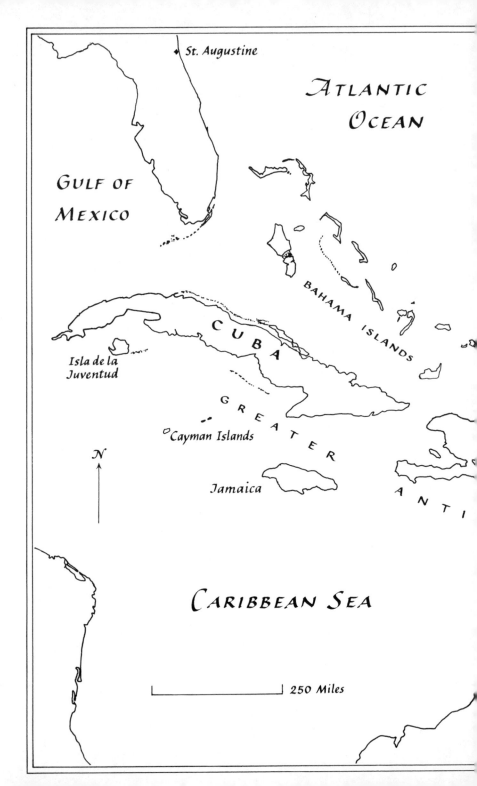

Once Mil Virgenes
(Virgin Islands)

Anguilla
St. Martin

St. Bartholomew

50 Miles

Santa Cruz
(St. Croix)

S. Cristobal
(Saba Is.)

S. Jorge
(St. Kitts)

Barbuda

S. Martin
(Nevis)

S. Maria
La Antigua

S. Anastasia
(St. Eustatius)

S. Maria de
Monserrate

LESSER
ANTILLES
(DETAIL)

S. Maria de
Guadalupe

Deseada

Todos los Santos

Mariagalante

HISPANIOLA

San Juan
Bautista
(Puerto Rico)

- LES

SEE
DETAIL

Dominica

Martinique

St. Lucia

LESSER ANTILLES

St. Vincent

Barbados

Aruba

Bonaire

Grenada

Curacao

Isla de
Margarita

Tobago

Trinidad

Sea of Lentils

Night falls; a slate gray light comes in through the windows and descends along the white wall of the gallery. Near the top of the wall, well above the man who holds the halberd, there are a half-dozen paintings, big, rectangular, insipidly colored, that hang a palm's length from the molded ceiling. The gallery is not wide, so to see the paintings in detail one has to lean back against one of the stone blocks of the wall opposite; even then it's an awkward distance: faces of virgins and saints appear distended, darkened by a sad arrogance, scarcely accessible in the dark shadows that curl among the roof beams. The halberdier rests one shoulder on the wall; in spite of his careless pose and the livery he wears, there is a certain loose elegance in the way he steps, wears a plume in his cap, tilts his head; he seems about thirty years old, perhaps younger, with a showy, thick moustache and short chestnut beard. A fly, perhaps made drowsy by the dusk, falls from the near window and gets tangled in one of his fuzzy eyelashes. Murmuring unintelligibly, the man swats hard at the insect, but the blow, too strong, pulls his shoulder from the wall, and as he retakes his position it slides along the whitewashed surface; now his legs, drawn off balance, stumble against the halberd, which hits the floor with a shattering report. As the confounded guard picks up his weapon, the far door opens just a crack and releases, behind a thread of warm and fetid air, an imperious admonition. The door, whose single plane displays a beautiful lock and eight shining olive-colored panels, closes quietly as a curtain an instant after the fly has traversed the opening.

Beyond it one can hardly breathe, such is the stench in the room; all attending dress in black, and the penumbra of incense and ash will barely show their features' outline, just the ivory of their bowed foreheads, the bunched folds of their collars, their hands stretched out across their jerkins, as prescribed by St. Ignatius Loyola in the *Spiritual Exercises*. Awake now, the insect loops above the twelve-lighted lamp whose wick no one has thought to trim; it flies quickly above the pious furniture, above the crystal urns, above the hushed and blurted sobs and sighs and prayers that seem to have escaped from some pot where old broths boil unwatched. Emerging from a whisper of hinges, a woman's face appears in a corner's blurry mist; beyond her eyes, in the room just opened, two bluish flames tremble on long candlesticks. "His Majesty is asking for the candle and the crucifix," she says dolefully. "Instantly, Highness," responds a silhouetted dignitary, rising to his feet. Above, the fly describes his gesture.

The bedroom is small and smells like a charnel house. The bed, raised on a platform, floats heavily between draperies of red silk and gold brocade. An ancient prelate, his sweating nose illumined fully by a candle at the headboard, kneels at a prie-dieu; he is reading the Passion according to Saint John, which he does not interrupt at the dignitary's entrance. His body hidden by the sheets, his head sunken in the curtained shadows, the man lies stinking and gasping; in spite of the half light, it is easy to perceive that the disease that is killing him has begun to strike along one leg, the right leg; a bloody-colored rust dribbles from his foot resting on a pillow, and at thigh level a sinister clot, fat as a poultice, stands loud against the linen's pallor; whatever the illness is, it has proceeded to infect his belly: the sheets bulge above an abscess as if sheltering a wineskin or a huge bubble. The dignitary waves the crucifix to shoo the fly away from the bed, then, from the prelate's reading candle he lights another, whose worn and dried-out wick crackles darkly, smokelessly. The dignitary pulls down the sheets, takes out an arm—like a fragment of some wooden image, worm-eaten from centuries upon an altar, or one of those martyrs' relics, dried and black-

4

ened, kept in urns in the adjacent room—and holding it carefully by the wrist, lifts it to the candle. He hears a groan and puts it back. "Wait a little while, the hour has not come," a mild voice says from deep within the bed. The prelate, touched perhaps by the dying man's lucidity, stops his droning; then, in the silence, he hears the frothy growling of a gut. As the dignitary places the crucifix and dead candle on a chest, the ghostly gentleman who keeps his vigil at the bed steps to the window and fiercely inhales the air that blows across the dusky plain. From the other side of the room, near the bed, a trickle of flowing liquids draws a moan from the man who lies there, but there is nothing in the room to explain this strange noise, the jar is on the table still, the three old men immobile, the woman flat against the door, her creamy eyelids closed as her lips spin out a mute and lacerating rosary.

The fly swoops low, it skitters along breeches and high boots, by the platform-cover's cordovan hide, to the edges of the drapery; it disappears inside the bed's dark opening. Out from within the canopy's gloom, the faint voice of the one they've called His Majesty begins reciting: "And standing by the cross of Jesus were his mother, and his mother's sister, Mary the wife of Cleophas, and Mary Magdalene. . . ." The prelate, clearing his throat, continues with him: "And when Jesus saw his mother, and the disciple whom he loved standing near, he said to his mother: 'Woman, behold your son!'" Doubtless these words are a comfort to the dying one, for his voice quickens as he proceeds; nevertheless, presently, taking for himself a verse of the Gospel, he repeats in desperation: "I thirst. I thirst. I thirst!" The gentleman steps from the window with a sigh, goes to the jar of holy water at the table, and then, leaning over the bed, he sprinkles the hyssop. Leaving the darkness, the fly soars upward; it perches upside down on the canopy's yellow border. The dying man's pupils, emaciated by suffering and fever, moisten as they fix upon the insect. "Ha! Now the hour has really come," he murmurs.

[II]

A KIND OF CORTEGE, slow and murmurous, proceeds along the mountain path. Before it walks a clump of skinny men, wasted, miserable, their privates scarcely covered by a cotton fig leaf. These dark brown, hairless men sing and clap listlessly as they walk through the grove, they shake their meager gourd bells, blow through heavy horns, waggle their hands from side to side, all falteringly; the bunches of their long hair, gathered at the nape, sway like mule tails in a train. An old man walks among them, his face painted in red and white; around his neck are strings of beads, shells, and hollow flutes of bone; his haunch is girdled by a wide belt, tightly woven, with a flat, oval stone at the center on which one can discern a pair of eyes, a mouth, a nose, these features shaped naively. The old man supports himself upon a handsome staff inlaid with shells, and his invalid gait preserves a kind of quiet hauteur, one might even call it an irreducible inflection of majesty. Ten or twelve women follow, their nipples exposed, clapping also and singing now and then; almost all of them are pregnant. Unlike the old man, they have about them an air of insult, ignominy . . . perhaps it is the sway of their breasts above their loaded bellies, perhaps their faces' dull indifference to the yellowish fluxes that run down their thighs to be licked by a runty, jumping dog. Next, walking alone, a completely naked man carries an upraised pole to which a crossbar has been nailed; stuck atop this improvised cross is a visored helmet with a faded yellow plume, hung from the crossbar are a steel breastplate, a shield, assorted straps and irons. The naked man has

6

been tortured, he has neither ears, nor a nose, nor lips; his head is a post set with a veil of horseflies. A scant distance from the maimed one, occupying more or less the center of the procession, comes a group made up of four exhausted youths and a white man with a reddish beard; the former carry two guayabo branches, at whose ends a skillfully woven netted hammock has been tied; barefoot, sweating and grimy, dressed in a tattered shirt, the red-haired man sinks spongily in his bed of cords, fanning himself with a bunch of heron feathers; his bombastic mien has the clumsy starch of vanity, of false majesty; a menacing crossbow rests upon his belly, and within his reach are a quiver filled with arrows and a long sword. Walking even with the hammock are two small girls with budding nipples who support a canopy of silvery yagruma leaves that creaks in the midday sun. Twenty and some porters close the column, bowed and mute, their swollen ankles wobbling; on their backs they carry tools—picks, hatchets, spades, hoes—and troughs, trays, baskets of yucca, yams, mamey, guanábana, tender hearts of palm, bundles of cassava; they bring restless little beasts enclosed in rustic cages, here you would see a parrot's florid plumage, there the iguana's stern and peeking eye, there the rodent's swinging tail.

The dark, hairless men are Taínos; the white man's name is Antón Babtista, a soldier who came to Hispaniola with Christopher Columbus's second voyage.

A FEW MINUTES EARLIER, when he saw the fly, his thinking had been confused and transcendental. Now, helped by the monotonous praying all around, he eases himself patiently out and away from life, overcome by an imperturbable resignation, as if the time it was taking him to die did not belong to him. In his thoughts there is a familiar and calm landscape: a wide river, gray, with naked banks; it slips through a meandering bed. It's afternoon, and beside the overlook there is a small autumnal forest, now bare, at whose entrance two boys on wooden horses joust happily, assailing each other with candles. A sudden wind from the east sweeps up the fallen leaves, piles them, whirls them, lifts them in a flutter of old gold and muted red. Nothing of the children can be perceived except their peals of laughter, delicate, removed, high, mixed up in the whirl of leaves and straw-colored dust that moves away to coil, twist, spin above the plain of olive trees, ripened grapevines, turbulent gullies, snow-roofed villages, gathered flocks, and bushels of summer grain, then to spend itself thunderously between the peaks on the high plateau. The leaves fall broken and dispersed upon the procession that marches toward the only visible gate of a walled city that looks, from the road, like a vast, sober pastry thrown out upon the mountain: a white building stands out above its belt of walls; further up, convent towers and church needles form a marzipan crown against the May sky. Bells from the city beckon the many lords and ladies who walk in the cortege. The bellmen must have disagreed among themselves, because some are calling to arms and others to prayer. A small mule with velvety haunches carries one of the boys who played in the autumn afternoon; his blond hair has grown and his jutting forehead and jaw make his face seem bland. A beetle-browed man, with the look of a veteran captain, walks beside him, his hand on the saddle horn; another man, with a handsome gait and a tapered black beard, carries the reins. The column halts; the boy, helped by the tough-looking man, dismounts and stands before a swarm of little girls who have come out of the laps of duennas, out of canopies and litters; then he dances along the road lined with orange scrub that leads to the city; behind him a singing train of pages, ladies, and young gentlemen, playing zithers and *vihuelas,* copies the boy's steps. Hangings and tapestries are laid out on the walls; the people wave standards, flags, handkerchiefs, but their vivid colors, like the lilting frontier ballad that the entire procession sings, are devoured slowly by the clamor of the bells; then the city blurs, films over until it disappears, crushed by the heavy beating of the clappers that swing back and forth and bang ceaselessly against their bronze casings.

The bell jangles a summons to the *Angelus Domini;* its last peal resounds in the bedchamber of the one who is dying; it sounds in the corridor guarded by the man with the halberd; it sounds in the parlors, cloisters, naves, and cellars of the monastery. Beneath habit and hose, knees numb from genuflection rise quickly to take up the night's ceremonial. The sun has already fallen below the mountains, and within this great construction of tile and masonry, set in the solitude of the bleak plateau, candlesticks and oil lamps are burning, lights that will last until dawn; on each side of the gallery, rows of tonsured heads stretch like snakes toward the refectory; spanning the arcades, above and below the stairways, squadrons of guards cross to take charge of the doors. With his greenish-white eyes, frozen like icicles, the dying man scrutinizes the frightened faces of those around him; he perceives in the distance the basilica's main altar, whose twinkling halo reaches him, through the door left open in the bedroom wall, like an ordered constellation of sparks; knowing the set ritual that each new hour carries, he feels the officious stepping of boots and sandals behind the walls, and this quiet scraping rubs his soul in a subtly irritating and unsettling way, as though he were trapped in the upper cone of an hourglass. The ras ras ras of the footsteps sends him over, trembling, into another corner of time, not of childhood games or the knights' entrance into Avila the Noble; nor into a dreamlike self-contemplation; rather he is now within his own skin and surrounded by hostile footsteps, and in a colicky, shuddering sweat. At last he dares to lift his head, and from the platform of the great hall of the Brussels Palace he looks out nervously at the pudgy faces of Flemish lords, at their scandalous dress, at their enormous pink hands that stick out from their lace cuffs like baby pig snouts; he looks askance toward where the burghers are assembled all reddened with wine and pride to contemplate him impudently with their little albino-lashed eyes as if he were a pope or a madman or a carnival king. The jokes and laughter stop when his father, helped by the prince of Orange, stands up; he sees him, weak and faltering, as he adjusts his spectacles and begins to leaf indecisively through his notebook. "I have had to suffer the trials of many wars, and I can affirm that I entered into each against my will. I have never waged them other than when forced to and in sorrow. Even today I regret that in my departure I cannot leave you at peace. I have not come here without feeling all the hardships of those wars. This you can judge easily by seeing me as I am. I have done what I could do, and I regret not having done it better. I now realize my limitation, my incapacity, and in my present state I see it as my duty to adopt this resolution: my son is now a man, and I trust that God will give him the strength to fulfill better than I the obligations imposed upon a king." Never before has he heard his father speak with this afflicted voice; wrapped up in those thick, dark garments, the old man moves his long jaws with the weary sadness of a spent war horse. "I ask you not to see in this abdication an attempt to flee from ordeals and dangers yet to come; believe me, I am moved only by my incapacity. In my place I leave you my son, and I entrust him to you. Lend him the love and obedience you have given me." *Lend him the love and obedience you have given me,* he thinks, while his horse, surrounded for a moment by frowning faces, shakes his head nervously and tugs at the reins. On approaching the gallery, he sees a worsening aspect to the faces in the crowd. The archers of the guard, taciturn, muttering profanities, goad the heavy white Percherons against the noisiest and most obstructive onlookers. He had delayed this trip out of fear of being contaminated by the Jerusalem of the North, adducing, among other motives, his mourning at the death of his uncle, Luis. But week after week, with obstinate regularity, his father wrote from Spain, urging a visit to the newly rich burghers of Antwerp. Well then, there he was, and it was not quite love and obedience that they were showing him, in spite of his regular smiling and saluting, which were half-hearted of course, for the Scheldt's foggy chill sat upon his breath and tinged the nausea brought on by all the beer and wine and brandy he had swallowed, trying to please everyone along his route into the city. The foreign merchants, to show just what they thought of him, had put up a half-dozen paltry, prudently erected triumphal arches. He had halted at each one to drink to the healths of England, Lombardy, Portugal, each time with the queasy knowledge that he raised his glass above the hats of heretics and crypto-Jews. Perhaps to remind him of the money that he owes them, the arch built by the Genoese merchants stretches sumptuously over the middle of the square, crisscrossed with effigies and allegorical paintings, and with fine brocades adorned with pregnant spheres from whose mouths spill colored gusts of smoke and fireworks like fistfuls of gold coins, lighting up the evening. A sudden blast of wind hits him full in the face; out from behind the whinnying and the flying armor comes a deafening roar that knocks him off his horse. From the ground, astonished, he watches as the flaming arch falls slowly down on people who run away with hands over ears, their capes and hair singed by fear and gunpowder. Beside him an archer lies spread-eagled, a nail stuck in his forehead and one eye hanging down his cheek. Abandoned,

11

helmetless, helpless, and stifled with fear, he hears a ferocious squawk from among the lamentations: "Down with Philip! See what comes with his Spanish Inquisition!"

But all that would have happened much earlier, when he had first felt himself hated by his Flemish subjects, and he had sworn not to accede to any of their demands on matters of faith, whatever the cost. Now he is again at the great hall of the Brussels Palace, hearing his father's woeful abdication, the discourse of a valetudinarian emperor, a hoary general overthrown by heaps of debt, of treason and bad blood, of heretical Bibles and pamphlets and almanacs. "Zealously preserve this union which you have never forsaken, defend and maintain justice. And above all, never let us be invaded by the heresies that surround our realms, and if ever this should happen, root them out. I know now that I've made many errors in my life, but I made them out of ignorance and never knowingly. Now I am sorry and I ask forgiveness." Overcome with sorrow, he leaves his chair and falls to his knees beside his father; he takes the old man's hands, swollen and twisted by the gout, and buries his sobbing face within them. He hears his father's quaking voice speak down at him: "My son, keep the Catholic faith in all its purity, respect the laws of the land as sacred and inviolable, and never harm your vassals' rights, and if some day by chance you should wish to seek, as I have done, a secluded life, would that you have a son on whom you may confer the scepter as joyfully as I now give you mine. *Would that you have a son on whom you may confer the scepter as joyfully as I now give you mine,* he sighs. The doctors have been examining Mary for more than a quarter of an hour. Sweating, choked with anxiety, he stretches his legs and rests his neck on the back of his chair. He stares at the door. Poor Mary! He has found her aged, sick, more ridiculous than ever. He had gone to meet her in Greenwich and, two days later, they left for Whitehall. He rode beside her royal litter and tried to be courteous, and when she cut off his small talk by wrapping herself up in furs for a nap, he let himself slide, alone, ill-humored, into a melancholia that floated that year above the English highways, while beside them the bland snows of April opened on the sooty huts of woodcutters and peasants, who with their arms folded over their ragged clothes, and hopping up and down, drew up a bit of spirit to shout out *God save the Queen*, whereupon they begged a crust of bread. His mood did not improve as he passed through London, and he resolved to return to Brussels as soon as he had impregnated Mary and had got ships and soldiers from her, enough to finish off the French. There must surely have been some respectful people among the many beggars in the streets, but for the most part they saluted the passing cortege through the usage of tradition alone. Mary was no longer a popular queen, and nobody remembered him anymore. On crossing London Bridge, out from among the little shops that cling to the rail, unexpectedly there came a jovial Spanish greeting. He rose in his stirrups; it was a disabled tinker, who waved his crutch above the tattered caps and bonnets, surely some old sailor from Asturias or Biscay whom the waves had pushed up the Thames. He thought about that man, and at Whitehall he talked to Mary to see if she could help him. But she was so happy to be reunited in her palace that perhaps she would forget. On that very day he realized that it would be impossible to recapture the mediocre happiness that had teased him three years earlier when, his timidity disguised by a red mantle and an Andalusian pony, he drank ale, hunted foxes, and kissed the ladies on the mouth, as was the wanton custom. Things had changed at court as well; there was talk of the reluctance of the lords to give back the Church's ancient landholdings, of tenants thrown out upon the roads, of the dozens of heretical sects that defied the prohibitions and called poor Mary *bloody,* of the market price of wool in Antwerp, of the high interest rates demanded by the moneylenders, of William Cecil's power over Parliament, of the price of sheep, of the clever resistance to the restoration of the Catholic faith . . . but, above all, there was talk of Elizabeth Tudor, and no one understood how, after her complicity in the Dudley plot, the queen had failed to get rid of her. Poor Mary! things go from bad to worse; a false note sounds in her chatter and her songs, an ill-omened gaiety. If only a son would come! The beds of Whitehall, and then those of Windsor Castle, had borne their febrile efforts at resolving the problem of succession. Night after night, looking away from her baggy, reddened eyes, he would climb atop her once and again, listen to her tired wheezing, feel the dig of her rings and nails in his shoulder blades; sometimes, kept awake by shame and disgust as he heard her fragile snoring, he would pray until dawn for an heir to outlive his weakling Spanish child, the one who devoured insects whole, and to push the Stuart who had married the French dauphin even further from the English throne; at other times, desperate, he wished for Mary's death so that he might betroth himself to Elizabeth Tudor, who owed her life to him and would immediately be made the queen. Ah, if Elizabeth would only show gratitude at his having interceded when her plot with Dudley was discovered! But there was Mary first of all; she ought to bear a child or die. An English child would ensure Spain's command in both Europe and the Indies, *his* command, and he would tip the scale toward the Catholic faith, *his* Catholic faith, with no big feudal lords, with no arrogant burghers, with no Cortes and no old feudal compacts to restrain him, with no more insolent conquistadors, with no emperor but one who was *his* child, nor any pope who was not *his* servant, and the whole world living in fine order, decently, piously, under *his* government and *his* religion, without the unspeakable chaos of heretics, without brazen Turks or idolatrous blacks, without pagan Indians, with the New World's gold and silver serving God alone, *his* God, for the salvation of *his* soul and *his* body. . . . Two little taps at the door and he squares his legs, fusses with his collar; he straightens in the chair. "Come in," he mumbles. Again the little taps. "Come in!" he commands. The oak slab opens respectfully and three doctors appear. The eldest, dressed in a hooded cloak, advances with upraised arms, lamenting in the Jewish way: Mary is not pregnant; her wish to give birth is what inflates her belly. The daughter of Catherine of Aragon is no more than a sick and desiccated pumpkin that will never produce even a seed. As soon as she died he could woo Elizabeth Tudor, but he shouldn't fool himself about his chances. So much for the English child. Then, a return to Brus-

sels. Once more the great hall with its noisy footsteps, the Flemings and their pig-snout hands, the emperor's broken voice, the abdication. "Say something, for God's sake," his father whispers from his beard and he sinks back into the upraised throne. "Get up," his father sputters, and he, scared, flustered, rises from the parquet, manages to stop trembling at the knees, and turns nervously to face the murmuring and coughing hall. "You are handing me a heavy burden," he stammers. "Nevertheless, obeying Your Majesty, as I have always done, as you ask me to, as Your Majesty asks me to, the governing of my province, of Your Majesty's province . . . I mean of those lands." A snort of laughter, barely muffled in a handkerchief, draws his look to the right of the platform. A corpulent Walloon, the medal of the Golden Fleece around his neck, dries an invisible tear with a tip of folded lace. Searching in anguish for the French words that he has memorized, he looks closely at the gentleman, whose grief is sharpening as he sees himself observed. "I would have liked to know French . . . sufficiently to express to the States, to the States and to the people, the concern and love that I hold . . . for them. But since it is not possible for me to do so . . . in French, and even less in Flemish, the bishop of Arras, who . . . who . . . will do it in my place." *Will do it in my place.* But who could do anything in his place? Who could sustain for a moment the enormous, devastating piety of his crown? Who could guide that exorbitant empire, that sluggish galleon foundering in mortgages and titles, up to the feet of the Lord? He had begged God to make his last night be a sweet one, to let none but his most pleasant recollections usher him toward death. At first, when he had seen himself a child playing in a mock tourney, and when his mule had been led by that Francisco Borgia whom he loved so much, it seemed to him that El Greco's angels would hold prizes and victorious allegories above his bed—why not San Quentin, Lepanto, Florida, Lisbon, Las Terceras, and above all the vindicating triumph of Antwerp? But the moth-eaten roll of his failures, of all that had brought him fear and shame, had begun to unfurl before him, and he knew somehow that the figure of the good daughter Isabel Clara Eugenia, there sniffling at the door, would straighten and reduce into that of Elizabeth Tudor, the renegade, the damned, the devil's concubine, whose devices and defiances he had suffered like a torment of smells, sparks, and burning brands, blowing in his ears through the course of forty years, and then into the room would fall the shadows of Drake and Hawkins, and Orange, and then his canopy would be scraped by the face of Ana, immured and cross-eyed, and then the pale bloodless heads of Egmont, Montigny, and the justice of Aragon, and the breast of Verdinegro, pierced by daggers, ah, and the ghost of his son Carlos, risen from the hell of intended parricides, what sorrow . . . and that malign confederacy, crowned by a thick violet cloud of which each vapored drop, a sinner's life consumed by fire, or strangled by the rope, or quartered on the rack, or pierced by steel or stake, would stay near to attend his death, immobile, grave, silent, as if at an auto-da-fé, and he, for the greater glory of God, would file past with the green candle in his hand, in that infamous bed of worms and lice, wrapped in those sheets all daubed with blood and sweat, with urine and shit. He would die raving, that was clear. Before him, hung on a lance tip, was the vinegar-soaked sponge that would set fire to his wounded lips, his interminable thirst.

Eloi. Eloi, lama sabacthani? the prelate chants, and the dying old man turns to look at the crucifix that the dignitary draws near his hand.

[IV]

THE TOWER'S UPPER ROOM at the castle—or for-
tress—of Adeje, in Tenerife, is square, to suit a cubical
structure; a spiral staircase passes through the central
space to vanish in a high hollow filled with light that opens up
among the roof beams; six or seven paces opposite the step that
spills into the room there is a large table, if one could call it that,
made of two stones, badly planed and of unequal size, crossed by
a wide, blackened slab whose polished surface fails to moderate
the harshness of the whole ensemble, starkly volcanic, savage,
pagan in appearance; spread on the slab there are big, dusty
books, scrolls, files tied with faded ribbons, a writing implement,
a seven-armed candelabra etched with rust and verdigris, and
an abacus made out of ivory, cobwebs, and bamboo. Behind the
table, on his feet, bent over slightly in his black silk tunic, we can
see, in flesh and blood, that dark-bearded man, transfigured
now by a shaft of light descending from the rafters, whose slow,
vaporous hand is stretching out like a reflection toward the
abacus's ribs; the figure is no wraith, in truth it seems like a
conjecture, the recollection of a name, still vague, inside the
memory of the old king who lies in his agony of death upon a
bed of putrefaction; this man, or name, or whatever it may be,
thickens, takes on substance as he begins to thrum the abacus's
beads with a lutenist's light dexterity, and the objects on the table
are reborn, summoned to a distant afternoon when Pedro de
Ponte, in his customary tunic, takes up his pen and moistens it,
then enters sums upon the pages of a heavy book with locks of
brass. He works with a mysterious zeal, unblinking, as though

the columns of numbers that he builds from top to bottom were amazing him continually, were leading him, dazzled, to the cryptic numeral that sounds Jehovah's name; his nose, sharp, long, and curved, follows the working fingers at short range and seems to sniff the busy murmur of the abacus, the subtle rustling descant of the pen. He shivers, lifts his gaze, and turns it to the low side-window; a wind from the Levant is darkening the sea, twisting and blurring the waves of the anchorage below the tower sunk into the barren overhang of rock; the wind bursts into the room, and Pedro de Ponte stands before gray gusts that bear the scent of bitter dates; suddenly, perhaps alarmed by rattling tapestries and picture frames, he shuts the window and he sighs; some papers have been blown onto the floor, but he ignores them, with his elbows leaning on the slab of stone.

It is impossible to read de Ponte's thoughts, furtive as they are, his slitted, half-shut eyes as unrevealing as a shroud, behind them not a quiver or a sign. In the memory of the old, dying king other faces and events take color, shape, and resonance; Pedro de Ponte, once recalled, begins to vaporize . . . and vanishes in the dust.

What could be the secret he concealed?

[V]

YOU MAY NOT KNOW IT but on leaving the Canaries
Don Pedro Menéndez de Avilés's armada met a heavy
storm, which split his flagship, the galleon *San Pelayo,*
from the body of the fleet. I was not aboard her; rather I lay low
inside a caravel transporting laborers and peasants to inhabit
Florida. The king, you see, had dressed me up with Santiago's
cross for exploits I'd performed in Italy against the Turk, and
my father would have kept me back there on the royal galleys,
where I'd shown my valor and good sense. Reasons enough
have I today to rue my disobedience! But what could one expect,
I was a youth of twenty-four and newly wedded to Don Pedro's
eldest daughter, and had the poor girl not been carried off by
pestilence I would have had the Captaincy of Florida with title of
marquis, for there was room for it within the terms of the
agreement that the king contracted with my father-in-law before our sailing, and more room yet within the old man's heart,
for I came of a good family and I was a very faithful son-in-law,
and he was wild with disappointment when my father had refused to let me go along.

The *Adelantado's* armada was very different from the others
that had set sail for the Indies. Wanting to follow him on the
adventure, many hidalgos from Asturias, Galicia, and Biscay
had signed as soldiers and even as sailors, so that by the time that
the ships and provisions had been gathered in Cádiz scarcely
any beggarly or low persons could be seen in any taverns, inns,
or wharves within the port, and the five hundred Negroes given
by His Majesty were never boarded, there being men of quality

enough for everything. At night, wrapped in my cape, I combed the city to make observations, and by the next day I had left my beard in a barber's basin and had dressed in such a way as to hide my real position as a captain and a knight of Santiago. I enrolled upon the caravel *Sant Antonio,* where my companions were a priest, fifty soldiers with an ensign in command, and a score of peasants, carpenters, and masons with their children and their wives, none of which persons knew me by any name but Pedro Tineo, an Asturian hidalgo with no history of war or sea voyaging who was heading for the New World to find out what fortune held in store for him. The ship's master was named Juan Ginete, from the Canaries, and he was said to be a knower of the Antillean isles as well as all the ports and cities of the Indies. He was eager to hoist anchor, for before she crossed the ocean the ship was going to make a stop at Las Palmas, where his mother lived, she whom he had left behind in sickness the preceding winter and of whom he had heard nothing since.

Not waiting for the Biscayan and Asturian squadrons, and in very good weather, we departed Cádiz on the twenty-ninth of June, the feast of Saint Peter and Saint Paul, which I judged to be a happy omen, for I had been christened for the first of these apostles, as also had my father-in-law, the *Adelantado.* We soon made out the outlines of Lanzarote and Fuerte Ventura on the horizon, and one week later we were moored in Grand Canary. I was tempted to present myself before Don Pedro and then beg him to take me into his service, but on reflection I resolved to wait until the trip had ended, since a boat was going back to Cádiz, and I feared that I'd be put on it, for the *Adelantado* had always favored the opinions of my father, who was a relative of his. I pretended to be seasick and stayed inside the caravel, where it was so hot that I got sick in earnest with a touch of fever.

On Sunday our eight ships left port to go out looking for Dominica, which is inhabited by Carib Indians, and then on to Puerto Rico, whence, well rested and provisioned, we would set out to take the forts and villages that the French Lutherans had built in Florida. Just before nightfall a quick breeze blew across our path and then shifted over to the northeast.

By sunrise we had neared a rainstorm, and as we could not see a single sail around us and I thought I'd heard the noise of cannon shots to leeward, I told the ship's master that I'd volunteer to climb up to a high spar and see if any ship of ours was foundering. Weakened with my sweats and fevers, I nearly flew from the halyards, for the wind was very brisk. When I got aloft I soon grew uneasy, for my counting hadn't registered the sails of either the *San Pelayo* or the tender at her side. Juan Ginete, very downcast at his mother's death, which they had told him about in port, thought that the ships must have collided and then sunk. But I, seeing how pale the ensign and the soldiers had become, declared that the *Adelantado*'s galleon was a new one, with a thousand-ton displacement, and there was no way that a feeble little tender could have damaged her, for she'd been made to fend off boardings from big galleons and pirate ships. And I argued hard, for those men knew nothing of the sea and, though brave, were terrified of death by drowning, and as they all had swords and daggers they were dangerous.

It wouldn't be long before Juan Ginete was to praise my judgment, for at the height of the storm the boat that sailed at our poop began to take on water. Her master, who knew his business, tried to keep her pointed straight ahead, the better to withstand the pounding waves, which had climbed to a height of three fathoms. The boat was very near us, but we couldn't cast an accurate line to her in such a wind. We were waving encouragement to them when we saw Captain Francisco Sánchez, sword in hand, with five of his Galician soldiers, walking toward the helm. Soon our worst fears were confirmed as the boat began to twist and turn, and then, half-capsized by the waves and with her middle under water, she moved off heavily toward the rising sun. "Pray for her, for they'll all die before they see the land—they've lost their heads," said Juan Ginete to the priest, and it was true that here was a time when the master had good reason to hold to his forlorn outlook.

THERE COULDN'T BE much work aboard the *Maria-galante*, other than to let oneself to be borne off to Cathay, Antón Babtista thought, dumbfounded, gawking at the deftness of the sailors at whom he had sneered just yesterday in Cádiz, where he'd seen them loiter, dull and nerveless as oxen at a waterwheel, in inns and taverns and the sunny ramparts of Santa Catalina castle. But now the boatswain shouted and everyone hopped to it, and a Moorish-looking lad moved sharply to avoid the Franciscan friar who would perform the first Mass ever on the isle of Ofir, and another boy with a heretic's face sidestepped a bundle of caps, tradable for gold nuggets, and ran to hoist the spritsail, while a sportive troop of stewards stamped and elbowed through the crowded main deck to take down the *señores* hidalgos' coats of arms, which had until then been hung at the gunwales to enlarge the aura of that never-before-seen armada provisioned by Seville's archdeacon and awarded to the Catholic kings, and on whose mastheads fluttered seventeen majestic standards with the Castle and the Lion.

Antón Babtista cast his glance out on September's gentle sky; the clouds, delicately strewn, embroidered a broad alley of very white lace that grew more subtle to the southwest. A good omen, thought Antón Babtista, and he drew in a satisfied mouthful of wind from the sea, but a clatter of farewells and cannon shots caused him to turn his head downwind: the Venetian galleys of the escort had begun to turn about, and from their graceful myriapodal forms, festooned with streamers, appeared handkerchiefs and powder flashes, and then skeins of black smoke that the sea breeze instantly unwound. A wish to memorize the shore's outline suddenly came to his heart; he jumped sharply from the cask of flour where he'd been sitting and, quickening his pace, went down a step to the main deck, flailing through a mob of workmen, masons, soldiers, carpenters, all struggling to reach the quarterdeck, which then was occupied by the hidalgos and the volunteer cavalry; pushing and shoving, squeezed and crammed, wholly overcome by a furious desperation, pummeled left and right, his clothing torn, he knew for certain that all was lost if he should miss a last glimpse of the coast of Spain, for surely then he'd not return. But the same idea had come over everyone aboard, and now the hidalgos, armed to the nines for the farewell, drew their swords and hurried to defend the taffrail, when an unexpected boom from the great cannon, together with the appearance of the Admiral's contorted visage at the entrance to the quarterdeck, miraculously quelled the riot.

"Don't you know I'm sick?" the Admiral said, reproachfully, pointing to the linen nightshirt underneath his overcoat.

Antón Babtista stared at the deck. Some of the workmen fell to their knees.

"What do you want?" the Admiral demanded.

"*Parleu, homes,*" offered Fra Pane in Catalan, for he could not make himself understood in Castilian, and he spread his arms in a tutelary gesture.

Antón Babtista raised his head, looked about him, and took a step forward.

"We want to see the land," he said. "We want to see it."

Up above, the vizored, helmeted hidalgos laughed in unison.

"You'll see no land until we reach the Canaries," said the Admiral.

Antón Babtista trembled; pleas, oaths, and lamentations rose up around him.

"Are you afraid?" the Admiral asked.

"I fought at Granada. I was an archer for King Don Ferdinand."

"Then you need fear nothing," the Admiral smiled, "by the

grace of God and of their Majesties, I am the Admiral of the Ocean Sea, and all those are my lands," he added, pointing to the waves, "and this my willing corsair," he stamped firmly on the deck.

"Let me look, my lord," Antón Babtista begged. "If I don't see land I know that I'll die far away."

The Admiral frowned and thought, his look held fast to the unhappy faces there before him.

"Topman, ahoy!" he shouted suddenly. "What do you see astern?"

"I see the Genoese galleys" came the distant answering voice.

"Do you see land?"

The silence froze Antón Babtista's hope.

"Land I now see."

"Climb up and see the land," the Admiral whispered in contempt. The door closed on his pallid smile.

Antón Babtista took a few steps toward the ratlines, then he vacillated and then stopped to gauge the crow's nest's distance. His stomach turned and he felt for a moment that he was falling toward the sky. Stricken with nausea and stung by the hidalgos' scorn, he hid like a beaten dog behind some biscuit crates.

⟦ V I I ⟧

AN END TO THE CONQUEST of Tenerife was achieved, in no small measure, with money lent by the Genoan merchant Cristóbal de Ponte; in payment the first governor-general, in distibuting the island's lands, ceded him the fertile-looking Daute and Garachio, and the haughty Adeje, in whose abrupt valleys, spiky with palms, the *guanche* chieftains had resided; to establish his *converso* line he gave his hand to Doña Ana, sister of Pedro de Vergara, the conquistador, called *the elder* in the chronicles, who became the acting governor of Tenerife; the marriage produced two sons. . . . Bartolomé and Pedro de Ponte would have passed their first years under the auspicious clamor of the great discoveries, the new and strange arrivals from the rising and the setting sun, and rarely would a ship return to Lisbon or Seville without its leaving there upon the archipelago something of its cargo of extraordinary tales, and now and then a parrot or a sheaf of silk, a bar of silver, a clutch of pepper or of pearls, a sack of moldy cassava stuffed with sweet potato seedlings; one can picture easily Cristóbal de Ponte, there in the epoch of the arrival of the sugar masters from Medina, taking his sons to mark the progress of his sugar mills; man of vision that he was, he would have willed the mills already to the boys, the Daute mill to Bartolomé and the Adeje mill to Pedro; founder of the most extended branch of the Pontes, great-grandson of the magnificent Mateo, who had as banker been inscribed in the Golden Book of the Republic, with cousins in England, Germany, and Flanders, Cristóbal de Ponte never changed his surname nor his sons' to *Puente;* with a tac-

25

iturn, wry smile he may perhaps have squelched his wife's suggestion that they adopt the name of the Vergaras; his sons were to be Pontes, and as such they would be drawn to the pursuit of trade there in those fortunate isles which he had found some years ago to be a bridge of gold—ponte d'oro—stretching out between three worlds, the vertex of a triangle whose resplendent lines extended toward the vault of heaven.

The sweet smoke of the sugarhouses, the fragrance of the sprouted vines brought in from distant Malvesie, the aroma of the tilled fallow land, of the pottery in the kiln, the resins burning in the night, the quicklime in the mortar, the slaked lime in the whitewash, everything in Tenerife smelled then of newness; the bellows at the forge blew out unending gusts of sparks and hammer blows, and the upland pines, the refuge of the last *manceyes,* came felled and rolling down to be refashioned into furniture and building frames; here a rope delimited a plaza, there a granary appeared, over there a church was built and a wall put up, with parapet and aperture, and everything increased and prospered and the rare wine of Icod was drunk above the din of the guitars and the dealing of the cards, and times were good for those who came in search of pleasure and enrichment.

In the beginning, though, Cristóbal de Ponte's venture was to founder like a galley without oarsmen; the *guanches* in captivity were few, the Negroes haggled from the Portuguese were even fewer, the hidalgos were abundant, and even more so those who claimed to be hidalgos; in the town halls, seething with Old Christian peasants, they collected genealogies, new bows and ceremonials were invented, new coats of arms designed, bends sinister described which generally took root in glory that derived from Covadonga or Roncesvalles; these arguments ended with a fierce assertion of pure blood, nobility, and lordship, with calloused hand upon a dagger's hilt; these farces, nonetheless, inspired by the glory of reconquest and the sting of having threadbare hose and empty stomach, did not provide the manpower to break the quarries' rocks, to bring the forests down, to mow the wheat. One desperate afternoon, perhaps, it may have been recorded that Cristóbal de Ponte had been absent from the Friday session of the Orotava council; we can picture a certain Catalan, named Soler, who covets the *converso*'s seat as *regidor*, as he starts a rumor of the latter's going off to Genoa for good, having taken the suspicious-looking boat that for some days had been seen hovering offshore; there is a historical basis to assume a rivalry, even an enmity, between the two, for the magnificent Mateo may have been one of the Genoans who robbed the Catalans of their hegemony in the Mediterranean by placing agents, in a slick maneuver, at the flanks, in Burgos, Córdoba, Valladolid, Seville, and Cádiz, to look upon the western ocean and to set themselves in business with the bold monarchs of Castile. But now let's follow in the footsteps of the inquiring party led by the imputative Soler, lantern in hand, beside the mayor, as they walk down the neglected road to Garachio; see them stop, a bit deflated, before de Ponte's unfinished house, barely illumined by an oil lamp; listen to them asking the bent, lumpy *guanche* servant girl if her mistress might be still awake, for they had come from a long way off to talk with her. This mission that the mayor led and that Soler encouraged would have discovered very little. Yes, Don Cristóbal had gone, that was quite certain, but he'd left no explanation other than a hushed good-bye and an exhortation to remake his old clothes into little caps and robes for Pedro and Bartolomé, and on no account to sell the seven-armed candelabra that had lit the Pontes' fortunes since the days of the magnificent Mateo. One week later, *mosén* Rodrigo Vivar, a knock-kneed Valencian who was certain he'd descended from the Cid and handled the meat traffic between Tenerife and Hierro, would swear to having recognized Cristóbal de Ponte on the poop of a hooker he himself had loaded with the count of La Gomera's goats and cheese. Doña Ana, almost certainly, would found fantasies on Cristóbal's course, knowing him to be astute and enterprising, so that now he came to her dressed in Molucca silks, while seasoning pastries, stews, and roasts with golden herbs and exquisite powders; of course she would have given no credence to the rumors that sent her husband following the winds that once

27

impelled that other Genoan, also named Cristóbal, who had just died in Valladolid.

The days must have passed lazily for Doña Ana; she would mark their going with the sweet impatience which in childhood she had felt as she awaited the ripening of the prickly pears, the grapes and watermelons in her father's fields; she would have stitched the days together with songs she'd improvised, perhaps, upon the verses of *Una morilla de bel catar,* or some other such distant lyric made for Moorish minstrel girls by tipsy, smiling predicants; the good Isabel, her Sevillan duenna, would grunt above the rustling of her distaff, for she'd spent her youth back in the days of *La Beltraneja* and the reconquest of Granada, and she'd deem worthy of remembrance only ballads of a martial or political cast, the ones the Catholic monarchs ordered sung in all the streets and highways; as she listened to her mistress's piquant lays, it is very likely that she meditated on the sorry consequence of marriage between *converso* and Old Christian.

The ship on which Cristóbal would return would first have been mistaken for a Portuguese caravel, one of those that sailed to Lisbon after having threaded through the islands hawking black slaves from Cape Verde or San Jorge; the ship's saluting volley would have stirred, as always, a pernicious, greedy curiosity. Without bothering to answer the salute, the whole town must have scurried down to jump in any nutshell that might float out to the ship; once there, parading in their patches and indented armor, they would have passed inspection over the poor Negroes handcuffed in a row, one local puffing out his cheeks, sunk from too much fasting, another rattling a nail-studded belt while fingering the buttocks, hard as helmets, of a slender, nervous black girl; those few who'd hoarded a half dozen of the *excelentes* minted in Granada ten years back, the first and last gold yet to glimmer on the island, would have been loath to make a show of them, for they'd fear the cadgers, taxmen, customs officers, tithe collectors, the whole band of leeches dressed in doublet and in cassock who could suck dry any purse that smelled of a transaction. But nothing of that order would happen now: lurching from among the Negroes, bronzed and arrowy, his right eye crossed and his left hand maimed, launching whip cracks right and left, bellowing, striding back and forth, turning, jumping to and fro, menacing, terrible, blaspheming and slave mongering, came Cristóbal de Ponte.

Doña Ana would have screamed to heaven as she watched the diminished figure of her husband disembark; he'd changed in more than his physique: as weeks went by she saw that something dangerous had corroded his insides, some dark, insidious thing that rent him from within, "like termites," she would note unhappily to Isabel as they sat stitching. Through the sailing master, a Venetian in the employ of Henry of England, she discovered that Don Cristóbal had leased the hooker for some ducats and a promissory note, diverting it from its explorations in order to set up commerce with the kings of Guinea; the Venetian, perhaps still excited by his own temerity, retailed a rapid-fire, arduous account of the fearsome shoals, the towers of foam, the forward lines of palm trees that quivered in the void like illimitable weathervanes, the enormous rivers whose waters, thick and yellow, spilled like oil throughout the littoral; it was there that he had seen the hippopotamus, the crocodile, and bulky, armored, short-legged unicorns that watered at the weedy, murky pools whose banks seemed as to float, to undulate, in such a devilish heat; one evening, as they went upstream, the boat was grounded in the mud; Don Cristóbal, restless with a fever, had held hard to the notion that he recognized the spot, particularly lush, and he convinced half of the men to come with him into the bush the following day, in single file, with a cannon, harquebus powder, and provisions for two weeks. . . . In the now silent boat the time dragged by with the malign monotony of those wretched, muddy waters, and only in the act of turning the hourglass could the Venetian find some notion of the passing of the hours; helped by the first rainstorm, the leaky hull rose up out of the muck, and the stay lines, which extended to both banks, became trapezes for macaques, huge rattan lattices, before the absent ones appeared, in four skiffs; bloodied and half dead, Don Cristóbal was brought in; he had the strength to mutter, as they set his shattered hand, that he had stormed a Portuguese fort upriver, and that they must send a party to bring back the slaves held there in dungeons by the traders waiting for the ships from Lisbon.

In any event, and in spite of the changes in her husband, Doña Ana would find cause to rejoice in that voyage, for it was on its account that wealth came pouring into the house at Garachio. Don Cristóbal, determined to combine the profession of moneylender with that of slaver, had sold the slaves on credit and accepted his neighbors' future harvests in lieu of payment; without losing a day, after having gauged the force of the water that flowed through his land, he had the remaining Negroes make for him, by dint of pillory and lash, two mills that had good grindstones; when the wheat was reaped and threshed, the milling done, and the accounts outstanding taken in kind, he sailed with the flour toward Grand Canary, where he not only sold the goods at his own price but also picked up orders to be filled with a new expedition he would make to Guinea, from which he would return with ninety slaves, eighteen hundred-weight of ivory, some gold, and an olive-eyed page, son of a Negress and a Portuguese, whom he had named Estebanico.

That might have been the origin of Cristóbal de Ponte's insular prosperity, give or take a few vicissitudes. We know with total certainty that his trading moved ahead before a favoring wind, extending, by the time they heard about the conquest of Peru, to the essential docksides of the Guadalquivir; this is confirmed by a contract, witnessed by the notary Alfonso de Barrera, obliging him to sell the goods of Suzardo and Sempronis, "Genoans residing in Seville," in any of the Canary Islands; with the money thus obtained, he would have purchased Negroes in the market at Cape Verde. The document does not spell out what Cristóbal de Ponte was supposed to do with the cargo; perhaps he was to head for the Canaries, perhaps Seville; the most likely thing is that he'd steer toward the Teide crest, whose crown of clouds was blackened by the woodsmoke of the mills and sugarhouses; in fact, from the canestalks that Pedro de Vera had imported to Grand Canary there would come the dense plantations that in no time were to reach the islands of La Palma and Tenerife; it was in those years that the archipelago started to become known as the *sugar islands,* so that it's almost certain that Don Cristóbal would have sold the slaves in his adoptive land, in places like the valley of La Orotava, where at that time there were three great sugarmills; of course the *converso,* without abandoning his wheat, would soon begin producing his own sugar, to be packed in cases urgently dispatched from mills at Daute and Adeje to the Genoans in Seville. Doña Ana, haggard and palpitating almost since the start of the commotion, would greet no more than four more harvests; she died on the evening of a Negro festival, holding the still chubby hands of Pedro and Bartolomé, beneath her husband's desolate gaze, the curate's orisons, and the heartfelt tears of Isabel; it should be added that her funeral was in every way the most ceremonious, as befit the sister of Vergara, *the elder,* who attended with his entourage as acting governor; on the widower's part the obsequy would have been honored with the rubicund attendance of a certain few audacious Bristol merchants, who, jaded and worn out by the latinizing funereal pomp, would have amused themselves by guessing at the outlays of the Canary sugar fleet.

His billowing success would not induce Don Cristóbal to abandon the triangular trading missions, whose vertex would continue to be Africa; knowing, more than anyone, that exports grew in direct proportion to the number of Negroes in the canefields, every so often, having made his calculations, he must have gone to sea again in the old caravel he'd bought for nearly nothing in Cape Verde. One tenebrous morning, governed by a wind from the Levant, he must have taken the caravel out upon the waves for no reason at all, or no apparent one, for it could not have been three months since he'd last sold slaves there on the islands; frowning, irresolute, and without a definite plan, with the Punta de Teno at his back, his eyes fixed on the horizon, he must have asked himself again and again what could have moved him to set sail; as night fell he would have recalled the far-off day of his first homecoming, the rowboats pulling up to the Venetian hooker, the gawkers on the dock, his wife's strange outcry as she saw him on the gangplank, the mayor's jumbled words about the rumor that he'd come back from the New World. . . . The New World, of course, the Indies, whatever you might call it, where Negroes could be sold for bags of pearls or silver bullion, where the coasts were so broad and bitten out with coves to hide in, where the islands made you almost silly, all named after brigantines and ponies; now he understood; from aboard his ship, without a route map, the New World, there, in the setting sun, was out for his reading like a damsel's favorable palm; that was why he'd cast away his moorings.

Overcome by inspiration, Don Cristóbal would have pictured himself already loading up the *Santa Ana* on the island of Hierro, buying, on credit, casks of powder and biscuit, lengths of chain; he'd return once more to Cape Verde or to Guinea, and from there, his holds full freighted, he would cross the ocean in a single stroke; at La Margarita he'd pretend to be a Portuguese, contracted by the Germans whom the emperor allowed to sell four thousand Negroes every year, and everything would work out splendidly . . . crooning with joy, Cristóbal de Ponte must have spun around to call out a starboard turn, a maneuver never to be carried out; a stealthy unexpected knife thrust from Estebanico, aimed at his neck before he turned around, would dig out his one good eye.

⟦ VIII ⟧

A PANG STUNG DEEP and made him shut his eyes. The thorny hours of his general confession gathered in his bowel like a feculence of pain which, if God the Father willed it, was to take a path of expiation through his blood. The voice of Brother Diego de Yepes, anointing his attention with the Passion's fiery unguent, grew distant like the spiral staircase of a pulpit on Good Friday that soars upward toward the steeple, while suddenly Diego's other voice grew near, the one that earlier had pardoned all his sins, every sin that the scepter and the orb had brought him to commit. Through his eyelids, now half opened, as he saw the friar signal the cross of absolution by his pillow, he learned that he had just repented something; perhaps it was the English springtime, cold and unsettling, when he had wished for Mary's death, so that he could marry Elizabeth Tudor. Now he caught a glimmer of compassion in the friar's pungent glance, if not meant for him then for his stinking, ulcerating body; he might perhaps have thought his sufferings comparable to those that had wasted Job's arms and legs down to the bone, though it could also be that they reminded him of the plagues that Moses had called down in Egypt on the transgressors of the Law.

"I beg Your Majesty's permission to retire," said Brother Diego, as he rose heavily from a chair drawn up against the headboard, "the time the doctors gave to us expired long ago."

"Ah, the doctors. . . . Well then, we'll begin again tomorrow. After the Mass I'll wait for you," he heard himself enunciate, now rapt in resurrecting words and gestures, "just one moment, though. There is a doubt that's gnawing me, and I want to hear your thoughts about it."

"If it concerns the soul, I will presume to offer counsel to Your Majesty."

"I've been thinking that I could have wiped out heresy once."

"Is Your Majesty quite sure of this?" Brother Diego asked uneasily.

"Not completely, not completely . . . I don't see the whole thing clearly."

"Then what was this chance that Your Majesty may have had?"

The confessor's query hung in suspense above the bed. Ah, if he had only not held Mary back from marching Elizabeth Tudor to the block! But, how could he destroy his chance of fathering an English son? How could he foresee that fragile girl's becoming a wet nurse to bulldogs? How could he imagine that that island, foggy with intrigues and revolts, beggared by confusion, was to claw its way to wealth behind a parvenu nobility that seized the Church's lands and had no scruple about signing contracts with the textile makers, Jewish bankers, arms procurers, pirates, the whole rotten crowd? How could he ever have foreseen that shaky crown's connivance with false princes and rebellious burghers, a gluttonous and lustful hydra that set fire to palaces and leveled altars, that wrecked the liturgy, all with the help of its damned printed Bibles?

"I didn't see it," he replied. "There was nothing I could do."

"If that's true, Your Majesty, there's no need to think about it, you're not responsible at all; God willed it thus; On the contrary, all Christendom should know that Spain was always first in fighting heresy," Brother Diego insisted.

"You're right. Perhaps it was just vanity that made me think my efforts by themselves might have sufficed to send the devil's work back into hell. This is another sin for you to pardon."

"That is no sin," Brother Diego smiled. "Your Majesty is too demanding of himself."

"One must demand more from the powerful than from the rest," he said quietly, beneath a sigh of satisfaction at his having made a phrase in the face of his infirmity. "It's easier for a camel to go through a needle's eye than for a rich man to enter in God's kingdom."

"Your Majesty has gained the gates of Heaven a thousand times by holding heresy at bay, decisively and at great expense, protecting all your subjects' souls. Think of the good you've done in sponsoring the vigilance of the Holy Office throughout Spain."

"I've tried to be a humble shepherd," he managed to say, as he heard his insides murmuring, simmering, mute and muffled, while they pulled his energy down to his bowels.

He closed his eyes. The voice of Brother Diego, pardoner of all his sins, receded, while the other one came back, the voice of the Diego come to anoint his hearing with the Passion's burning oil.

"Pilate saith unto them, Take ye him and crucify him: for I find no fault in him," the monk intoned.

Was that damnable belief now taking northern Europe not the credo of the Antichrist, the word that would confuse the world before the trumpets came to sound the Judgment?

A harrowing contraction pinned him to the bed.

To keep from crying out, he drew his meager strength into a single thought: he had done everything he could to overcome the Antichrist; what's more, he had subdued him on the frontiers of the realm. He'd be rewarded for this sacrifice.

〚 I X 〛

WE CAME UPON ANOTHER STORM on the twentieth of July, this one ten times stronger than the last and the equal of which I had never seen. The sky went dark at mid-morning, with a very sudden wind and turbid sea, and soon, tossed between the thunderclaps and towers of water, we lost sight of all the ships remaining in the fleet. I advised Juan Ginete, who had come to respect me by then as a man of substance and a veteran at sea, to unload the second deck, which had been stacked with casks, provisions, and other stores. We were at least eighty men on board, but of them we could count no more than twenty who weren't seasick. The ensign Núñez, who was very strong and steadfast, had collapsed on a straw mattress, no matter how he would have liked to stand erect, and so had the sergeant and many of the soldiers, all of them moaning and complaining of their weakness as their mouths and nostrils streamed with whatever had been in their stomachs. While these laments were breaking out below, we healthy ones heaved overboard such things as boxes of biscuit and salt fish, four of our six cannon, barrels of oil and wine and water, tackle, iron bullets and cannonballs, thick cables, and, one by one, the seven millstones that we were bringing for our settlement. The caravel lightened at these losses, but not enough; the waves kept washing over her, entering at the poop and leaving by the bowsprit, pummeling the planks and taking with them much of what they found along the way. I went up to the master and told him what we'd done was not enough, that our lives were forfeit if we didn't sacrifice the whole load; he agreed, but then confessed to me his fear of telling this to people whose belongings and whose armaments would be thrown over; I assured him that I, along with two of the best Asturian soldiers, would stand at his side, and the pilot and the sailors would also back him up, for they knew about dangers and shipwrecks, and taking me at my word he consented and we went together with our weapons ready to where the others were, and they, on hearing him speak firmly and sensibly, accepted their misfortune with such good grace that even the most seasick stood and threw whatever they had owned into the sea, though many of them wept.

The storm lasted four days, and just as we were most beset and near to foundering, when the caravel could stand no more, the wind began to calm down and then it changed direction and the sun appeared between the clouds. Astonished to come out alive from that catastrophe, we sank to our knees and praised the Lord for having saved us. But the sobbing and the oaths began again quite soon, for we had been pushed so far that neither Juan Ginete nor his pilot had the least idea of our whereabouts, the astrolabe and everything that he had kept in the binnacle having been lost to the waves. The master came to blows with the pilot over his carelessness, and hit him quite hard, when the lookout spotted something floating on our lee. We aimed our prow toward that point, thinking that it must be the remains of one of our ships, for we saw no sign of them anywhere, but it turned out to be the roof of an Indian hut, which is called a *bujío* or *bohío*. A little later we found boards and branches, and later birds, and so it was that on the fifth of August, Sunday, on the Feast of Our Lady of the Snows, we recognized the coast of Isla Deseada to our starboard, soon to be left astern.

We took to port at Dominica on Monday night, at about nine o'clock, and with the anchor cast and the full moon's light, and given our great need, the master sent out a boat with six sailors to look for water. They came back with brimming jars and a turtle that had more than twenty eggs inside its belly. They went ashore four times the next day, and with a bar of soap lent to me by the priest I managed to wash my body and my clothes.

Having taken on a fair amount of water and wood, as well as some shellfish, and having found no signs of our armada, but some signs indeed of Indians, who were Caribs, cannibals, we set sail toward the northeast and passed along the isles of Santos, Guadalupe, and the Virgins.

On the ninth of August, at dusk, we glimpsed the land of San Juan de Puerto Rico. Because of the many shoals that faced that part of the island, Juan Ginete had the sails furled to keep us still and, using good judgment, waited until dawn. We came into port at two in the afternoon and, once within, we had scarcely passed before the fort that looked out above the promontory when we saw, to our great joy, all the ships that we had sailed with, including the flagship and her tender. It seemed as though a battle had been won in those calm waters, so heavy were the volleys and the shouting and the music of our welcome. I went up to the master and the ensign to have them lower a boat and, as the caravel cast her anchors, I was taken over to the flagship to see my father-in-law.

Don Pedro received me as a son, with tears on his beard and a grand embrace and, after thanking God at our having found each other, he took me by the arm and led me into his chamber. There, in time with his devouring roasted birds, jerked meat, and sugarcane, of which he was a devotee, he explained how worried he had been on my account, for he'd known that I had traveled hidden in the caravel, there being nothing in the fleet that could be kept from him. Out of respect for my parents he had pretended not to know what I had done, but he'd kept the post of *maestre de campo* open for me, for it was there to be held by no one else. I kissed his hand to thank him for the favor, and promised that I'd give him no occasion to regret it.

The storm had damaged all the ships. The most ruined of them was the flagship, being closest to the land when hit. The winds had pulled out her entire foremast with its rigging, as well as the yards atop the mainmast, and a good deal of the gunwales. The San Pelayo nearly foundered, for when the weight of all the masts and rigging fell down on the port rail it was necessary, with the storm raging strongest, to cut the lines with hatchet blows to keep the hull from capsizing. My father-in-law told me that thirty men and seven priests had already deserted for the mountains, frightened by the dangerous seas. The governor refused to go after them, arguing that in Puerto Rico everyone who wished to stay was welcome, that the lure of gold and silver in Nueva España, Nueva Granada, and Peru had depopulated the island, especially of cassocks. He also refused to provide the fifty soldiers and twenty-four horses that my father-in-law's royal decree specified for our expedition. Nonetheless, the following day, against his will, threatened at sword point, he was forced to accede to this mandate.

With the money that he brought, which was his own and not the king's, the *Adelantado* bought a boat for carrying his new command and their mounts. Days later, when, with the ships now outfitted, we had set sail for Florida, one of the *Adelantado's* carpenters drilled a hole in the boat, and it began taking water. After the provisions, arms, and horses were jettisoned, the boat turned back toward land and beached on one of the sandbars off the coast. I wanted to go back and give those scoundrels a lesson, but the *Adelantado* smiled and shrugged his shoulders.

"You'll see a lot of rotten dealings like this one in the Antillean ports," he said to me. "Here everyone works for himself and no one helps his neighbor. They rob His Majesty of his one-fifth, they defame the honorable, and they disobey all laws and contracts that might not favor them. Heretics pass through these waters in more safety and contentedness than good Spaniards do, for the former strike their deals with the town councilors, while the latter wander about hungry and in need, because the *Casa de Contratación* doesn't provide the fleets that it ought to, and many things are lacking."

When we had glimpsed the mountains of Santo Domingo, we met up with two galleons of the fleet accompanied by a French vessel, a hooker. A hurricane had thrown the galleons into the doldrums, beyond Brazil, and after months of mishaps and privations they had set out on a return trip from Cartagena. Two days later they had come upon the hooker and another French ship on their way to Florida to reinforce the Lutherans under de

Ledoniel, who had landed and built the fort of Carlefor in those lands. Advised by the galleons' commander to abandon their mission, for King Philip would not permit it, they had surrendered to him, but the heavier ship had escaped that night. The *Adelantado* told Don Estéban Álvarez, that being the name of the galleons' captain, who was from Asturias, about the conquests and settlements that we were set to begin in Florida, and he asked for some Frenchmen to tell him where Carlefor lay. Don Estéban obliged my father-in-law, with whom he had sailed in the Indies fleet, and sent over two soldiers who said they were Catholic and who, being Gascons, spoke our language. One of them had gone with de Ledoniel on his first voyage and the other was a youth of about twenty, very frightened and somber, who was sick and would soon die. After a supper at which we tasted the wines and cheeses that the heretics took with them, which were very piquant and delicious, we said good-bye to Don Estéban with no more delay than what it took to write letters to the king, to the governor of Santo Domingo, who was supposed to provide us with four hundred men, and to the captains Menéndez Márquez and Alas, who commanded the galleons from Asturias and Biscay which were to join our armada.

In order to chase down the Frenchmen's galleon before it could land men to swell the forces at Carlefor, the *Adelantado* ordered a turn to the north, to enter a very dangerous channel through which, according to the pilots, none had ever sailed. The waves were washing over us and a sudden wind came up that nearly wrecked us at every turn, seeing which, and seeing also the soldiers' and sailors' fright, the *Adelantado* had the clergy recite their best prayers and sermons, which they all did with the greatest devotion, for ahead they saw a sandbar where the waves were breaking thunderously. When night came, and along with it an increased risk of shipwreck, my father-in-law had the sails furled and anchors cast. With the first light, throwing out the sounding lines every minute, we crossed the terrible reefs and entered the Bahama Channel, with no untoward events except for three stiff blows against the bottom which I expected at the time to split the *San Pelayo*'s keel. Taking advantage of a calm that overtook us that afternoon, we launched a boat and went from one ship to another. In the course of his inspection the *Adelantado* replaced one ship's master and two infantry captains, who had wanted to go back to Santo Domingo, and he gave jars of wine to those who had been sensible and brave. We ate supper on the admiral's ship, which was under the command of my cousin Diego Flores de Valdés, and we agreed that the arming should begin and the shot, powder, and artillery should be distributed among the ships, for in two days, if the wind came up, we would see the coast of Florida. During the supper, my cousin Diego Flores behaved quite coldly toward me, for I had offended him by being named *maestre,* a position he regarded as being one step away from *Adelantado,* and he'd let himself entertain the illusion of obtaining both titles. My father-in-law didn't act surprised, but rather drew us aside to tell us that the governing of our conquest required a head and two arms, one by land and one by sea, and those arms were my cousin Diego Flores and I, for in everything that was a seagoing matter he could rely on the admiral, and on land he had the *maestre.* But Diego Flores wasn't content with that, since the ocean had been crossed, and it was the land that lay ahead.

That very night, as we returned to the flagship, God showed us a mystery in the heavens; at about eleven o'clock a comet appeared above our heads, and it shone like the sun. It hurried toward the west, its flight through the firmament lasting long enough to say two credos. We took this phenomenon as a favorable sign.

For the safety and well-being of all, the *Adelantado* had each man fire three shots, the last one with a ball, at a target set up on the decks, since many of our men, who were were not even soldiers or were new ones, had never lain their hands upon a harquebus. When the exercise ended, our sails swelled suddenly and we moved along in very good spirits. Soon we left Grand Bahama behind and went out into the channel, entering a weedy current which, judging by the charts, would take us to Florida. During the night, with a few sails still set, we let ourselves be carried along, and the Frenchman thought that by morning we would glimpse the spot where Carlefor lay. He proved himself a good pilot, for at dawn we saw a spit of land and, just beyond, a very fine bay with a river that my father-in-law named for Saint Augustine, whose day it was.

At midday, with the envy showing on my cousin's face, the *Adelantado* ordered me to land upon the beach with fifty soldiers and begin looking for heretics or Indians who might tell me where to find Carlefor, for the Frenchman wavered, now saying it was to the north and now to the south. I marveled at the smooth coastline and the absence of rocks and shoals, for there was nothing but sand, and after imploring God's help I left ten harquebusiers to guard the longboat while we spread out looking for some branches good enough for bonfires to attract the Indians. But they didn't come, so I decided to head inland and, at a distance of about three leagues from the beach, I stumbled on a village hidden in the palms and thickets. Among those receiving us was a long-faced Indian who wore a broad-brimmed hat with a crimson plume. Another wore new green shoes, and another, who had a sweet, cajoling manner, wore a cape and sword. On seeing those bare bodies decked with so much pomp, some of the soldiers mocked them, but I scolded the men for their bad behavior, for we had to take care not to offend the people we needed as our friends. The Indians signaled with their hands to tell me that there were ships and swordsmen nearby, toward the north, and that they were numerous and traded with them. I gave them a few trifles that I had brought with me and, in spite of their embraces and fond gestures urging me to spend the night in the village, I kept two pieces of impure gold that the hatted one had given me and started back quickly to the beach, arriving before dark.

The *Adelantado* was very glad to hear what we had found and, pairing up the ships, ordered them to hoist anchor and head north. The next day, almost at nightfall, we spotted four very large enemy ships to our lee near the mouth of a river. The *Adelantado* devised an excellent plan of attack, consisting in the *San Pelayo*'s engaging with the Lutherans' flagship while my cousin Diego Flores came up against their admiral's ship; our tender, along with the caravels and boats, which carried all of our impedimenta, would withdraw and wait further out to sea. In a good wind, we anchored beside the heretics at about ten o'clock, with swords drawn and cords lighted. Don Pedro, wishing to see if they would surrender without a fight, since we were at a disadvantage, accosted the Frenchmen:

"What nation?"

"France!" a voice replied, in our language.

"What is your business here?"

"We bring men and arms to a fort that the king of France has built in these lands, and to another that he is yet to make," they answered from their flagship.

"Are you Catholics or Lutherans?"

They answered that they were all adherents of the new religion, and that their general was named Juan Ribao.

"This armada sails to serve the king of Spain, and I am Pedro Menéndez de Avilés, its commander, come to destroy all Lutherans I find by sea or land, being so instructed by His Majesty, and I shall do so when I take your ship."

The Frenchmen answered him with japes and vulgar noises.

"If you're a brave man, take us now," said one.

My father-in-law, infuriated, for he was quite punctilious about his honor, called for the grappling hooks. But the Lutherans, seeing that the combat was upon them, cut the hooks off as soon as they landed, and fled with the wind in their foresails. We gave them chase as quickly as we could, and the *Adelantado* had us shoot at them with the half-culverin at the bow.

"Stop, you scoundrels, in the name of King Philip," he shouted, and with the same gun he fired another great shot, and so five or six, which we later learned had wrecked their flagship's poop and killed eight men.

Leading our entire armada, we chased them for several days, but a menacing wind with heavy rain sprang up, and the *Adelantado* decided that we should return to St. Augustine, where we had anchored on the Eve of Our Lady, in September.

It had rained so much in St. Augustine that the river overflowed and much of the coast had been erased. Paying no attention to the water, my father-in-law landed three hundred soldiers under the command of Captain López Patiño, so that on the next day, as dawn was breaking, they would be familiar enough with the land to choose a sheltered and secure place for our entrenchment, as the Indian village was quite close upon us. The captain was most diligent and reliable, for during the night he convinced the chief, who was the Indian with the hat, to make a big hut for us upon a dune that overlooked the beach, and so it was that, by the afternoon, we had a roof above us and a moat surrounding, and a good embankment, and plenty of firewood, the wood we found there being good for nothing else.

On seeing this, and seeing too the many Indians who greeted our ships with shouts and gestures, the *Adelantado* decided to disembark, which he did with flags unfurled, to the music of drums and trumpets, followed by his captains and ensigns, all gallantly dressed, and then two hundred soldiers and artillery. A priest who had spent the night ashore had put together a procession of Indians and he, with the cross held high, came up to meet us singing the *Te Deum*. Kneeling in the sand, we kissed the cross one by one, after which Don Pedro drew himself up and took possession of those lands in His Majesty's name, while his knights and captains all acclaimed him as perpetual *Adelantado*. The Indians, like monkeys, set about carefully repeating the ceremony that they had witnessed. Some of our men were scandalized by this, and wanted to kill them, but Don Pedro stopped this punishment from being dealt them, indicating to the men who had drawn their swords that the actions of these new and docile subjects of His Majesty were not a mockery, but rather an indication of the respect in which they held us, and of their desire to please.

My father-in-law dispatched Juan Ginete's caravel to Havana and Santo Domingo to report on everything we had found and to gather the forces needed to defend St. Augustine, for the French had plenty of men in the vicinity. But one morning, after a three-day downpour that left the fort surrounded by water and looking like an island, he resolved to take Carlefor from the

Frenchmen with the soldiers that he had. While he was taking them in longboats to the dry land he addressed them:

"Although we're not at war with France, we must hit the Lutherans with blood and fire, for they give no peace to us nor we to them. They keep us from planting the Holy Word in this and other provinces, in order to extend their evil sect. We are five hundred soldiers; it seems to me that we are enough to take the fort that they've built fifteen leagues from here. We'll march through the swamps and surely take them by surprise, for they won't expect to be attacked in such high water and such wind. We must form two parties of harquebusiers, one of pikemen, and take ration for eight days in our knapsacks. We march without boys to help us, carrying our own arms, divided into ten companies with their flags. Where we find a forest, we'll hatchet out a road to let us through and show us the way back, but even if we should find none we shall not be lost, for I have with me a compass and a Frenchman who was there as Carlefor was being built and who knows the land about it two leagues round."

An increase in the daily ration of biscuit and bacon was not enough to quell the grumbling, for many soldiers' spirits fell when they saw themselves so close to war. The *Adelantado* put out a huge supper and spoke to them again, promising to give them his share of the Frenchmen's gold, which the Indians said was plentiful and good. Soon the trumpets, drums and fifes resounded, and we started on our march, with St. Augustine remaining under Don Bartolomé, the *Adelantado*'s brother. Remaining there as well, though furious, was my cousin Diego Flores, whose job it was to guard our ships from any attack by sea that the Frenchmen might devise.

We walked for a good four days with the water never below our waists nor the mud below our kneecaps. I was traveling with the rear guard beside Villaroel, the sergeant major, to keep our men from running off, when I got the word from my father-in-law to come ahead, for he had reached the fort. I found him stuck in a lagoon and looking tired, but when he saw us he addressed us resolutely:

"Carlefor lies beyond those trees," and he pointed to a thicket that lay on the right. "Tonight there will be a storm and we'll attack under its cover," he added, lifting his arm toward the clouds, heavy as carracks, that passed over us. "The two of you have behaved well, and you'll come with me in the vanguard."

At nightfall the wind howled like a pack of dogs and the rain fell thick. The *Adelantado* ordered a prayer said, and when it ended he told each captain what his place was in the fight and where to attack. The shadows were so thick that we used our weapon points to tell if we were running against wood or darkness. The water reached our nipples, and each step we took, always against the current, made us think that we'd left our flesh down in the mud. Soon the men stopped moving, and we had to pass the night in the lagoon, racked by cramps and terrified. At dawn my father-in-law sent for me, and with great difficulty I went up to him. He had the Frenchman with him, as well as five or six captains, outside the lagoon on a hill in only a foot of water.

"The fort is there three gunshots away," he said to me, his voice hoarse and ill-humored, for he had wanted to attack the previous night. "You and Martín Ochoa will go up and scout it."

After taking a swallow from the wineskin that Castañeda, my father-in-law's captain of the guards, held out to me, I went off with Ensign Ochoa toward the miserable pine trees that the Gascon's hand was pointing to. The land there was raised a bit, but still difficult to cross because of all the fallen trees. It was then that, after a few steps, the pinewoods having ended, we saw the roiling, overflowing river that spilled over into the marshes where we'd spent the night.

"The French ships that we saw before were sitting in this river's mouth," said Ochoa. "That's how Carlefor is supplied."

"Look," I said, pointing to a dozen houses that stood upon some bleak outcroppings at the treeline. "Forward!" I whispered.

❲ X ❳

A BOON, A BOON! I see the land!" sang out the aged pilot from the *Mariagalante*'s top.

Some minutes earlier, the old man thought that he had seen a silhouetted island floating, as in dreams, in the quiet half-light that foretells the dawn; despite his age he had clambered up the ratlines as nimbly as a cabin boy, knowing that behind on deck he left a watch that had been deadened by a month of sailing. Antón Babtista, sprawled on the foredeck, his bed since they had sighted the Canaries, was among the first to open his eyes, stand up, and run toward the prow anchor chains; it seemed to him then that the ship was sliding into a dark pit held open by an angel of the Final Judgment below a vault of pallid stars that kept collapsing as he looked, and he drew his wits together with a shiver and a quick sign of the cross; but the sailor standing at his side began to holler Land! and then he started prancing with an almost impossible joy, and very soon the news went flying out above the hulls and halyards of the fleet, and the whole sea swelled with jubilation and sincere thankfulness to God.

Antón Babtista was surprised at having made it safe and sound to the Indies. Each day that the trip lasted fed his discontent a little more, made him curse the hour in which he'd pocketed the gold coins that his captain, a hidalgo raised in Barcelona, had advanced him toward a slippery wage of one thousand maravedís a month; damn cheap payment for a life, he'd grunted to himself, remembering the lousy, reamed-out whore inside whose tattered costume he had left the money.

47

When will you learn, Antón, you halfwit? he asked himself each time the *Mariagalante*'s heavy pitching made his gut evacuate and sent him kneeling to the rail, leaking bilious curds from either end. Are you ever going to smarten up, you idiot? he would think, when, to amuse themselves, the hidalgos tossed him in a blanket on the poop, and he hung, bristling like a cat, above the void of darkened waves. Will you ever come around, Antón you fathead, numbskull, dolt? What differences does it make to you to reach the Isle of Ofir, or Cathay, or the Earthly Paradise itself? What's your rush to grovel at the feet of Prester John or the Great Khan? Antón, Antón, the grandees told you back beneath Granada's walls that you'd get rich; instead you got a scalding of hot grease to straighten out your back. Antón, Antón Babtista, my good man, you weren't meant to be a soldier, there is no sea anywhere more brilliant than the Ebro, and no better job than that of boilermaker in the shadow of La Seo. . . .
When the cantilena of the cabin boy—*Blessed be the Light | and the Holiest True Cross | and the Lord of Truth | and the Holy Trinity*—awakened him at dawn, he was sure that he would not survive to hear the *Salve Regina* at day's end, and the biscuit he bit into became dust between his teeth, and the rancid bacon and the slug of turbid water that he downed converted quickly into gagging, belching, and his skin had yellowed, and his teeth had loosened, and in his fever he could manage just to whimper that the Admiral was the lord of Purgatory, nothing less, since he must have died weeks ago of nausea and ill-treatment.

And yet the isle was there, no doubt about it, just off to the portside, and with it God's requital for a prolonged passage marred by hazard, scarcity, and wavering course; it sprung up in the black-and-white illumination of the dawn, still colorless, its contours undefined; and the hidalgos' horses, roped haphazardly upon the main deck, smelt the gray and vaporific beaches, and pawed and whinnied in their joy; and the roosters caged along the rails heard the awakening of woods and plains, and crowed incessantly; and then the Admiral, feeling a bit like Noah, stepped out grandly on the quarterdeck and freed a dove from his cupped hand, which overflew the ship and headed resolutely toward the island, you shall have the name Dominica, because today is Sunday, day of rest and homage to Our Lord, and Antón Babtista, like each one of the some thousand men who had sailed out with the fleet, kneeled and sang songs hoarsened with emotion, then took up fervently the introit to the Mass of unconsecrated hosts that Friar Buil had hurriedly set up. But when the *Agnus Dei* came, there was no sailor, soldier, workman, knight, or artisan still following the Franciscan's wretched Latin: the sun's rays began to scatter on la Dominica's peaks, and tonalities never seen before in autumn, not even in the Andalusian orchards, were born beneath their gaze; the island dressed from top to toe in fervent, humid green, flecked with a greenness of ripe lemons, glittering emerald green, lime green that verged on black, a green of almond trees, gold-green of oranges from the East. To the astonishment of everyone on board, the dove returned with a twig in its beak; it seemed like laurel, but it smelled of clove.

The sails of the *Gallega,* the *Colina,* and the fourteen caravels had billowed softly like silk curtains in the breeze. Their prows set schools of fish to scattering as they sailed in the *Mariagalante'*s wake into the turquoise sea, and beams hung heavily with eager men went gliding past la Dominica's craggy coast. There was no anchorage at all. The isle was like the top of some enormous, gorgeous tree that jutted from the waves. Discouraged at the silence and the immobility of the men who'd crammed themselves agains the portside rail, Antón Babtista elbowed out a spot between a doctor from Seville, named Chanca, and a scraggly Indian, one of the ones that the Admiral had brought back to amaze their Majesties at the end of his portentous voyage. Biting a lip that was blistered by thirst, he saw the minutes pass, charged with the deliberate flight of parrots, unknown fragrances, and fruits whose juicy red and purple pulp the birds were pecking, almost within his reach. The Admiral, holding the ceremonious smile that he'd put on when he freed the dove, called for a change of course, to head directly toward a neighboring island, visible since daybreak; he named it Mariagalante, to everyone's approval, since it was both fortunate and fitting to do honor to the old ship that willy-nilly, thought Antón Babtista, had performed the mission for which she had been leased from Antonio de Torres, her master and a worthy man as well.

As the island rose off the port beam, everyone moved to the leeward. Antón Babtista, knocked down flat upon the deck, pushed aside the greave of a hidalgo dressed up in his armor and poked his head out through the scupper hole; he liked what he saw: an inlet, with waters of surpassing clarity, a good spot to heave an anchor.

And to many it seemed fanciful to tread on land again, there, at least, on that little beach of fat-grained sand on which the Admiral took possession, in their Majesties' names, of distant islands that had grown like green pearls from the waves. The Sevillan doctor, as he stepped below the frondy canopy, composed in his imagination all the sentences of the report that he would send home to the Court with the first ship: and there was an astonishing thick growth of wood; that variety of trees being unknown to us, some of them bearing fruit and some others flowers; there were wild fruits of various kinds, some of which our men, not very prudently, tasted; and upon only touching them with their tongues, their mouths and cheeks became swollen, and they suffered such a great heat and pain that they seemed by their actions as if they were crazy, and this happened to a certain Antón Babtista, an Aragonese soldier, who was by me, and I cured him with cool water. We found no signs of any people living on this island, and concluded it was uninhabited. We remained there two long hours, for it was already near evening when we landed, and on the following morning we left for another very large island, situated below this one and at a distance of about seven or eight leagues and the Admiral gave it the good name of Santa María de Guadalupe, of which virgin he was a devotee. We approached it under the side of a great mountain that seemed almost to reach the skies, in the middle of which rose a peak higher than all the rest of the mountains near it, and from which many streams came out and diverged into different channels, especially toward that part to which we were proceeding. At about three leagues' distance from it, we could see an immense fall of water that appeared to us of the breadth of an ox, that came rolling down from such a height that it looked as if it were falling from the sky. It could be seen from that great distance, and it occasioned many wagers to be laid on board the ships, some people saying it was nothing else but a series of white rocks, while others maintained that it was a great volume of falling water. When we came nearer, it showed itself distinctly, and it was the latter. The Admiral ordered a light caravel to run along the coast to search for a harbor. The captain of this small vessel put into land in a boat, and seeing some houses leapt on shore and went up to them, the inhabitants fleeing in sight of our men. There he took two parrots, very large and quite different from the parrots we had before seen. He found also a great quantity of cotton, both spun and already prepared for spinning, and four or five men's arm and leg bones from which they make arrowheads. When we saw these bones we immediately suspected that we were then among the Caribbee islands, whose inhabitants eat human flesh. On the port side we could see four islands which the Admiral named Todos los Santos, and to starboard was the unending coast of Guadalupe, which seemed to us to be about twenty-five leagues in length. On the part toward which we moved it appeared all made of very high mountains, and on the part we left there were extensive plains; on the shore were a few small villages whose inhabitants fled as soon as they saw the sails of our ships. That night the Admiral resolved that some of the men should land at the break of day in order to talk with the natives, and to learn, if possible, what sort of people they were. One of the parties returned at the dinner hour with a boy about fourteen years of age. Another detachment brought in a little boy whom a man was leading by the hand, but he left him and fled; other detachments remained away longer and brought in several women natives of this island, together with other women who came willingly because they were captives there. The captain of another detachment, Diego Márquez of Seville, not knowing that we already had information about the inhabitants of this island, advanced farther away into the interior and was lost. He and his men could not find their way back to the coast until after four days. We thought they had been killed and eaten up by the people called Caribbees, for we could not account for their long absence in any other way, since there were among them pilots who, by their knowledge of the stars, could navigate either to or from Spain. The Admiral sent out four parties of fifty men each to look for them with horns and lanterns, and there were times in which we feared for the two hundred more than for the first group. But thank God the two hundred returned safely, though very tired and hungry, and without having found a trace of those who had disappeared. On the first day of our landing several men and women came on the beach, down to the water's edge, and gazed at the ships in astonishment at so novel a sight, but when a boat with some of our men was sent ashore, in order to speak with them, they cried aloud *taíno, taíno,* which is as much as to say *good,* and waited for the landing of the sailors, standing, however, by the boat in such manner that they might escape from our men when they wanted to do so. The result was that none of those men could be persuaded to join us, and only two of them were taken by force and led away. More than twenty of the female captives were taken with their own consent, and a few of the native women, by surprise, and forcibly carried off. Several of the boys, who were captives, came to us, fleeing from the natives of the island who had taken them prisoners in their own country, and they said that there were few natives there because they had gone off in ten large canoes to attack the neighboring islands. There were houses made of straw, and a considerable quantity of cotton, already spun and prepared for spinning, and many cotton blankets so well woven as to be in no way inferior to similar ones made in our country. We inquired of the women who were prisoners of the inhabitants of this island, what sort of people these islanders were, and they replied, Caribbees. As soon as these women learned that we abhor such kind of people because of their evil practice of eating human flesh, they felt delighted. And after that, if any man or woman belonging to the Caribbees was forcibly brought forward by our men, they informed us (but in a secret way) whether he or she belonged to that kind of people, evincing at the same time by their dread of their conquerors that those poor women pertained to a vanquished nation, though they well knew that they were then safe in our company. We were able to distinguish which of the women were natives of this island and which captives, by the distinction that a Caribbee woman wore on each leg two bands or rings of woven cotton, one fastened around the knee and the other around the ankle, by this means making the calves of their legs look big and the above-mentioned parts small, which I imagine they do because they believe this sort of adornment makes them pretty and graceful: by that peculiarity we distinguish them. The three islands we have seen are of the Caribbees: this one on which we are is called by the natives *Turuqueira,* the other, which was the first we saw, is named *Cayre,* and the third, on which the Admiral sank the royal pennant, is named *Ayay.* There is a general resemblance among the natives of these three islands, as if they were of the same lineage. They do no harm to one another, but each and all of them wage war against the inhabitants of the other neighboring islands, and for this purpose sometimes they go as far as a hundred and fifty leagues in their canoes. Their arms are arrows, in place of iron weapons, and as they have no iron, some of them point their arrows with a sharpened piece of tortoiseshell, and others make their arrowheads of fish spines, which are naturally barbed like coarse saws. These arms are dangerous weapons only to naked people like the Indians, causing death or severe injury, but to men of our nation they are not much to be feared. In their wars upon the inhabitants of the neighboring islands, these people capture as many of the women as they can, especially those who are young and handsome, and keep them as body servants and concubines. The captive women told us that the Caribbee men use them with such cruelty as would scarcely be believed, and that they eat the children which they bear to them, only bringing up those which they have with their native wives. Such of their male enemies as they can take away alive, they bring here to their homes to make a feast of them, and those who are killed in battle they eat up after the fighting is over. They claim that the flesh of man is so good to eat that nothing can be compared to it in the world; and this is pretty evident, for of the human bones we found in their houses everything that could be gnawed had already been gnawed, so that nothing else remained of them but what was too hard to be eaten. When the Caribbees take any boys as prisoners of war, they remove their organs, fatten the boys until they grow to manhood and then, when they wish to make a great feast, they kill and eat them, for they say the flesh of boys and women is not good to eat. Three boys thus mutilated came fleeing to us when we visited the houses. And after another four days the captain from Seville returned, who had been lost with his men, of whose return we had abandoned hope, because other detachments had gone three times out to look for them. Neither this group nor the others found any native inhabitants, either because they were few in those regions or because they had gone off to attack other islands. Our men came back so worn that it was painful to look at them; we asked how they had become lost, and they said that the thickness of the trees was such that the sailors had climbed them to get their bearing from the polestar, and they never could find it, and if they hadn't come upon the sea they would never have returned. Shortly before leaving Santa María de Guadalupe, the soldier whom I had cured of his swelling from eating of the wild fruits found the planks of a ship washed upon the coastal rocks, and it was thought that they were remnants of the wreck of the *Santa María,* which the Admiral had lost in Hispaniola during his first voyage, and that the currents had brought here. Shortly before weighing anchor, the Admiral ordered the destruction of the Caribbees' canoes used in assaulting the islands of the good Indians, whose women said that they were large islands and lay to the northwest. We had spent so much time on the island waiting for the lost men that the Admiral made measurements and spoke greatly with the pilots about the route taken and yet to take toward Hispaniola, for he was drawing in the islands we had seen now upon a very large navigational chart. With the fleet there was a certain Juan de la Cosa who also made a chart of his own, which differed greatly from the Admiral's, and they never agreed on this, though most of the pilots said that the Admiral's was correct, and not Juan de la Cosa's. But the Admiral's map would be lost, not on this his second voyage but rather years afterward, along with others that he had made with his own hands, and the chart of Juan de la Cosa remained, even though it was not correct about the shapes of those islands or the distances between them. The Admiral's rightness was seen many years later, because in Constantinople there was discovered a world map made in the year of Our Lord 1513, made by a turk named Piri Reis, and this cosmographer said that he had taken the shapes, placements, and names of these islands from the Admiral's navigational chart, which had been found on a Christian ship that his people had captured, on which there was a pilot who had sailed on this voyage with the Admiral. There was Santa María de Guadalupe, which everyone called Guadalupe, and the isles had names very similar to those by which we knew them, as Guadalupe was *Vadluk,* Mariagalante was *Galanda,* Santa Cruz was *Samokristo* and San Juan Bautista was *San Cuvano Batisdo* and many others went like that; and this world map of Piri Reis became very famous for the reason I have just mentioned, and also because it appears below a large and very distant western land, which was always frozen and covered with snow, which no one knows anything about, and which was not on the Admiral's chart, and it is a mystery and a marvel that it should be there because neither was it on the charts of Vespucci, the Cabots, Magellan, or El Cano, and nobody can explain its discovery.

We left that island of Santa Cruz eight days after our arrival there. Then on the following day another island was seen, not very large, which must have been at a distance of twelve leagues; he named the new island Santa María de Monserrate, and we went along its coast, and the Indian women who came with us said that it was uninhabited, that the Caribbees had wiped it out, and therefore we did not stop there. Then that afternoon we saw another, which the Admiral decided to call Santa María la Redonda, and it was a rounded rock, small and leaning, under half a league in length; that night, near that island that I just mentioned, we found some shoals, fearing which we dropped anchor, not wishing to proceed until the day. When morning came, we saw another island, quite large, and it received the name of Santa María la Antigua, who is the Virgin of the Seville Cathedral, and the Admiral's protectoress. We stopped at none of these islands, for we were traveling quickly to relieve those who had stayed in Fort Navidad, for they must have been in dire need ever since the Admiral left them in Hispaniola. The next day at suppertime we reached an island that seemed quite populated in that it had many tilled fields. We went there and anchored off the coast, and the Admiral sent out a boat to the land, with a detachment of men to try to take some captives and see what kind of people they were and to get information about the route to Hispaniola. We took five or six women there, most of them already captives, as on the other island, because this island belonged also to the Caribbees. When the boat came back to the ships with its captives, we observed that there came along the coast a canoe in which there were four men, two women, and a boy, and as soon as they saw the fleet they began to marvel and stare dumbly, and did not stop being thus entranced for more than an hour, during which they did not move from where they were, at about two gunshots distance from us. Then our men in the boat went up to them, by the shore, for the amazement that they must have felt had kept them from seeing anyone until they were very near to them, and they could not flee very well although they tried hard to do so; but our men hurried so that they could not escape. The Caribbees, once they saw that flight would not avail them, daringly took up their bows, the women as well; and I say daringly because they were no more than four men and two women, and ours were more than twenty-five, of which they wounded two, one with two arrows in the chest and the other with one in the side, and if they hadn't been carrying shields and wearing breastplates, and hadn't come upon them quickly and overturned their canoe, most of them would have been stuck with arrows. And after the canoe had been capsized, they kept swimming in the water, sometimes standing, because there were some shoals there, and our men had a difficult time in taking them, for they still shot arrows when they could, and with all that only one could be taken and only after having been badly wounded by a lance, and they brought him thus wounded to the ships. But his wound was so bad that his entrails were spilling out and I said that he could not be saved; and this Antón Babtista of whom I have spoken took the Caribbee around the waist and threw him overboard, but these barbarians are so bold that they neither surrender nor admit defeat, and so the afore-mentioned captive began to swim toward land with the power of but one arm and one hand, as with the other he pressed his entrails to keep them from falling out; and the boat captured him again halfway there and took him back to the ship, and there they tied his arms and legs together and threw him into the water again, but this didn't work, for the Caribbee untied the bonds and they had to shoot many arrows into him to kill him. And their women are just as fierce, they are like Libyan lion-esses, and a very beautiful girl, whom the Admiral would give as a slave to Michele de Cuneo, being naked as is their usage, moved Cuneo to want to take pleasure of her, but the girl refused and fought with her nails and teeth so hard that four men were needed to subdue her and tie her to the mast; there Cuneo whipped her with a rope, and the girl let out a huge outcry until she fainted, and only then could Cuneo have his way with her; later he said that he had come to terms with her, and he was overjoyed because she was as if taught in an academy of whoring. The difference between these Indians and the oth-ers in dress is that the Caribbees have very long hair, while the others are shorn and have their heads dressed in a hundred different ways, some painted with crosses and various figures, each one done at the bearer's whim, and effected with sharp-ened reeds. All of them, the Caribbees as well as the others, are beardless people, and it is a miracle to find one who is not. These Caribbees that we took had their eyebrows and lashes dyed, and it seems to me that they do it for ornament, and to make them seem more frightful to us. We then left from Santa Cruz on that day, and we had been there but six or seven hours. On the morning of the next day we came upon a place that seemed different from any we had seen, more than forty tall and discontinuous islands, most of them bare. It seemed like land that would contain metals, and we saw mountains of purple and other diverse and brilliant colors. The Indian women said that they were uninhabited islands, and the Admiral named them Santa Ursula and the Eleven Thousand Virgins, who were all Cornish navigatrices and good patronesses of sailors. On the next afternoon we came in sight of the island the natives call *Burenquen,* whose coast we followed all day long. It was judged to be some thirty leagues on that side, and the Admiral named it San Juan Bautista. This island is very beautiful and fertile seeming; the Caribbees come here to conquer, and they carry off many people. The island's natives do not have canoes, nor do they know how to travel by sea, but, according to the Caribbees that we took, they use bows as they themselves do, and if by chance they defeat the attacking Caribbees, they eat them just as they would have been eaten. We were two days in one of this island's harbors, but we were never able to take any captives, for they all fled in fear. All of these islands were discovered along this route to Hispaniola, for until this point the Admiral had seen none of them on his other voyage; all are very beautiful and have very fine land, but the one they called *Burenquen* seemed the best of all of them. There is certain to be land toward the east as well, for we saw some birds that they call stringtailed, which are marine birds of prey and do not rest or sleep upon the sea; from which all judged that there was land in that direction which is east of us along the route to Spain and which we did not explore so as not to turn around. And that day, before nightfall, we caught sight of more land, and the Indian women that we carried began singing and swaying, and it was the great island of *Haytí,* for that is what the Indians call Hispaniola, and there our voyage ended.

⟦ XI ⟧

A Y, JESUS!'' his father had blurted as he died, his look fixed on the selfsame cross that good Toledo, for the second time now, brought Philip in his bed. Soon his suppurating hands would clench upon the traces left by that imposing man, the man whom he had most loved, respected, admired, mourned. . . . He had been in Brussels when they told him of his father's death, caught up in a war he never understood, that had no conquerors or conquered, where he might wear the laurels of St. Quentin on one day, while that same day the duke of Guisa swept down suddenly upon Calais, to strip the English of their last remaining foothold on French soil. Wars had turned out to be much more complicated than he had supposed, much less glorious: vanity, sacrilege, betrayal, bloody skirmishing, and, above all, debt, with the reins of power in the bankers' hands, with Jews tugging on the left, Genoans in the middle, and Fuggers on the right.

What would happen to him with his father gone? A frigid wind had set him shuddering; it knocked him down into his chair, helpless, wilted like those autumn leaves that palace gardeners swept up into piles along the edges of the lawns to be burned off together and then blown away as ashes in the wind. He thought for a moment of concluding peace with France and then, under Princess Juana's regency, he might abdicate to Carlos, his unlucky son. He could retire to Yuste, as his father had, and there he could forget the world. Mary was no impediment; the last dispatch from London, sent by Feria, his ambassador, had made her out as almost dead, shut up within her chambers, jaundiced with a fever, frightened by conspiracies and her own darkening aloneness. It was then, in the Royal Chapel, as the priest raised up the Consecrated Host, that he first glimpsed his earthly mission: martyrdom, quiet martyrdom, persevering martyrdom; he would look for a region in Castile that radiated peace and quiet grandeur, and there he'd build a basilica to suit his need and taste, a monastery out from which he'd rule as none had ruled before: he'd take upon himself, like a self-mortifying lash, responsibility for everything that happened in his realm, each subject's life and destiny; his office would become a tabernacle where daily he would consummate a living sacrifice, his body and his blood become the bread and wine of his redemption.

Some weeks, before, as he arranged the details of his burial, he remembered that within the archives he had kept a chronicle of his father's funeral. He had the document brought up to him, and Brother Diego himself, who was revisiting the painful stations of the cross, had read it to him at his bedside. "Leading the long procession were the priests and monks, the cantors of the Royal Chapel, the prelates, bishops, and deputies from Flanders, two hundred paupers dressed in tunics and black hoods, court constables, grooms, and pages. Then came a boat covered with imperial insignias; after that there was a sea with two beacons and two sea monsters, then a horse in yellow, gray, and violet harness upon which Saint James rode. Each dominion of the emperor's was represented by a corsair dressed in mourning; then came the mace bearers and the dignitaries; the duke of Alba and the grandees finished the procession."

Hearing those distant words revived for him the details of the funeral. The eagles embroidered on the black standards regained their luster for a moment, he could hear the trumpets' music and the Legion's martial tread; it filled the room, dissolving the expectant faces of the death watch, the fog of snuff and resin that hung there in Santa Gudula's yawning nave, pressing out against the arch and ceiling . . . as his memories returned, he decided that in death he'd have his body wrapped inside a sheet tied with an ordinary rope that held two sticks to form a cross.

〚 X I I 〛

B Y   T H E   T I M E   T H A T interest in sugar from the Canaries
had declined, owing to its oversupply and the competition
from the islands of America and of the Barbary Shariff,
Cristóbal de Ponte would have grown old and many years would
have passed since he'd made his last voyage on the *Santa Ana;*
the reversal could not have taken him by surprise, as had the fell
stroke of Estebanico—who, inscrutable to the end, would have
died forthwith strung up from a topmast—as in the first year of
his blindness he would say to his son Pedro, the favorite, that he
ought to burn away a part of the Adeje cornfields and then plant
Malvesie grapes there upon the ashes; this substitution, whose
economic yield would soon surpass what the sugar had brought,
would not occur by chance, but rather through his viticultural
practices, commercial contacts, and a drawn-out argument
among the isle's most active landholders, divided for and against
the implantation of the Grecian vine; the introduction of this
lucky crop should be regarded as a part of the Canary Islands'
total picture in the first third of the century, before the Crown
imposed restrictive measures to cut back the tender mercantile
shoots aimed toward America, France, and England, which had
meant an appreciable traffic in flour, sugar, dragon's blood,
orchil, hides, silk, and even fabrics as diverse as taffeta, satin,
and velvet. Cristóbal de Ponte, who would never have lost the
ambition and initiative of youth, must have been first to experi-
ment with those vines from far away and first to feel between
his then-unfurnished gums the bursting of those dusty, sweet-
skinned grapes, as fat as plums, whose juices would ferment to

one of the best wines of the era; it seems likely that his cousin, Giacomo de Ponte, a naturalized Englishman whose ambition led him not just into Devon's high commercial circles but might even have brought him into contact with the area's nobility through the marriage of his daughter to Sir Walter Raleigh of Fardell, would have hurried to broadcast, for a reasonable commission, the excellence of the wines of Tenerife; in any event, recommended or not by his *cugino inglese,* Cristóbal de Ponte would have received, in the mansion at Garachio, on one of those afternoons, perhaps, in which his bones cooked in the hot wind from the Levant, a foreigner with a hoarsened voice whose clothes smelled of sargassum and who from the door announced himself to the decrepit Isabel as William Hawkins, sailor, armorer, and merchant from the port of Plymouth.

And so would have begun a close commercial friendship, characterized by that mysterious gloom that hovers over all late-blooming contacts, especially those between two people who are feeling that they've lost their souls.

[XIII]

W E STOLE IN SECRET up to the Lutherans' houses.
We made out the first of them, a short one built of logs
and mud, and proceeded alongside it trying to hear
some sound within, but it seemed deserted. When we reached
the second house we turned left to find an enormous fallen pine.
From there, hidden behind the branches, we saw the sturdy
stockades and watchtowers of Carlefor. The morning light reflected off its front.

"In faith, *maestre*," Ochoa murmured, "scaling that wall is
going to cost us a lot of men."

I said nothing, but Ochoa seemed quite right to me.

Quickly we turned back to report to the *Adelantado*, but as we
approached the houses we saw a fat soldier leaving one of them,
stretching, with a hunk of bread in his hand. He was not wearing
a helmet, but he did wear a breastplate and he carried a sword.
Since we couldn't hide, we went right up to him.

"Who's there?" the Frenchman asked, with his mouth full.

"France," Ochoa answered, stepping forward.

As we drew near, the man realized that we were not of his
nation, but when I saw how surprised he was, I came at him with
my sword and hit him such a quick blow to the neck that he fell
down backward without trying to defend himself. He looked at
me with the eyes of a startled ox, and trying to cry out, he
opened and closed his mouth without producing anything but
choked breaths and clots of blood and biscuit. Ochoa pulled him
up and pinned his arms.

"Kill him, *maestre*," he said to me as he wrestled with the man. "If he yells, we're lost."

I had killed many men in combat, but never a defenseless one, since in His Majesty's galleys we healed the wounded Turks to trade them for our own. My sword had stuck right through the poor man's neck, and the simple act of withdrawing it repelled me.

"Kill him, *maestre!*" Ochoa insisted.

Someone jumped up beside me, shoved me away, and split the Frenchman's head with a single chop. It was my cousin Diego Flores, and I was astounded, since I had thought that he'd stayed back at the bay of St. Augustine.

"If you can't stand a bloodstain, you've picked the wrong profession," he said to me under his breath, without Ochoa's having heard.

"Santiago! Attack them!" a voice roared out behind me. I turned around and, half-stupefied, without thinking to pull my sword from the Lutheran's neck, I saw the *Adelantado* charging uphill before the vanguard.

"Victory! Santiago! Victory!" my father-in-law cried. "Death to the Lutherans!"

I pulled myself out of my daze and, after pulling out my sword, ran up beside him. Three Frenchmen came out of the last house, wakened surely by my father-in-law's shouting. They were unarmed, and they fell with pikes stuck through them. When we reached the fort's entrance, the gate opened a bit. But I wedged my sword into the crack, worked open the wooden slab with my shoulder, and jumped over a body to get inside of the fort.

"Help the *maestre!*" someone said.

I looked back and saw the soldier on the ground take aim at me with his crossbow. No shot came from that weapon, however, which stayed mute, but rather from Villaroel's smoking harquebus, which I saw in the porthole at the gate.

The Frenchmen, astonished by so much shouting and thunder, stuck their heads through the windows and came out on the flooded esplanade that stretched out before the gate. They came half-dressed, in their shirtsleeves, and some of them brandished their swords weakly, without showing any more martial aspect than their women, who ran shrieking through the plaza and the galleries, from one corner to another, their arms upraised or filled with children, almost all disheveled and barefoot.

The men died like pigs, many still naked underneath their tables and cots, others spread-eagled in the stable's mud amid taunts and whinnies. Some managed to flee along the granary roof, dropping on the other side of the stockade. When I got there, I saw that they were trying to escape in a boat that they'd shoved out from the dock. Their general, Renato de Ledoniel, went with them, and before he could disappear downriver Ochoa broke his arm with a musket shot.

"We'll settle accounts with you!" Ledoniel shouted in Spanish.

We were set to jump over the fence and take one of the boats that they left behind on the dock, but halfway aboard I was stopped by the *Adelantado*'s voice.

"Let them go. The Lutherans on shipboard ought to know what's happened here."

"Then you don't want to exterminate them all?" I asked, with a certain insolence, when I came down from the granary.

His face turned very grave, for as I have already said, my father-in-law was punctilious.

"Well, let's be clear, my dear *maestre*. First it makes you sick to kill a heretic and now you're giving me lessons in war. Do you think I can give the Frenchmen a good fight after the days of privation that my men have just been through? Tomorrow you'll see half the troop wake up with rheums, catarrhs, fevers, colics, and shits. Let the heretics think things over; it wouldn't be strange if they chose to surrender their arms."

And upon hearing a sudden commotion in the granary, which turned out to be the scurrying of soldiers after a little band of Lutherans, the *Adelantado* went off, leaving me resolved never to say another word to him about one of his orders.

By midmorning there had been so many duels and quarrels, burnings, rapes, and gunshots that the *Adelantado* assembled the thirty men of his guard along with all of his captains.

"Disarm your soldiers and take them out of here, or you'll see the unraveling of my army," he told the captains. "Make your camp in the houses outside the stockade and in the dock buildings, and you'll be provided there with all you need. Keep no one near you but your ensigns, sergeants, and men you trust, and hang anyone who disobeys, without hesitation. I'll back you up from here."

I saw in the gestures and murmurings of certain captains some signs that they were unhappy at what had just been said. One of them, San Vicente, an elegant man, roused himself to protest.

"Don Pedro de Avilés has promised us plentiful riches and pleasures," he said, rising with his hand on his hip, ready to draw his sword. "Is this how his excellency rewards the blows we have struck on his behalf? It would seem to me more fitting to thank the soldiers. . . ."

A crossbow shot sent San Vicente's helmet flying, and it landed rattling in a corner.

Some of the captains jumped up with their hands on their swords; others rushed up to San Vicente, who, white as a sack of flour, picked himself off the floor and touched his forehead, where there was some blood.

"Your worship must excuse my clumsiness," said Castañeda calmly, stepping out from behind a table piled with armaments. "I was playing with one of these Lutheran contrivances, and I'd never trade my red crossbow for ten of them, but now look what I've done," he added, seizing the weapon by its stock and hurling it through the window.

"Control yourselves, gentlemen, and keep your swords in their sheaths, for we're all men of good will here, and nothing serious has happened," the *Adelantado* said, and he got up from his chair to go to San Vicente, whom he took by the head, the better to see his wound. "Captain," he said, turning toward Castañeda, "I swear you really ought to be more careful. Apologize again to the brave knight San Vicente, and give him an embrace, for I value him most highly and you nearly broke his head."

Castañeda, showing signs of great contrition, hugged San

Vicente so strongly that their breastplates clanged as though they'd fallen on the floor.

"Ho, Gabrielillo!" Don Pedro called to his servant. "Bring out the good wines that you took from the Frenchmen's store, and we'll raise our glasses to the glory of King Philip."

And that was the end of the incident.

On leaving the room I came upon Diego Flores and, seizing his arm, I stopped him.

"You owe me satisfaction for what you said this morning," I said. "And this seems the right time for me to claim it."

"You are rather slow to understand, Don Pedro. Don't you see that the *Adelantado* was doubting your ability as a soldier when he sent word for me to join the vanguard?"

"Then," I replied, furious, "do me the favor of drawing your sword, so that we can tell with steel which one of us is better."

"As you like. I'll wait for you at midnight at the very place of your weakness, then you can try to purge your fear with blood."

"By the wounds of Christ, what's going on here?" the *Adelantado* suddenly exclaimed, having heard us through his window. "Go get some rest and save your bravado for fighting the heretics; there are many hundreds of them left to overcome. You're still my *maestre* and you my admiral," he added, scolding us like children at war over a piece of candy, "but you're novices in spite of your campaigns, and if I ordered you separately to face the enemy it was so that you could shine before your captains and soldiers, because they're going to have to respect you if I get sick or wounded. You, Don Pedro, have gone resolutely up against the Lutherans, and you, Don Diego, have fought astutely and fiercely. Try in the future to copy each other, because both qualities are necessary. Now make up," he said, extending the handle of his sword, "and swear never again to use your arms against each other."

Approaching the window, and without looking at one another, we held out our right hands above the sword's hilt.

"I swear," said Diego Flores, resentfully.

"I swear," I repeated, knowing that sooner or later we would face each other down.

67

We went away by separate routes.

The following day, far from what one might have expected, the troop departed without any untoward event. Since the sun had come out and the Frenchmen were beginning to stink, it was easy to convince the soldiers to take the bodies by their hands and feet and drag them out of the enclosure, then throw them into the river, all of which quickly turned into a great amusement, as three carts with kegs of wine, loaves of bread, hams, and cheeses were taken to the dock, and what's more, the *Adelantado*'s musicians had been sent there. Don Pedro was surprised to hear them playing airs from Cádiz, since the fifes, bagpipes, and tabors suited some *seguidillas* for guitars that they had brought over with them, and although he was not going to say anything about it, I noted that it bothered him to see those hardy Cantabrian boys stepping, clapping, and bending like Andalusians, whom he had always regarded as effeminate wastrels. Before leaving to change the guards, he charged me with investigating the rumor that the Lutherans hadn't fought because they were all infected with the plague. I went at this task so thoroughly that after a little more than an hour the commotion had died down, with only the clerics' preaching and the supplicating prayers and vows being heard, and in truth it was hard to believe that those pious men kneeling there in the drizzle were the same ones who, a little while back, had delighted in tossing one hundred and forty dead heretics into the current, who had drunk and gobbled wagonloads of refreshment, who had swayed to the rhythm of the songs, who had stripped off their clothes to waggle their members at the Frenchwomen.

By afternoon some of them were stiff with rheumatism, others swollen with indigestion, while the rest complained of coughing and nausea, and begged the *Adelantado* to let them sleep in the forest, since they had suffered so many ills of both body and spirit at the sight of that damned stockade.

After loading a boat at the dock, and also a two-masted bark which, already caulked, was filled with all the arms and provisions we had found at Carlefor, as well as the women and children who had survived, the *Adelantado* sent them sailing downriver along with some artillery and forty soldiers. As the captains were not happy with these boats because of the few soldiers that they carried, Don Pedro said to them:

"Don't worry; there's no reason for it. If you meet any Lutheran warships at the river's mouth or along the coast toward St. Augustine, have the smallest children placed inside the cannons, so that their heads stick out and can be seen; be careful that they're all males, because King Philip's generals shouldn't be known as woman killers."

The captains, convinced by my father-in-law's reasoning, ceased their complaining and cast off, to the great anguish of the Lutheran women, who had read the meaning of the gestures.

Remaining in Carlefor, to be taken by land with the body of the troop, were four Catholic Frenchmen and a Portuguese who said that he was a Hieronymite friar. The *Adelantado* had already talked with them, but to see if they were truthful he ordered them to go with his chaplain to have their faith and consciences examined. I was eating supper with my father-in-law when López Patiño asked permission to interrupt us.

"Speak, *señor*," the *Adelantado* said contentedly. "Eat here with me if you haven't done so yet."

"I thank your excellency for the invitation, but I've already eaten. I came only to tell you that the Portuguese is a friar and three of the Frenchmen are Catholics, but the fourth doesn't even know the *Ave María*."

"Is he eager to be baptized and swear to the true faith?"

"He asks for nothing else, *señor*."

"Let him be baptized, then, and afterward, for being a liar, he shall have his tongue cut out," the *Adelantado* decreed. "Wait," he added, stopping the captain, "perhaps you should just whip the rascal a bit. We want him to make his words understood in Heaven."

I could not tell easily when, in governing those lands, one ought to use severity and when leniency, and seeing a ripe occasion, I confessed this uncertainty to my father-in law.

"I couldn't explain it to you, Don Pedro," he said to me after thinking for a while, "since many times I don't know myself whether I'm doing right or wrong, whether I should spare a life or cut it down, whether I should be benevolent or be a scourge, and I swear I think the same thing happens to the king, because the only one who knows the measure of all things is the Creator. Now then, if you should come to govern this province in my daughter's name, do as I do, proceed according to your own lights and look always toward the glory of Spain; try to abide by the Holy Commandments and the commands and orders of your superiors, but only to the extent that this favors your mission. I warn you that you will kill here, fornicate with Indians and blacks; you'll steal and bear false witness against your friends, and you'll commit many other repugnant crimes, for the maintaining of the order demanded by our Church, which is the marrow of our kingdom, will force you into it. But anyway, don't go running to the confessor, because it will turn you into a lost soul; rather keep your sins within your own conscience and repent them every day, and pray to God for a good death. That's all I can tell you."

And with a wrinkled frown, and wobbling a bit, the *Adelantado* left the table without finishing his supper and without even bidding me good night.

⟦ XIV ⟧

TOLLING, TOLLING . . .
   Bells tolling through his last night. The bronze voices beat out a drowsy vigil of pangs and starts that had been his sleep for weeks. Now he felt no pain at all, but fright; in a while this would recede, giving way to pain, then fright again, then pain, and so on for as long as God desired. If there were only a way that the pendulum of suffering could be unhinged, to allow a single unexpected hour of truce, without faces, names, or bad surprises; only an hour, a touch of Lazarus's finger dipped in water to allay the rich man's thirst. But wasn't he then Lazarus himself, dying, covered everywhere with sores? One hour, Lord, just one! I beg a single hour, one small hour! . . . The sound of the heavy bells stopped. He peered out through half-opened eyes and saw no more slack shadows there to serve his agony. He looked around expectantly; he was all alone within his chamber at San Lorenzo el Real, before a stack of files and folders, his gouty leg stretched lightly out to rest upon a chair. He wondered if he ought to call for Eraso or Idiáquez; one of them perhaps might tell him what was happening. Perhaps he'd gone to sleep after eating plums, he'd never stomached them; perhaps his sickness, his prostration, had been nothing but a nightmare. Or perhaps the Lord had heard him and had stopped his torment for the moment. He looked for a tray on the table, for a pile of plum skins and pits, but saw nothing there but papers, heaps of papers that he didn't bother to identify. Then, intruding on his little prayer of thanks, the bells again began to toll. They were not the bells that for some weeks he'd

heard above his bed, the bells for souls in Purgatory; rather they were a jubilant erupting carillon of doves and towers, a wedding peal, or for some great victory of the faith, a prince's or infanta's baptism. He thought whether to call for Eraso or Idiáquez. He decided upon Eraso, the faithful one; no not Eraso, for he'd been carried off by plague at the Cortes of Aragon; if he called for him, would he appear? But he'd had enough of deaths, enough of dead men. He stood up, with some effort, although, encouragingly, with much less than he'd expected. He took his cane and, scarcely limping, walked in the direction of the gallery door, and opened it. A halberdier with bushy brows and chestnut beard stood negligent guard.

"Those bells, can you tell me what they mean?"

The man, surprised, gesticulated in the air; he took his shoulder from the wall, then tripped and dropped his halberd to the floor, where it landed with a shattering report.

"Can't you hear them?"

The guard picked up his weapon, mumbled an obscenity, and then resumed his careless pose.

"Can't you hear them?" he repeated angrily. "The bells. . . ."

It was then that he remembered:

As God ordains whatever should occur, and as His ends are not for men to know, but yet beneficent for being His, whatever might have happened is what serves His glory and the betterment of souls. The failure, then, of the Armada that we sent against the English does not call for lamentation, but rejoicing. The deaths and losses that occurred, no matter what their number, we should greet with happiness and not with weeping; the churches and the monasteries of the realm shall thank the Lord, and every show of mourning shall be banned.

So that joyous flight of clappers had been brought on at his own behest, proclaimed triumphantly through village, town, and city. It had been his way of showing his humility to God, his willingness to bend before His will. Ah, but at the cost of so much suffering.

He closed the door and went back to his work table. As he resettled his aching leg upon the chair, it occurred to him that the Lord was asking him to run through the days of those he'd spent as king that most resembled Calvary. He breathed a sigh of resignation and then put his hand, as if in yet another torment that he had to bear, into the mass of documents concerning the Armada. His trembling fingers touched the woeful pile: here a debt, there an accusation, there a frightening dispatch. He mustered up the will to finger through a vaguely annotated day-book, recorded in a minute hand; quickly he scanned the opening lines; it was the diary of the duke of Medina Sidonia, that unlucky wretch. He tried to put the notebook down, but his hands and eyes were governed by a febrile longing for a moral martyrdom, and after a cold shiver had passed entirely through him, he let himself submit to God the Father's plan, just as Christ must surely have submitted to the Cross.

Once a page was read, the paper withered, cracked, caught fire, and disappeared in a burst of flame, to leave a residue of moaning ashes, drowning gasps, ships drifting aimlessly, roaring rocky outcrops, frozen gales, garbled prayers, and ugly curses, promises to God and Satan drowned out by the blast, the thunder, and the darkened rain, and over all that evil came the coarse, vulgar laughter of Elizabeth Tudor. Before all of his five senses passed the ill-preserved conserves that the provisioners had sold, the barrels built of new-cut wood that made the water putrefy, the treachery, incompetence, capriciousness, the fear, improvisation, and temerity, but always, within each detail, defeat, and death, there was the scent of veiled recrimination toward himself, and it was this that made him suffer most, in truth this was his only torment, how to make them understand, Lord, that if You had willed it so, the heretics would have been smashed at sea, then swept away among the ruins of London, for a poor shepherd having You to guide his hand could overcome a pack of wolves, how could he make them understand so obvious a truth, he had said publicly that he could fight with men but not against the elements, and his words had not been understood; far from being coined out of his pride, they had come from his humility and his obedience, and therefore, to make them unmistakable, he decreed a joyful ringing of the bells at the disaster, the disaster that had shown the splendor of

Divine Providence to all men living and to come, for England had not conquered nor had Spain been overcome, but rather God had worked His will upon all things.

The night was coming on. The window's slatelike light now scarcely let him see the letters' outlines. With a tired resolve he read on to the end of Pedro de Valdés's final letter, reeking of stupid arrogance, then held it toward the corner of the table, where it made a sudden yellow flame. Just at that moment the festive bells stopped ringing and a sharp silence like a needle's prick informed him that his hour's reprieve had ended. Certainly he'd felt no pain or upset while he had been working, but the martyrdom had never ceased, and it was plain to him that God the Father would not take the bitter chalice from his lips. A heavy bell announced the *Angelus Domini,* and he knew that he would have to resume the Purgatory of his bed. Over the heaped-up ashes on the table, he cast a look out toward the walls and corners of the room that he so loved and that had seen so many of his vigils: there, in the depths, he saw a clump of painful silhouettes whose features he could not discern in the penumbra, only the blurry pallor of their hands and foreheads bent down over stiffened collars. The door to his bedroom opened slowly in a whisper of hinges, and the outline of his daughter Isabel Clara Eugenia occupied the doorway's hollow: "His Majesty is asking for the candle and the crucifix," she said, sobbing.

Now, urging him to leave the study, each stroke of the bell came on him like a hammer blow upon the nails of his excruciation, to drive them deeper in his fibers, to bore into and to break his bones. With a brave effort he managed to lower his leg from the chair where it had rested, and with the help of his cane he passed through the expectant mourners. As he reached his stinking bedroom he pitied the scabby rag doll who lay looking hopelessly around, with a crucifix in one hand and a lighted candle in the other, imploring death to end his agony of sores and diarrhea. He sat down on the bed and stretched out upon the sunken, hollow carcass.

[XV]

IT WOULD NOT BE until after the peace of Cateau-Cam-
brésis that relations between the houses of de Ponte and
Hawkins—now carried on by their progeny, of course—
would emerge from what could be called their heroic period.
There are signs enough, however, to lead one to conclude that
an important traffic was established, in those obscure years,
between Adeje and Plymouth, carried out by rapid thirty- or
forty-ton packets, often piloted by William Hawkins himself, or
by one or another of his sons Will and John. And so the taste for
Don Cristóbal's wine, and for everything that went into the
planting of malvesie vines in Tenerife, quickly took root in
England thanks to its extraordinary quality, Hawkins's spon-
sorship—his voyages to Guinea and Brazil were still remembered—and the efforts of Giacomo de Ponte, if indeed he ever
made any. In London it was known as sherry, sack, malvasia, or
just simply as canary; it could be drunk, without fear of significant adulteration, in The Ox and The Bell, two inns on the well-
traveled road from London Bridge to Bishop's Gate, and in The
Mermaid, a reputable tavern near St. Paul's, frequented by merchants, theater folk, and sportive gentlemen, who used to whit-
tle their feats of gourmandizing on the benches, tables, pitchers,
and beams; well into another century, during the Jacobean
reign, people were admiring still the following inscription,
carved modestly upon a wooden tablet:

One capon 2s2d
Sauce 4d

```
Canary wine, four gallons .......................... 7s8d
Anchovies & more wine ............................ 2s6d
Bread ........................................... gratis
```

The tavernkeeper, a crypto-Catholic who delighted in twisting everything that happened in order to promote uncertainty, attributed that grand consumption of canary wine to Sir John Falstaff.

What is certain is that the malvesie's renown stopped only at the frontier of poor Scotland, and that at the deaths of Don Cristóbal and William Hawkins, which happened just a few months apart, certain intruders more than simply stuck their noses into the canary wine trade, first of all the house of Hickman & Castlyn, of London, which even before the war had posted a certain William Edge as agent in Tenerife, knowing that the island's wine production reached a total of twelve thousand barrels; Hawkins and Don Cristóbal both made impossible efforts to hold on to a monopoly of malvesie, but Tenerife, overnight, became a giant vineyard, and districts like Icod were now adding *de los vinos* to the names they'd registered in the old parchments. Perhaps, on one of his visits to Garachio, Hawkins might have spoken to Don Cristóbal about one of his more celebrated voyages; and perhaps the latter, in reply, confided the source of all the flour mills, the sugarhouses, vineyards, canefields, wine cellars, wharves, and warehouses that his sons Pedro and Bartolomé administered; but it is certain that one William Edge, of the house of Hickman & Castlyn, never did suspect that all those holdings were acquired through a handful of Negroes brought to Tenerife some fifty years before.

⟦ XVI ⟧

S O T H E R E Y O U A R E, Antón Babtista, feeling like a duke
from the vantage of your lousy hammock, your feet mold-
ering with sores and chiggers, your loins festooned with
pustules that all the arboreal waters of the guayacán will never
cure; there you are, shooing mosquitoes and sweating out the
midday fever, underneath the pallium of branches that you've
improvised to overhang your miserable pomp; there you are,
Antón Babtista, lord and master of unhappy Indians, lord of
fear, lord of iron and bad dreams, master of death. Who could
ever have predicted, years before, with the hidalgos laughing as
they tossed you in a blanket, that you'd come to be their equal?
Back then, it was you who called yourself an idiot, a dolt, and
cursed the hour that you cast your fate before these western
skies. Do you recall your promise to the Virgin of Guadalupe?
You had just come ashore. You walked terrified among the
shouts and gunshots of the landing party. But nobody had
answered. Nothing remained of Fort Navidad except the ribs
and rigging, wasted and burnt, of the old ship *Santa María*.
Every man who stayed behind had died. That was learned later.
You promised to wall yourself within a monastery for the re-
mainder of your life if the Virgin would contrive a way to get
you quickly back to Spain. Really, Antón, anyone who hadn't
seen you whining on your knees would not believe it.

Do you remember the early days at Isabela? How much effort
the Admiral spent in tacking, with the north coast in his view,
along those ten or a dozen leagues; more than three weeks, as
long as a trip to Spain, just to find that bosky cove, no more than

an anchorage and a little clearing where the cabins would be raised, always at daybreak a gray string of prayers and a dead man on the leeward rail. You arrived healthy and intact, but famished, and if it hadn't been for Chanca, the doctor, who stuck his finger down your throat to make you vomit up a poisonous wad of yucca, you would not be strutting about now all puffed up and lordly before the Indians that Roldán parceled out, nor would you own any lands in Jaraguá, nor have impregnated any young girls, nor sliced off anyone's nose, or hand, or ear. You repaid Chanca miserably, taking the shirt right off his back and running off to look for gold at Cibao with Alonso de Ojeda's party. What a man, that Ojeda. You felt safe with him, even though he was a hidalgo. Barely four and a half feet of a man above his buskins, but four feet of nerve and enterprise, four feet of guttiness and mad desire to get the blood to spurt. Every stream and canebrake that you left behind, every step you hazarded through rough and elevated scrublands helped to banish fear and to restore your hope. Nothing could match the feel of grass and gravel under the esparto of your sandals. You were built to walk across the world on foot, no mules and horses for you, and even less the shipboard's undulating planks, with their horrid yawning distances. With your crossbow on your shoulder, a scrap of meat to chew on, and your ambition in the lead you thought yourself the only master of your fate, a valiant man among the brave, and you did not hesitate to kill. You liked to play the braggart then, you swore upon the wounds of Christ, or on the mantle of the Virgin of Pilar, on Saint James's steed, and you made up tales of the Alhambra, or of dueling with a Moorish cavalier within the Generalife garden, or of the night when you were on the verge of carrying off the Abencerraje himself; only Alonso de Ojeda dared to put the lie to you and ridicule your boasting pantomime, and then you'd leave the campfire with your tail between your legs, for there were many with the fleet who'd seen Ojeda pirouette and jump up with his lame foot on the gangplank jutting from Giralda tower, fifty yards above the glassy Guadalquivir; you slept on the ground, face up and sulking, but you fell asleep with fortune as your blanket, while a shooting star slipped through the firmament like a silver spur. Do you recall, Antón Babtista, when you saw the evening star turn somersaults, and it was just a firefly?

The sun came mild and early and it swallowed up the misty banks bunched in between the ridges of the cordillera. A natural world of solid green, crammed with fruits and parrots, was opening before your gaze, and one of Ojeda's Indians answered the questions of your pointed finger, *caoba, jutía, mamey,* and the Indian laughed like a child on hearing you pronounce those sonorous words that you then made your own, that you raided and deflowered, that you repeated endlessly as in a ritual of propitiation to stake out your new dominion over forms and colors and the gentle spirits dwelling on the mountain. Now the ragged path, formed by bare feet passing to and fro, turned left abruptly between high stone walls, crossed a spring that ran with cold and tenuous water, and entered a small copse of palms, blue flowers, and bird songs. Then, unexpectedly, right below, like a calm, indulgent prophesy, the Vega Real, as the Admiral would name it, spread out: league upon league of still and tender valley, fresh with streams and groves, black earth and greening fields of potato, yucca, maize, alongside villages with huts whose roofs were made of palm fronds. There you stuffed yourself with cassava and the meat of juicy, long-tailed rabbits that lay basking in the trees; you ate the plump roots that when you roasted them were just like chestnuts; you ate, with some mistrust, the roe of the iguana and a leg of one of those chubby little dogs that never learn to bark; you swallowed half a dozen of the fish they called guabinas; you choked on magical tobacco smoke, and stretched out, sated, sleeping in an ebony's shade. On waking, in the afternoon, as Ojeda marveled at the huge gold nuggets that the Indians kept bringing him, you relaxed beside a girl whose crotch was tight and musky; then you grabbed another one, who was still nursing, and, nearly throttling her, began to suckle like a calf until you left her dry. That was real living, not like the days of want and prayer aboard the *Mariagalante;* you would sigh with pleasure, hidden in the canefields by the river, as you pecked between the legs of a young girl whose breasts were hard and salty as two olive pits.

With trembling knees, heavy gut, and empty testicles you rejoined Ojeda's party for the trip back to give the Admiral the good news: deep within the huge valley, which seemed more like a patch of heaven, ran a noble sierra that the Indians said was Cibao; water scrambled down its slopes in streams and torrents that delivered gold from their own rocky beds. News this promising was exactly what they needed in the wretched Isabella, where those whose noses weren't running, as was the Admiral's, had been shitting blood and puking bile, and the Franciscans never stopped their shuttling, viaticum in hand, from one cabin to another, and the beleaguered Chanca witnessed the exhaustion of his miraculous powders and ointments, and the crosses grew like weeds in the field behind the settlement. But Ojeda's ardent report put everyone on a war footing, even those who just one day before had begged aloud to be confessed. Only the dead, and the grumbling sentries posted on the ships and lookouts by the Admiral, stayed behind. Do you recall, Antón, that joyous morning when the march to Cibao began? With flag unfurled and beating drum you crossed the strip of flatland, mottled with stumpy shrubs and bushes, that lay between the mountains and the sea; the hidalgos and the horsemen, their lances set, rode up in front, as straight as towers, white tunics crossed with red above their iron coats of mail, the saracen corselet and the burnished Toledo cuirass, here and there the color of a coat-of-arms, a bandolier, a plume above a crested helmet, trumpet to the wind; behind them came the Admiral with his retinue, the captains and the masters of the caravels, Chanca the doctor and Friar Buil astride their mules, Franciscans holding crosses made of tree limbs, intoning hymns of praise to God the Father, then the bowmen, and the infantry with their hackbuts and their partisans, with their shields and knapsacks on their backs; then, hard put to keep in step, pressing to maintain a martial posture, came a troop of woodchoppers, carpenters, bricklayers, smiths, diggers and stonemasons, transporting on their shoulders all the tools that they would use in felling forests, building forts and mills, working gold and precious stones and woods; finally, lagging behind among the sailors and the sick, there came the peasants with their hoes and seedbags, the stewards and their donkeys with the bulging saddlebags and casks of wine, oil, garbanzos, sacks of flour, pots and pans. Along the spine of the sierra, when the Indian trail began to narrow and darken, the Admiral sent out the hidalgos to expand the road. Do you remember your astonishment, Antón Babtista, in seeing them cut through the matted underbrush with sword and hatchet, and then take up pick and shovel to break down the upswells on the mountain pass? You had never seen any hidalgo work up a sweat and spit on his hands before, and yet they laughed and joked, and pretended to be opening a breach within the Moorish ranks. The Admiral, with his mania for naming everything, had called that place the Pass of the Hidalgos, which just increased your hatred of that haughty cavalry, strongly built and muscular from so much riding into combat in their armor; they, too, could work if the desire came over them, and it wasn't killing them to have to use their hands, as you had thought it would; they could be like you, but you could never aspire to be one of them; they could make you give them all the gold you might secure at Cibao, and nothing would happen, for the world is made in such a way as to keep the slave forever slaving and the commoner a commoner for life, and a joiner's son may come to be a soldier or a priest, but he'll never, you thought bitterly, put on a bishop's robe or wear the cross of Calatrava, not even in the Indies. What makes a hidalgo different from you? Well, my friend, a hidalgo owns land and has tenants to work it and to pay him tribute, and he was born a hidalgo, and so was his father, who was not a tinker, as your own father had been. But what's to keep you from taking all the gold you can manage to pilfer and buying a good hundred acres, and then forcing as many Indians to work for you? Why shouldn't their Majesties decide to create some new hidalgos in their lands beyond the sea? There are enough islands in these parts to make a thousand rosaries . . . and this was how you went on flattering your greedy expectations, Antón, when the Admiral, hallucinating from the sea of verdant flora that spread out before his view, asserted that this valley must portend the nearness of the Earthly Paradise.

But Cibao was not Cipangu, as the Admiral had suspected, maybe it was Saba, yes, surely that it was, and just in case, he had them build a fort on the high ground above the river, and then he set out with his troops back toward the coast. You stayed behind, Antón, under the command of the foul-tempered Pedro de Margarit; fifty men in all, not counting the hidalgos. Those days in Cibao would seem so long to you, your waist bent and hurting from the moat-digging and the cutting down and planing of the trees, whose hearts would blunt the hatchet's blade, and from all the carrying of logs and heavy stones. You were in the land of Caonabó, and everyone said he was the chief who led the massacre at Fort Navidad. Was it stockades that he couldn't stand? you asked yourself, when your terror took control and chilled you all night long. You begged piteously to be put in charge of the corral, where you knew the Indians wouldn't dare to go. But suddenly there were no Indians. Something important must have happened to them, given over as they were to snooping all about, to trading gold dust for a worn-out shoe, a little bell, an old shirt, a cap, an inkstand to be spilled out on their pointy heads one drop at a time, as if the liquid were some priceless balsam. It was obvious: Caonabó was going to attack. But then, fortuitously, rotten weather intervened; it rained in buckets and the cordillera's rugged slope became a turbulent red torrent, and the inundated moat seemed boiling in the downpour, and the river, abandoning its bed, brought in a swollen Indian or two, a palm roof, a fat ceiba tree. Provisions grew scarce, and to cap the misfortune, the wood began to ooze and drip through the joints' eroded mortar, and the cassava loaves turned into moldy wafers, and the yuccas lost their hair, to show a pinkish, flabby skin, and the ears of maize went overnight from green to black, and the yams and the potatoes burst like blisters and began to stink like corpses. We must send to the Admiral for help, said *mosén* Pedro de Margarit one pallid, drizzly morning, letting out a muted oath that seemed more like a fart emitted from the mouth. Here was your chance, Antón, to leave that rat hole, and you volunteered to go. You spurned the offer of a mangy nag that once belonged to a hidalgo who died choked in phlegm, but you took the company of an Indian, one of those whom Chief Guacanagarí had awarded to the Admiral. Do you remember the mud holes, the impossible fords, the rheums and catarrhs? Thank God the Indian turned out to be acquainted with those flooded mountains, those arroyos that had now become broad rivers that the *Mariagalante* could have negotiated easily.

At Isabela it was clear and sunny, although the two hundred cabins seethed with discontent. True, the sugar and the vines were doing well, and the melons and the cucumbers had ripened, and on the day that you arrived they reaped the wheat's first fruits, but still the wine and the grain and the biscuit and, in general, everything they'd brought from Spain had all run out, and the graveyard now was harboring more dead men than there were living ones within the settlement.

Do you remember, Antón, the matter of the nuggets? It was the only time you ever spoke directly to the Admiral, so how could you forget? Giving you not even a quarter-hour to get the mud and hunger off your back, he sent out Alonso de Ojeda, your old captain, to look for you. You were in Chanca's cabin, waiting for him to come in from his routine consolation of the moribund; you couldn't stop your coughing and your trembling, and you spat out mossy gobs that had been sticking in your throat like leeches. Ojeda's greeting was to ask if *mosén* Pedro and his men had collected any gold to speak of. You told about the heavy rains, and the flood, while Ojeda scrutinized your miserable garments and then turned your gripsack inside out. Then, not saying a word, he booted you into the street and dragged you to the Admiral's house.

"This is the man come back from Cibao," Ojeda said. "I know him. He's a brute."

The Admiral, thin and sallow, stood leaning over a table, and scarcely raised his glance from the parchment that lay half-unrolled before him; he had a compass in his right hand and in the other hand a ruler.

"I'll bring water from the river by means of a canal," he murmured, looking down at the parchment. "Here we'll have a square, and here a church, of stone, and the governor's palace here, and over here a fort; we'll build stone houses on this street . . . , and I'll build a good, strong wall. What's your name?" he said suddenly, and he fixed his glance upon your startled eyes.

"Antón Babtista, Admiral, *señor* . . . *mosén* Pedro sent me to bring help."

"He brought no gold," Ojeda said. "He may have hidden it inside a bush."

"I have no gold," you blurted in alarm. "As God is my witness, I have only hunger and disease."

Then the Admiral walked up to you, lay his hands upon your shoulders, and pierced you with a look so grave and leaden that you felt it sink down to your feet like a sounding in deep water.

"You've brought back gold from Cibao," he said, looking at you all the time. "You've brought back gold, a lot of it."

"I've brought back nothing, nothing," you whined, terrified. He took his hands from your shoulders and you sank down to your knees.

"A lout," Ojeda said, "a liar ready for the hangman," he continued, as the Admiral, with his head down and his hand upon his sword, paced round the table.

"Don't torture me!" you pleaded. "I'm telling you the truth. I haven't hidden anything. I'm telling all I know. I've only seen the nuggets and the gold dust that the Indians bring into the fort. If there are mines in Cibao, then I swear no Spaniard has ever seen them."

"But there are mines," said the Admiral softly, almost tenderly. "The richest, most abundant mines; mines to suit a king's desire, my desire, and the desires of the men who came here with me and who right now weep like women in their desire to return to Spain."

"Oh, my God!" was all you answered, not managing to pull

your eyes from those perfervid pupils that seemed to burn there and to smoke like Indian tobacco.

"Isabela will become to these dominions all that Rome has been to Europe," the Admiral continued, placing his finger in the center of the parchment. "But who is there to build my palace of eternal stone, or my high officials' houses, or the church, the mills, the walls . . . when everyone is studying to find a way to play me false, to mutiny and sail off in the ships?"

Ojeda walked over to a bundle that lay in a corner; with a brusque gesture he lifted the filthy blanket that had covered it.

What you saw there made you jump, and you moved backward, openmouthed.

"Here's the gold that *mosén* Pedro de Margarit sent with you," said Ojeda. "There is plenty of gold in Cibao, gold from mines, gold that Spaniards have discovered. Do you understand now, you dolt?"

"Don't humiliate him," said the Admiral, in a whisper. "He's a simple man, and I find him serviceable."

"Will I be rewarded?" you dared to ask, and you ducked as if to take a blow.

"With your life," Ojeda said.

But the Admiral went over to the corner, leaned down gently and picked up a nugget worth at least twelve castellanos.

"It's yours."

And that was the beginning of your gold, Antón Babtista, and of your anguish. Because until then you had moved freely, never thinking much about anything you left behind or took along with you. That nugget, big as a fruit, possessed your sleep and your thought as well, and the fear of losing it would never leave you. You hid it, you buried it, you gave it to a Franciscan for safekeeping, you asked him for it back, and you could only start to live again when you had lost it on a roll of the dice.

⟦ XVII ⟧

I KNEW ALREADY FROM the Gascon's mouth that the Hieronymite friar was a necromancer and physician. He had
come ashore two months earlier from the flagship of Hawkins the Englishman, whose ships had taken on water and firewood at Carlefor, and had stayed at his own request, intending
to collect herbs and study Florida's nature. Before proceeding
on his voyage to England, Hawkins had left the Frenchmen a
ship on which they could return if they wished, for neither their
reinforcements nor Juan Ribao's ship had yet arrived, and the
Hieronymite friar was supposed to return by that ship when he
had finished his investigations. The Gascon told me that de
Ledoniel had received the friar well and had lent him some men
to help gather plants and roots, as that was all that he had done
since his arrival, and had given him one of the best houses in
Carlefor, for which he paid with a gold coin every week.

My curiosity being aroused by what the Gascon said, for I
couldn't understand why a friar would stay to live among heretics, no matter how great his urge to find out about the trees and
herbs of Florida, I rang for the soldier who guarded him and
ordered him brought to me to talk. When he came into the
room, I was surprised by his youth and his martial bearing, since
I had thought that he'd be a graybeard in a cassock, but he was a
man of about my years, in long riding boots and a tightly drawn
jerkin.

"What do I call you?" I asked him familiarly, pointing to a
stool in front of the *Adelantado*'s chair, to which I had moved in
order to seem more lordly.

Without accepting the seat, and with a cool superiority, he said to me:

"I don't see how my name can be of much use to your excellency. Has the *maestre* had me summoned just for that?"

I was red faced, for he was a friar and a doctor and I shouldn't have been so familiar with him, but not seeing my way out of the situation, I commanded:

"Soldier, jail this man for his insolence."

The *Adelantado* scolded me for this the next day, so strongly that I thought he might take the post of *maestre* away from me.

"Who are you to jail men who are under my protection? God help me! I don't know how you ever got into the Order of Saint James. If you want to rule in my house, *señor* Don Pedro de Valdés, wait at least until I die. Do you think that the friar and the four Frenchmen earned my pardon with the color of their beards? For God's sake, no! One of them is learned and an astrologer, and he will be quite useful to us, and I'm thinking about sending the others to this Ribao out there in his ships to convince him to quit these coasts forever."

These and other things as well the *Adelantado* said to me, pacing restlessly back and forth across the room. When the reprimand was over, he stopped in front of the window and stood there looking at the Lutherans' scorched church, on the other side of the courtyard.

"You'll go yourself to release the Portuguese," he said, turning around. "Be courteous; he's a man of breeding and knowledge. If he responds to you, get close to him and earn his confidence quickly, because I'm going to leave Carlefor in two days, and I'll need to know where the gold mines are and if the Lutherans with Ribao are as spineless as the ones we found here, and . . ." the *Adelantado* stopped and stood there stammering and looking fierce, as though he couldn't find the right words. "And damn it! Ask him if the stars are with us!"

"The stars, sir?"

"The horoscope, Don Pedro, the horoscope," he said, impatiently.

"But, sir. . . ."

"Go on! You don't know a damned thing about war."

I found the friar sleeping on a platform, his cape folded into a pillow and his face as untroubled as if he were in his own bedroom.

"*Señor* friar," I called to him softly. "*Señor* doctor. . . . *Señor* astrologer," I kept calling to him, to no effect. "*Caballero* . . . ," I tried, and then he opened his eyes.

"Ah, the *señor maestre*," he said, getting himself up and stretching his bones happily.

"How has your worship slept?"

"I dreamed I was carving an enormous turkey," he sighed.

"Your worship is free to go wherever he pleases."

Straightening his clothes, without even looking at me, he stepped out of the cell.

"Miserable weather," he exclaimed on walking into the drizzle and mud of the courtyard. "I swear that your lord Avilés certainly knew how to pick the weather for his campaign. If he had attacked the French a week earlier, the result might have been different."

"If the *caballero* will permit me, I would say to him that they wouldn't have defeated us even in fair weather. In my opinion the Lutherans are cowards, in a storm or out of one."

"Watch out for that puddle," he cautioned me, and he jumped quickly, landing on his feet just beyond the washed-out spot. "Don't follow my example, *señor maestre,* for surely you're burdened by some meal in your stomach, where I have nothing to weigh on me at all."

Accepting his advice, but irritated by it, I walked around the wide puddle, which was in the center of the courtyard, giving the excuse of a pike-wound in my ankle.

"The *señor maestre* was saying that the Lutherans are cowards," he said, continuing the conversation as we approached the fort's principal houses, "but I don't agree. Look at the ones in Flanders, for example."

"I was speaking mainly of the French," I answered.

"Ah, then, you mean to say something quite different. The

Frenchmen may be cowards, but not everyone who follows the new faith."

"The *caballero* might prefer to call it the new heresy."

"Yes, certainly, the new heresy," he said, stopping in front of the unhinged door of a substantial house beside the little church's atrium. "Nevertheless, I am not in total agreement with the *señor maestre*. If the Frenchmen of Carlefor had been cowards, they wouldn't have let themselves be slain for their religion; they would have gone over to the Catholic faith to save their skins."

"What cannot be denied, *caballero*, is that they are bad soldiers, and that if the ones under Ribao are of the same order, there won't be any left to return to France."

"I see that the *señor maestre* wears the habit of Santiago," he said, brushing my cross with his finger, "and I don't know why I think he got it fighting against the Turks."

"In the royal galleys," I declared, with pride.

"Well the *señor maestre* will learn that a quarrel with them is a different thing from one with the heretics, whom I know well after having lived here for two months."

"The *caballero* must be a lucky man, because they've kept him well here, and lodged him in a good house."

"I have no complaints about them, *señor maestre*. From General Laudonière down to the humblest soldier they have treated me considerately and respected my faith, and if I didn't go back to Europe with Hawkins's ships it was because they offered to help me finish looking at certain rare plants and bushes, while serving as their doctor at the same time, for the one that they had brought here died. As for this house, I paid for it," he said, showing me, with a courtly gesture, the burnt planks of the façade. "I am not a man of war and so I don't know if they are good or bad soldiers, but in the matters that concern me in this life I assure you that their belief is firm and they will die defending it."

"The *caballero* isn't talking like an Old Christian," I said, impulsively. "It must be the time he's lived and sailed among heretics."

"The *señor maestre* forgets that since I'm not a Spaniard I don't think like one. John Hawkins is a pious man, and more than once I've heard words from him in praise and obedience to King Philip, whom he served in the last war against France. As for me, I haven't come to Florida to cut the throats of Huguenots nor to conquer it, no matter how good a Christian I might be or how schooled in my doctrine, to which your own clergy have testified."

"I heard a different story from the Gascon," I said, trying to frighten him, for my heart told me that he was a friar unreconciled to God and the Holy Father.

"Everyone does what he can to save his hide. If the *señor maestre* is speaking about the man who guided the *Adelantado* to this place, I say I have never seen him before, and if he has denounced me it is his word against mine, and your worship will know whose to believe. And if I may be of any use, you now know where I live, and Rodrigo de Alentejo, your servant, will always be ready to help."

"If the *caballero* would wait a moment," I stopped him, remembering that my father-in-law wanted something from him. "It seems to me that I have annoyed him, and along with my apologies I would ask him for a favor."

"Quite the contrary. I am indebted to the *señor maestre* for the dream I had about the turkey and for his excellent company. Tell me exactly what I can do."

"I found out that the *caballero* is a doctor and I thought that perhaps he might be versed in astrology."

"Ah, the *señor maestre* would like to know the future," he said, smiling and kicking open the door with one foot. "Come into my house, then, and I'll see what I can do."

"I want to know what's in store for us in Florida," I said, crossing the threshold.

The house, before the fight, must have seemed half pharmacy and half magician's cabinet. Now it was little more than naked planks and blackened beams, the floor a mottle of straw and burnt tatters, torn and crumpled manuscripts, shattered flasks and bottles, preserved animals, rosaries of fangs, rare roots and nuts, infamous decks of cards with figures of a naked Christ and bare-breasted virgins. Startled by this vileness, I backed away, crossing myself.

"The *señor maestre* has nothing to fear, for these unspeakable things, brought here by someone I don't know, have been exorcized," said Don Rodrigo, reaching out with his foot to nudge a two-headed lizard, whose monstrous shape stood out from among a half-dozen red acorns. "Let's sit down on that bench; it may have lost its back but it still has its seat."

"What a shame that the *caballero* has lost his magician's tools."

"I never had any, because I'm not a magician. But anyway I've lost the notes I took about this region's plants and animals."

"And haven't you lost any gold?" I asked him, pointedly.

"Ah, the gold," he sighed. "I thought its luster would have come out earlier. Some time ago the Indians here obtained it in a land that they called Apalache, but they don't have a nugget left; they traded it for hats, clothes, and baubles, and General Laudonière must surely have taken it with him when he departed."

"Where are these lands of Apalache?"

"They're far away, quite far away. There is no gold in Florida."

"I find it difficult to share the *caballero*'s opinion on that subject, for what could Ribao's fleet have come here for? Why would he build one fort and even think about another? Why challenge the justified wrath of the king of Spain?"

"There's no gold here, *señor maestre*," he said sharply, and then, in a quieter tone, but dark and complaining: "I'm tired of these jungles; I only want to go home. Is the *Adelantado* thinking about sending the women and children he captured back to the king of France?"

I said that my father-in-law intended to do just that.

"Have the good grace to advise him to let me go with them, and I'll thank you as long as I live. They're sure to put in at the Canaries, perhaps at the Terceiras, and there's traffic from both places to Lisbon, where my monastery is."

"I don't think the *Adelantado* is going to release the *caballero*, from whom he expects some service in the conquest."

"I'm ready to pay my passage, *señor maestre*."

"The *caballero* has buried some gold, then?" I asked suspiciously.

"Can the *Adelantado* buy a long life with gold?" he shot back, and without waiting for an answer he drew his head up next to mine and whispered: "The *señor maestre* must have heard of the Fountain of Eternal Youth. Isn't that true?"

"Many Spaniards have died in vain looking for it," I whispered. "But I can assure the *caballero* that the *Adelantado* does not believe in its existence."

"Do *you?*" he said, looking me in the eye.

I shrugged my shoulders and backed away a bit, annoyed at the unexpected familiarity of his behavior, for it must have implied some possible bribery or dishonest complicity. I felt short of breath, as though the impure vapors given off by that blasphemous Lutheran deck of cards were inflaming my throat.

"You're right," he said to me, after laughing softly. "There are no such fountains anywhere in Florida."

"Well then?"

He got up from the bench and, rooting around among the pieces of an earthenware pitcher, he took out a fistful of dark, dry leaves, which looked like fig leaves.

"They're from a tree that the Indians call the *palame*," he said, returning to the bench. "It grows on the coastal lands surrounding the great southern swamps and along the route to *Nueva España,* but only in the pools and waterholes. Anyone who drinks from them feels his vigor reborn for a few hours; that's how much medicinal power the roots have. Well, after mixing, boiling, settling, and drying, I have produced from its sap, along with the fatal humors of certain snakes, some powders more valuable than ten hundredweight of gold. Anyone who tries it in his wine will not only hold back age but will grow a few years younger. I'll give the *Adelantado,* a man entered in years, two ounces of this powder as the price of my passage."

"What about our souls, *caballero?* Won't they be lost?"

"It wasn't Satan who created the good things of this world, *señor maestre,* but the Almighty, so that men could enjoy them. I wouldn't have taken them myself if it had been otherwise."

"You?"

"Would you believe me if I told you that I was born in your grandfather's time?"

"Don't lie," I exclaimed, confused. "The Gascon didn't tell me about any of that."

"It's easy to guess why not," he smiled. "If he had, you'd have burned him for a witch."

"I hope to Heaven that you're right," I said, retreating toward the doorway. "I'll tell the *Adelantado* about it, and you'll answer to him and to Our Lord."

"Tell him also that a few days ago, before his arrival, a very big star halted in the middle of the heavens, frightening the Indians and the Frenchmen; tell him that the chief's wife gave birth to monkeys and some strange storms began to level the earth; tell him that a bolt of lightning fell on the Lutherans' church and that another killed de Laudonière's horse and stableboy, that his gold turned to ashes and the sword that Admiral Coligny gave him began to writhe one morning like a serpent; tell him, *maestre*, that from all the signs I've mentioned, and others that I will not, I know that his armies will succeed in Florida."

Bowing quickly to him, I took my leave and ran to see my father-in-law, who was amazed, and well disposed to deal with the friar. Before half an hour had passed, I was back at his house.

"Well, you've come back quickly; I didn't expect you until tomorrow," he said, with a happy look.

"When will the *caballero* provide the powders that he's mentioned?" I asked from the door.

"On the night before my ship leaves. Your lordships may verify the effects."

"Hurry up, because we'll have to start marching toward the coast, and that's where you'll board your ship. But if you're lying, the *Adelantado* told me to inform you that you'll be stoned to death."

⟦ XVIII ⟧

W HO WAS PEDRO DE PONTE? About him we have
nothing more than the chimerical biography of Don
Cristóbal, plus a few facts about his life, not many,
drawn from town council minutes, reports, genealogies, and
trials; for example, there's the fact that twenty years before Don
Cristóbal died, Pedro had dominion over all the holdings at
Adeje, with those at Garachio going to Bartolomé, the first born;
we know too that both the brothers were married to the daughters of the bachelor Alonso Belmonte, *converso,* lieutenant of the
captain general, *regidor* of Tenerife. . . . But it would be better to
lay out a small chronology:

circa 1505   Born in Garachio, Tenerife.

1514   Mother, Ana de Vergara, dies.

1528   Marries Catalina de las Cuevas, daughter of Alonso
Belmonte and Inés de las Cuevas.

1529   Appears before the Inquisitor Luis de Padilla to
declare his genealogy, as ordered, because of his
descending from a "lineage of the confessed."

1530   Birth of Niculoso de Ponte, his first son.

1532   Receives the lands at Adeje from his father, along
with their engines, mills, and storehouses.

1533   Birth of Alonso de Ponte, second son.

1535   Birth of Inés de Ponte, his first daughter, who would
marry the marquis of Lanzarote. Thereafter there
were seven daughters born, two of whom would die in

infancy, and a son who died while studying at Salamanca.

1537   The emperor Charles V appoints him *regidor* of Tenerife, taking the place of the licentiate Cristóbal Valcárcel, who had disappeared.

1538   Leases Hierro island to the count of La Gomera, with the object of providing meat for the whole archipelago. There are shipments of five hundred head of cattle.

circa 1550   Regarded as the richest man in the Canaries. Exports wine and sugar to England, wheat and cloth to the New World.

1552   Father, Cristóbal de Ponte, dies.

1553   Requests permission from Philip of Austria, then charged with the Castilian monarchy, to construct a stronghold at Adeje; request accompanied by neighbor's testimony concerning pillaging and arson perpetrated by French corsairs.

1555   Receives, through royal decree promulgated on May 2, the right to build the stronghold.

1556   Given, at Philip II's coronation, the honor of guarding the royal pennant.

1557   Ruling princess Doña Juana bestows title of *regidor* upon his son Niculoso.

1558   Assigns to Angla de Santana, as permanent agent, the Portuguese Enrique Nuñes. Employs Juan Martínez, pilot of Cádiz, who sails through the Antilles.

1559   Sends son Niculoso to the Court, where he acquires permanent status in his post as *regidor;* this involves a donation of many ducats. Transfers his agent Enrique Nuñes to Cape Verde Islands.

1560   Testifies on the behalf of Thomas Nicholas, Edge's successor as representative of Hickman & Castlyn, who had been accused by the tribunals of the Holy Office. Has an interview with John Hawkins, son of William Hawkins of Plymouth.

There is no need to go on, at least not for the moment; the last entry is of real importance, as we shall see:

November 1560: The *Peter*'s rigging, white and twisted like a conch, appears above the overcast horizon that winter brings to the scanty populace of Tenerife's western coast. Pedro de Ponte, leaving his account books and his abacus, walks over to the tower window and looks out in the direction of John Hawkins's ship, still distant. Bathed in the leaden light, his beard has lost its blackness and resembles now a clump of seaweed. No muscle of his face betrays emotion, but from his glowing eyes come fervors, furtive glimmerings, and shades of patient circumspection. The ship is now in view; he scans its bulky hull as if to calculate the value of its flag, artillery, and destination. The slightest glance at his life's history would show that he is a man of great reserve, the kind who likes to hunt from blinds; contrary to what we've found with Don Cristóbal, there is no archival record of his ever having made a voyage, fought a battle, or had an adventure; he gives one the impression of having always been right there, entirely wrapped up in the routine bustle that his tower residence affords; one might compare him to a spider, invisible behind his threaded pits and balustrades, who waits in febrile torpor for his captive to arrive for an appointment ineluctably divined.

What does Pedro de Ponte hope to get from the young Hawkins? Why does he lie in wait?

We ought to check some of the data in his chronology for what they might reveal, for example the entry dated 1559: "Transfers his agent Enrique Nuñes to Cape Verde Islands." The only business done there is slaving. Given the relative abundance of slaves in Tenerife, we may suppose that Pedro de Ponte, his profit making having reached its limit, would try to find another line of goods, exportable to the New World, and would then take up Don Cristóbal's venture from just the point at which he'd caught the flashing of Estebanico's knife. Now his testifying to the effect of Thomas Nicholas's innocence demands our attention; this was a trial convened by the Inquisition, and he, descending as he had from a "lineage of the confessed," must certainly have gauged the risks of his appearing there. Why would he be so vehement in desiring Nicholas's freedom? It's true that by this time the enmity of Spain and England had already begun to show itself; one could imagine, then, that Pedro de Ponte, intent on breaking up the trade monopoly, would think of having recourse to britannic ships and crews and captains, thus to avoid the dangers of a more direct participation. Perhaps Thomas Nicholas, the only influential Englishman in Tenerife, would commit himself to setting up the operation; in any event, in his position representing Hickman & Castlyn, he would be well enough acquainted with more than a dozen captains out of Bristol, Dartmouth, even London, who might be inclined to risk their necks in the acquiring of a sleek and sonorous purse of gold. Why not assume that Nicholas, before his run-in with the Inquisition, had been seduced by Pedro de Ponte and everything he offered? Must we even read the memorandum that the Inquisitor Padilla wrote concerning him, to wit: "Thomas Nicholas, in Tenerife, is the agent of Iquemán y Castelín, residents of London, who deal in cloth, linen and fustian and in other things that come from Flanders. . . ." And to summarize the rest, it says that in 1557 he acquired the post of William Edge, deceased, and took up residence in La Laguna, that he was denounced by two sisters known as *las morenas,* who made his shirts and handkerchiefs, and that of the charges that these women made, the following stand out: he does not attend Mass, he touts the value of his Lutheran sect above that of the true religion, he declares the spiritual activities of the friars to have no purpose other than to "get more widows pregnant," he calls virginity the road to hell, and he likes to sing indecent songs.

It's clear what sort of man Nicholas was, but *las morenas* stopped him cold in a stroke of evil fortune, unanticipated, that would wreck de Ponte's plans.

And yet the case is still unclear; more proofs are needed. Here's where our investigation starts.

Nicholas was arrested in Grand Canary. Having been told that the Inquisition in Tenerife had its eye on him, he jumped the first boat that was available to take him to the neighboring isle. Once there, he sought out Edward Kingsmill ("Duarte Quincemil"), the Hickman & Castlyn representative in Grand Canary, who furnished him the means of making his escape to Seville. But only with the means; the Holy Office, spread throughout the archipelago, caught him as he headed for the docks dressed as a nun. From his hasty movements they surmised that Nicholas believed himself answerable to something more than just beguiling *las morenas* and not practicing a Counter-Reformation brand of Christianity; he was a foreigner, after all, and the charges against him would only get him—and in fact did get him—a few months in prison; fleeing this was hardly worth the liquidation of his Tenerife operation, with a loss, declared in London, of fourteen thousand ducats, almost what an East India merchantman was worth; Nicholas knew himself to be accountable for a greater crime, and Kingsmill knew it, too. All this bears out the theory of his complicity with Pedro de Ponte. Is it worth our while to take a look at Kingsmill? It would not take long to do: when they searched his house, the Inquisitors found a few anomalies, for which he came before the courts just after Nicholas; the trial record has been lost, but we know that he was given a stiff fine and banished from the islands. That's how things stood, and would it be too much to say that the legal actions brought against these two agents cast suspicion on the doings of Hickman & Castlyn in the archipelago, and maybe even suggest a joint venture with Pedro de Ponte? And who were Hickman & Castlyn?

It is known that they, in old King Henry's time, had built up a house of trade in the shadow of the Merchant Adventurers Company, whose profits in Flanders alone were counted in millions of ducats annually; their house had been established with a capital of two hundred and forty shares convertible to twenty-five pounds each, but thanks to the enormous mass of wool then rendered by the English countryside, it soon became a model of the so-called chartered companies; its influence was such that, when its governor in Antwerp decided that it was bad for business to allow the Holy Office to set its courts up there, he defied the emperor Charles's pressure and got him to pull back the Inquisition's viridescent cross. But we're talking about Anthony Hickman and Edward Castlyn; made wealthy by their shares in Merchants and the windfall sales in cloth, they chose a western route and hit on favorable markets in Seville and Lisbon, and in the Canaries shortly after; this was the era of Wyndham's startling, celebrated voyage, and Hickman and Castlyn caught a touch of the African fever that it carried home; they quickly put up money for the voyage of John Lok, whose memorable homecoming—a parade of two hundred elephant tusks—would nourish both their dreams forever. The Portuguese, of course, did not look meekly on these incursions in the sources of their own wealth, and dispatches went out every day and night from Lisbon bearing haughty protests, arrogant messages, and the flat order to fire on all English ships caught sailing up or down the coast of Africa; in London, following a reflective pause, the Crown Council decided that it would face those risks and give assistance to a group, still secret, that was called the Guinea Club; it was not until later that Spanish and Portuguese agents could report on this daring and exclusive syndicate of investors; if their names appeared distorted in the Iberian spies' haphazard spelling, the messages' cramped handwriting yields up the names of Anthony Hickman and Edward Castlyn. The voyages that the Guinea Club conceived beneath the clattering of wine decanters met, in general, with spectacular success; the painstaking Richard Hakluyt, in his never sufficiently studied *Principal Navigations,* left a record of the optimism that these expeditions raised in the halls of commerce, where, like potted daylilies, they cheered the foggy and phlegmatic dens; and elsewhere actors, saltimbanques and mountebanks at carnivals, and emblems at the inns and hostelries began to feature Africa's beguiling natural world, and it is well known that, for a moderate tip, the keeper of a straw-strewn chamber in the Tower of London would display to a long line of visitors a zoo consisting of a dromedary, a crocodile, three monkeys, and a weathered lion who did nothing else but sniffle inconsolably above his artificial tail of yellow yarn.

99

In view of all this, it is likely that Hickman & Castlyn would have felt tempted by Pedro de Ponte's slave-trading project, which their enthusiastic agent had no doubt brought up to London.

What were the details of this project?

Who were Enrique Nuñes and Juan Martínez?

Again we must have recourse to the Inquisition's rotted files. Enrique Nuñes came from a family of Portuguese *marranos* who had settled into Antwerp; a dissolute and violent youth, he was thrown out of his job at Merchants' headquarters for having hurled an inkstand at the governor and for punching a Hanseatic delegate in the heat of an argument; thanks to the influence of his brother, doctor Heitor Nuñes, he was hired as a bookkeeper in Hickman & Castlyn's Antwerp office; later he was sent to Tenerife to take over the accounts left by the late William Edge and to stay on the island until the arrival of a successor, to whom he would deliver the office, and return to Antwerp; but that was not how things turned out, for when Thomas Nicholas arrived, Nuñes left the employ of Hickman & Castlyn, putting himself at the service of Pedro de Ponte, whom he had visited before in the tower at Adeje; before he left for Angla de Santana he was seen frequenting the *morenas'* house, in Nicholas's company, as well as in the taverns and in other centers of dubious activity; he met secretly in Angla with an envoy of the Barbary shariff, and six months later sailed abruptly to Cape Verde; there he died soon after of a sword thrust dealt him by a certain Captain Veiga, commander of the Portuguese armada that protected trade in ivory, slaves, and spices.

So much for the life of Enrique Nuñes, a tempestuous man, a man for the new times. Such a man was his brother, too, the famous doctor Heitor Nuñes, though he was much luckier: born in Evora, he lived and studied medicine in Antwerp, where he picked up an enormous international clientele by treating syphilis and gout with quite some skill, being one of the first to use guayaco wood in healing; intending to learn herbal medicine and the practices of sorcerers and oriental sages, he went on a lengthy voyage to India and the Moluccas—he may have even gone as far as China—from which he came home splendidly rejuvenated and with a portentous store of powders, seeds, dried flowers, and roots; called to England for a consultation about Mary Tudor's chances of conceiving, he was the only doctor who would tell the Crown Council bluntly that her case was hopeless; in London, where he then stayed on to reside, he joined the Royal College of Surgeons, and there is a record of his having performed, in Saint Bartholomew's Hospital, what seems to have been an operation of cosmetic surgery on a very wealthy and decrepit lady of the court; he must have picked up some unheard-of medical techniques while visiting the Orient (hypnosis? acupuncture?), for he's given credit for performing painless amputations, tooth extractions, births, and abscess lancings; a friend of the exalted Cecil, of the count of Pembroke, of Lord Robert Dudley, of Sir William Chester, and of others among the sponsors of John Hawkins's second American incursion, he sailed out on that voyage intending to find out if there were any truth to the legend of the Fountain of Eternal Youth; in Florida he must have sniffed out some fairly promising leads, because he left the expedition and remained behind in the struggling colony of Huguenots that had been founded there by René de Laudonière; Menéndez de Avilés, as we know, wiped out that beachhead with a cold and odious fury, but Nuñes escaped the butchery by passing—we have no choice but to imagine this imposture—as the able, fast-talking Hieronymite friar who appears, like a grain of pepper, in Pedro de Valdes's flavorless chronicle; on his return to London, he married Eleanor Freire—*la belle Freire* in the era's little social world—sister of the famous spy Bernardo Luis; beginning in 1568, as well as practicing medicine among the poor, he lent his efforts toward the wholesale vending of perfumes and drugs; the fame of his soirées reached the court of Czar Ivan IV, who took a lively interest in the wines and dishes that were served there, and was pleased at doctor Nuñes's eagerness to serve as envoy of the Muscovy Company, then but recently established; his age had always been a mystery, but despite his vigor he could now be seen to have declined in spirits and to shrink from accepting unavoidable invitations, and this was taken to mean that he was entering old age; in his later years his activity was largely political, though not lacking, certainly, in elements of gnostic mysticism; some have implicated him in the poisoning of Don John of Austria, and he has been mentioned as having been involved in the unspeakable blackmailing of Alessandro Farnesio, the duke of Parma, in the stormy days of the Invincible Armada; but such indictments are far from having any credible foundation. It is apparent, nonetheless, that Nuñes carried on an epistolary friendship with the great globe-trotters and anti-Spanish conspirators of the time, people such as the doctor Rodrigo Lopes, Jerónimo Pardo, the celebrated fugitive Antonio Pérez, Gonsalvo Anes (alias Benjamin George, alias Gonsalvo George, alias Dunstan Anes), the unfortunate Portuguese pretender Don Antonio, and Alvaro Mendes, son of the sumptuous duke of Naxos, known as *el Nasi,* whom he succeeded as leader of the western *marranos* and as owner of the diamond mines in the kingdom of Nasinga, which, contrary to popular belief, bear no relation to the mines of King Solomon.

And what's the point of all this?

We must go back to Cape Verde, where Enrique Nuñes's body lies, a foot of steel betwixt his breast and shoulder blade.

What was Nuñes's mission in Cape Verde? Why had be been posted first at Angla? What did he hope to get out of the Barbary shariff?

Let's take it one step at a time. In the first place, we would do well to remember that the shariff is a worthy representative of the Saadian dynasty, which has just overthrown the decadent Merinides and proclaimed a Jihad against the Portuguese invaders; Mohamed el-Mandi directs, successfully, an Islamic rebirth, uniting all the nations. Nomadic troops, ardent and veiled, made up of Riffian converts and moriscos exiled from Granada, are riding through the desert, their spirits inflamed by the *baraka,* the sacred emanation of the Morabites; Mohamed el-Mandi gives no respite to the Portuguese, whose commissioned agencies in black Africa deplete the gold and slaves brought in by caravans that stop in Gao, in Dienne, in legendary Tomboctou; but the descendant of the Prophet needs some arms to fight on equal terms, some hackbuts and a few artillery pieces to be carried on a camel's back and pointed at the coastal forts. We can easily suppose, then, that Nuñes, led at night by the Mohammedan spies in Angla, held a meeting at a secluded oasis with a *cherif* in the total confidence of Mohamed el-Mandi, to whom he offered arms in exchange for slaves brought in from Tomboctou. Well, for one reason or another the negotiations between Nuñes and the shariff broke down, as we surmise from the former's unexpected trip to the Cape Verde Islands; of course it would be rash to try to establish a reason for this failure, but it should be stated that when the renegade Djuder fell on Tomboctou before a column of harquebusiers, he found women there who cursed in Portuguese and spoke passionately of a *rumi,* come from the north some time before, who had claimed to be a friend of the sultan of Marrakesh. Who could that *rumi* have been? Why not Enrique Nuñes, who with the excuse of gathering slaves in person meant to discover the source of the gold that came to Tomboctou, and then pass on the secret for a price? Then Nuñes—or the *rumi* they remembered—must have offended the place's rigid hospitality by slinking in among the harem beds of one or another pasha, bey, or potentate in the pearl of the desert; there would have been a price put on his head, and he would have had no other choice but to escape the salt walls of the city in a flight we can envision as having been heroic and thirsty. When he returned to Angla de Santana, he surely would have sent word on to Pedro de Ponte of his diplomatic failure, without going into many details, and there awaited a reply. Of course Pedro de Ponte could do nothing other than what in fact he did: write to his agent telling him to go to the Cape Verde Islands. Since hackbuts were abundant there, he would have instructed Nuñes to try his hand at bribing some captain of the Portuguese fleet. Evidently Don Manoel Veiga was a loyal subject, brought up in the school of Prince Henry the Navigator. How could he deprive His Majesty of his half million pieces of ebony, what would become of Portugal if her captains let themselves succumb to such temptations? He unsheathed his sword, ran Nuñes through with it, crossed himself, and put the matter out of mind.

One thing is obscure, however: Who put up the hackbuts? It was said that Hickman & Castlyn were up to their ears in Pedro de Ponte's project, but that hypothesis will not withstand sober analysis: Hickman & Castlyn traded with Seville and, without a doubt, their rolls of fine cloth were bought there by Genoans who, disguised behind good Spanish names, sent them off to the New World through the loading docks of the *Casa de Contratación*, along with gangs of Negroes purchased FOB Seville; Hickman & Castlyn also maintained offices in Lisbon, which would mean that their fabrics crossed the Cape Bojador and Cape Blanco currents to arrive at Cape Verde, where they were partially unloaded and where there were a few men who, for a good price in gold, had managed to squeeze out a slaving license from the king of Spain; the remaining cloth resumed its journey, passed round the stormy Cape of Good Hope, picked up the southwest monsoon at Mozambique, and reached, after many days of tribulation, a Goa that was run as the Jesuit center for the missions to the Orient, and from there, among the peaceful cassocks, chasubles, and prayers, it left for God knows where. Were Hickman & Castlyn going to risk losing such laborious and stable earnings on the basis of de Ponte's ballyhoo? Of course not.

The hackbuts, then, must have been forwarded by Nicholas on his own account; he would have got them from the English ships that handled the Canary wine and sugar traffic; he would have paid for them with accounts receivable that Edge had left behind, or maybe with de Ponte's molasses and malvesie wine. This last is the most probable, and it would have been the only tangible thing risked in the three-cornered buying and selling operation: hackbuts in Tenerife; slaves in the Barbary states; gold, silver, pearls, and hides in the Caribbean. On the strength of a fat commission, Nicholas would make himself responsible to Pedro de Ponte, behind the backs of Hickman & Castlyn, in the matter of recruiting one of the sea captains whose services the

London merchants regularly bought; the hackbuts were easily obtained, as the peace with France had stockpiled thousands in the armorers' stores; they would go to Tenerife tucked in among the lengths of cloth, to be unloaded at the proper time on the Adeje dock. As soon as he got word from Nuñes, Pedro de Ponte planned to ship the arms out to the Barbary coast aboard the broad, flat-bottomed boat he used from time to time to carry cattle from the isle of Hierro; and that's the way it was: Nuñes would receive the shipment in some solitary anchorage and, when the formalities were over, he would entrust them to the strong backs of el-Mandi's camels, with a hackbut priced at one slave or one and a half.

How would the cargo get to the Caribbean?

It was agreed that English ships would take it. Yes, but which ones? The same ones that brought the hackbuts? They were too light for such a run; furthermore, no Briton until then—with the anomalous exception of some lost explorer—had ever crossed the threshold of that sea. Pedro de Ponte, there in his tower, must have wracked his brain to come up with a man who had enough experience, skill, and courage to embark on such a dangerous and lengthy voyage; we can imagine him, nestled in his black tunic, scrutinizing the names that Nicholas had given him, over a cup of malvesie, while Nuñes paces nervously: ah, if only Lok and Wyndham hadn't died. Towerson has settled back to live off his investments, young Martin Frobisher might do if only he were not so set on seeking out the Northwest Passage. . . . Inés, with the pitcher of wine, would come up to the big stone table to refill the cups, what's become of old William Hawkins's sons? And Pedro de Ponte, lifting his curvate nose from the paper on which he'd scribbled and erased so many names, would look at her deliberately, with that unblinking manner that he had, and then Inés would know that her words, gleaned from her memories of childhood, had won her father's approbation.

Yes, truly, any of the Hawkinses could be the one to sail to Africa and America, Nicholas would say, in his halting Spanish, as he congratulated Inés upon her perspicacity. The two brothers, once the war had ended, had gone back to Plymouth to take charge of the family business. They traded now with the ports on the channel's other side, though William, the elder, was prone to rheums and rarely left the office. In the end, John Hawkins was the right man for the job—the most ambitious, the most daring; he had taken a Hanseatic hooker as a prize, *Peter* was the ship's name, and Nicholas had seen it anchored at Plymouth a few months earlier, beside the pinnace that had taken him to Tenerife. They could order a few rolls of cheap cloth from him as a way of getting close enough to sound him out, said Nicholas, to Pedro de Ponte's silent acquiescence.

So John Hawkins was the man, but how would he manage to get there and back? How would he slip between the hostile currents, reefs, fortresses, and seventy-gun galleons?

Very simple: Juan Martínez would go with him. Do we know anything about *him*? Very little, but it's enough to know that he was a pilot from Cádiz who had served in the fleets of Portugal and Spain; under contract to Pedro de Ponte, he had just returned from a hasty voyage through the Caribbean coasts and islands, his maps and port charts all corrected, his notebooks replete with observations, requests of every sort, names of towns and people needing slaves. Yes, the sea Columbus had discovered was a total enterprise, just like the world itself. . . . But the world seemed to collapse one morning when Pedro de Ponte, still in his sleeping cap, opened a letter that his daughter handed him to read, which told of Nuñes's ruinous murder in Cape Verde.

And things weren't going well in Tenerife, as we already know: Nicholas, summoned to appear before the Holy Office, had taken fright and run away, only to be captured ignominiously, then tried, and jailed. One quiet night the hackbuts came, but that had no importance anymore; without the Negroes there was nothing to be done.

Yet even in those days de Ponte's gloom would find some respite: his son Niculoso, the first born, would come back from Madrid to tell him that His Majesty, responding to their contributions, had seen fit to make him Tenerife's *regidor* for life.

Perhaps this news stirred up some hope in Pedro de Ponte; the fact is that an idea, more feverish every hour, took hold of his hands, his eyes; soon he was glued to the window and had his food brought up to him; all was not lost; he could still gamble and win. The game had taken a much more difficult turn, but if he could make Hawkins think that to assault a Portuguese slave ship was yet a patriotic act, the deal was done. It was pure piracy, of course, and nothing less, but with some luck, and with the stars just right, well, let's give it a try.

⟦ XIX ⟧

AND NOW HERE IS John Hawkins, William Hawkins's second son, leaning out over the *Peter*'s rail to contemplate the Teide's gray-brown rock on the horizon, here he is, asking himself if, the war with France having ended, there might be a definitive resumption of the trade with Tenerife, the business that his father used to do, exchanging good cloth for good wine, not dealing in those paltry bundles of twill that Pedro de Ponte had just ordered and that would get him no more than ten or twelve tons, if that, of watered-down canary, for let's not forget that in England now Elizabeth, who every day seems more heretical, more reforming in all manner of things—though she herself seems unaware of it—is becoming the protectoress of an important economic power made up of new owners of the Church's expropriated lands, sheep raisers, cloth makers, wholesalers, merchants, brokers, armorers, and mariners who leap the oceans to set up new markets and explore and fight and sack and even, lately, colonize, yes, a new sort of men, men given to everything, men hated by the decrepit dying Spanish king, "that rabble," he had called them without comprehending, *without comprehending* them; nor does John Hawkins rightly know himself exactly what will come of this new sort, at least he doesn't think of the whole picture, for he's thinking of the contraband in wine and not about America or Africa; and just now as he looks out past the railing of the *Peter*, his gilded war prize, he discerns the tower at Adeje and starts remembering the Pontes: Don Cristóbal, the old man about whose death he hasn't heard, Don Pedro of the dark brown beard, father of the daring Niculoso, of Alonso the dreamer, of the knowing Inés, who must be twenty-five now and may not yet have married the marquis of Lanzarote; yes, he thinks of her before the rest, he sees her running in the Teide's harshest afternoon, he finds her in his recollection of his first, now distant, trip to Tenerife. At that journey's start the adverse winds had forced his father's ship back to the dock three times, and the old man, blind with rage, had said that all those false starts were absurd, absurd, and shut himself inside his cabin with a leg of mutton and a keg of ale, leaving the two brothers, John and Will, to bear the foolery of waving for the fourth time to the idlers on the dock and to endure once more the mocking children angling at the Fisher's Nose, who, when they saw them coming back again, yelled out in piping, whistling voices: "Westward, ye Hawkins!"; but then at once the wind had changed, becoming favorable, reasonable, amiable, and his brother Will and he thought they could make it to the Sound right then, each jostling for the wheel, and the men began to smile and to obey them, calling them chips off the old block; and when he felt the waters of the Sound beneath the planks the old man started talking to the pilot of his trips to Guinea and Brazil, so they heard his blustery exaggerations and enjoyed themselves, and every now and then he looked at them with his small, gray, watery eyes and patted their heads with his large, tarry, saltpetered hands; and days later, perhaps only to please them, for he was in a pleasuring mood, he set their course to run hard by the Barbary Coast, and out upon the sands and ledges they could see, small in the distance, the white-mantled horsemen who believed in Allah, still as scarecrows made of eggshell, except for one who reared his horse and raised his lance; and happy, then, they sailed southwest, urged on by a hot, sandy wind, and one morning there appeared above the starboard beam, its top sliced through by clouds, a purplish gray-brown rock, the Teide, and the two brothers asked their father if they could climb it, and the old man, who was almost sober on that morning, replied quite seriously that giants and dragons lived among the Teide's crests, and that he'd seen a giant jam a tree trunk as if it were a goosefeather into the left eye of a dragon, who had managed, just before his howling death, to disembowel the giant with his green and scaly tail; they asked again if they could climb the slope, and the old man said he'd seen a sleeping giant, fatter far than the one who'd killed the dragon, who couldn't be awakened by whatever noise or tickling one devised, because giants of that size sleep six months at a time, and single days are useless to them even for a nap, and that huge giant slept in peace, not bothered by the birds that lived in his white beard and fed their nestlings there, of course this was a good giant, at least when sleeping and with birds on him he seemed good, and tranquil, and a little worn, but one can never quite be sure what giants will do. The next day they landed at a place called Garachio, a wild and rock-strewn place of cliffs, ravines, and granite columns, and then, at the taciturn old blind man's house, they visited the caves where wine was stored, and there the air was as fresh and soothing as on a spring night; and when his father palated the wine that the old man's son, Don Pedro, drew from a cask and offered him, he nodded as though sleeping, as though listening to music, and he quietly agreed, *aye aye;* despite the daunting dark brown beard, young John had dared to ask Don Pedro whether, since it was so near, and it would take so little time, his brother Will and he might climb the mountain; at first Don Pedro hadn't understood, and told him to enunciate more slowly, as his English wasn't very good, and he had tried to speak both slow and loud as if to a deaf person, and then Don Pedro understood, and he said yes, while Don Cristóbal and their father closed the deal, the children, his own and Don Bartolomé's, with John and Will, would climb the mountain, and Don Pedro's voice was cavernous and his beard, perhaps, had taken on that color from his drinking so much malvesie, and his voice was so much like the voice of that Italian pilot of his father's who had hanged himself after a game of ninepins; the next day everything was ready very early for the outing, there even were three Negroes to carry the leather knapsacks with the food and weather gear, and he, Will, Niculoso, Alonso, and, most of all, Inés were happy and excited after breakfast, bouncing around in all directions, until Don Pedro blew a whistle that he wore around his neck; first they climbed through prickly pears, orange trees, and palms, and then through grapevines, pines, and every now and then they came upon a looming, sacred, terrifying tree that was called *drago*, as it looked just like a dragon, so said Niculoso, and maybe they *turned into* dragons after dark, and Niculoso said they could, but never into giants; those steep pine forests had once been the *guanches'* home and there they'd held the Spaniards off and ambushed them again and again, and they spoke a language of just whistles, because a whistle carries further than a voice up on a mountain, no matter how you shout, and the secret language had been lost, and they wanted to find out if some old *guanche* was still there to answer them, but all they got back was the echo of their shouts and whistles, bounced to them through the naked mountainsides; that night they slept bundled in hides and sheepskins, tucked into the *guanche* caves, which were really one cave with its ceiling blackened by torch and candle flame, and they made a fire and they ate and sang, and Will danced stiffly with Inés, and they all laughed and laughed to see Will dance, and when everything turned quiet Don Pedro poked the fire and began spinning out old stories, about the times before the Spaniards came when the island had belonged to a great king called Tinerfe, who had ten sons, though only nine inherited the island and divided it among themselves, because the tenth son was a bastard and got nothing but a cave to live in, this one? well, that's right, this very one, and that poor kingdom was the only thing the tenth son left to his own son, whose name was Zebensui, who was a proud and strong and valiant *guanche,* mortified at having to live on brittle corn cakes that his cousin, the king of Anaga, used to send him every year, and that was why Zebensui started stealing others' livestock, and complaints came raining in upon the nine kings of the island, and especially on Bencomo, who was the richest and the noblest of the cousins, and so one day King Bencomo set out traveling and found the cave of Zebensui, who sat eating a kid that he'd just stolen from another's herd, a poor man's, and Zebensui made an offer to the king of water and some corn cakes, which was all he had, and Bencomo ate the corn cakes, dipping them in his cupped hand just like the poorest of the poor, and afterward he said I liked the corn cakes very much, cousin Zebensui, because with salt or without it I prefer their taste to that of someone else's food, which is unsavory, and if your feeling poor should one day influence you to change your ways, then I am sure that you will find that you are rich, and saying that he went off to leave Zebensui to think about what he had said, and when Zebensui left the cave, this very cave, to find Bencomo and to ask forgiveness, he couldn't find him anywhere, so he went to see his cousin, the king of Tegueste, who then witnessed his repentance, and the king of Tegueste, pleased with that, put on a lavish welcome and appointed him head shepherd of his hacienda and his herds, which were so teeming that a hundred shepherds couldn't keep them. When the tale of Zebensui had been told, they all lay down beneath the animal skins, and as it happened he slept near Don Pedro; he fell asleep quite soon, because he was so tired from the climb, but something woke him with a start in the middle of the night, and it was Don Pedro, who got out from beneath his sheepskin covers to leave the cave, and he thought that perhaps he'd gone to see that the Negroes, out in the open air, still kept watch at the cave's entrance, but then he heard a streaming sound so heavy that it bathed the mountain and the silence; he heard a noise and looked over to the spot where Inés was, and she too was awake and looked at him above the embers, the small, softly dying flames, and her face shone like a fruit both orange and apple, and they shared a laugh at Don Pedro's endless streaming, and he fell back on the skins and pretended he was sleeping when Don Pedro came inside again, and he kept this up until he heard Don Pedro snoring, then he got up and walked deliberately toward the fire, until he felt the heat rise to his cheeks, exactly as he'd felt when Inés had looked at him and they had laughed at Don Pedro's running faucet; and then he left the cave himself, and it was very cold and the holes in the clouds had big stars in them, and everything was black below, and he thought he had the urge so he opened up his fly, and his jet was

not as strong as Don Pedro's, not by half, and he bore down hard
in the thought that perhaps Inés could hear him, and if she
could he'd want to splash and steam against the rocks just like a
horse, and not make just a little trickle, which he did, and then
he heard a noise, and then a sigh, but he didn't turn around, he
kept still, trembling, his fly open; and at breakfast he tried to
give Inés a nudge, but she ran off to Niculoso and wouldn't even
look at him and when the roasted meats and cheese and corn
cakes were all eaten, Don Pedro started once again to talk of
guanches, and he kept on looking at Inés until she would look
back, not smiling but with the peculiar unblinking look that Don
Pedro sometimes wore, that he had worn, for instance, when
Will asked him whether the Negroes had been taken from another's herd, and Don Pedro hadn't answered but had gazed out
at the sea, above the islands' shadows in the misty backdrop, his
face unstrung as though with sorrow or with longing, his eyes
big, brilliant, fixed upon the distance; when they resumed their
climb they left the trees behind, below, and the stones got slippery and their breathing quick, and they kept on going all
morning and ate lunch among the clouds where it was hard to
make a fire because everything was drenched, and they stopped
higher up, now breathing heavily, especially Will and he, though
Niculoso coughed and Alonso and Bartolomé were sniffling
and the black and gray and white stones sniffled too, and Don
Pedro's beard was dripping as though made of dark brown
moss, and Inés seemed almost dry, like a polished fruit in that
region of mists and sulphurous vapors, and they walked along a
red lava path and he kept looking at her, looking at her, and
then he stopped because Don Pedro had transfixed him with
that look of his, and he could see that Don Pedro's face was
puffing up and he was growing bags beneath his eyes and
wrinkles on his brow and at the corners of his eyes, and his
shoulders sagged and his chest had bent and sunk below his
black silk tunic, and the beard had thinned and now seemed
poor and blotchy, and he was frightened for a moment, being
there among those Pontes, his father had told him once that
Don Cristóbal was a Jew who knew about sorcery and could read

the future in the stars, and now Don Pedro had become almost like Don Cristóbal, leaning on the very same gold-handled cane, although his eyes looked at him big and shiny like Inés's eyes; Inés of the crimson bodice, of the radiant face both orange and apple, an impossible but ripened fruit, Inés of the mouth accentuated by libidinous down, a lip of wine from Malvesie; up above his head the strange Adeje tower room seemed to flash and yearn, and a shudder seized the brocades hanging at the bed and the magnificent tapestries, and it was the wind from the Levant, wind blowing papers from the great stone table, setting the beads dancing on the abacus of ivory and bamboo, rippling charts of planets and of zodiacs, snuffing the candelabra's seven flames, welcome John, how good to see you, we've been waiting for you for so long.

⟦ X X ⟧

THE *Adelantado* appointed as commander of the fort the sergeant-major Villaroel, who remained there with the soldiers we had brought. At dawn a Mass was said, and after he bade farewell and warned everyone to sleep with one eye open, because the Lutherans could attack, my father-in-law had two large crosses, which he had ordered built, mounted on the watchtowers, and the coats of arms of France and of Admiral Gaspar, which could still be seen above the gate, were changed for those of Spain, with the cross of Caravaca above a crown. He also announced that the stockade, now blessed, would be called nothing but San Mateo, on whose day we had taken it from the Lutheran Frenchmen. By ten in the morning the *Adelantado* was on the road, with only thirty-five men: López Patiño, Gabrielillo, the Portuguese Hieronymite, I, and then Castañeda leading the guards. After much travail in the swamp we reached St. Augustine. Since Gabrielillo went ahead during the final stretch, we were received handsomely, for those who didn't weep for joy were laughing upon our victory, and everyone hailed us and wanted to know all about the troop.

St. Augustine's appearance had changed mightily in those two weeks; with the high ground leveled back a league around, and a good supply of wood sawed down, a town had been put up behind the fort, whose defenses had been improved, and a dock was built, and though the stonecutters and masons were daunted by the absence of ashlar, they had, along with their laborers, taken to improving the poor croplands worked by the

Indians, who could be seen by the dozens walking from one place to another, already baptized and dressed, with loads on their backs. And of these Indians the *Adelantado* said they were the poorest he had seen anywhere in the Indies, and also the flightiest and most thick-headed, and would be no good for any work because they were more fond of pleasure than effort.

That night, after supper, and after Don Bartolomé, Diego Flores and the chaplain López de Mendoza had gone to bed, the *Adelantado* sent me to find the Hieronymite, telling me to make sure that he brought his powders, since they would be demanded as soon as the man came into the room, at which point I had better be holding a dagger to his throat.

I went directly to the Portuguese's quarters, where I found him packing his clothing and equipment into a few trunks that the *Adelantado* had given him. He greeted me nicely and went right on stuffing his seeds and notebooks into the trunks, but I said to him:

"You must come with me, Don Rodrigo, because Don Pedro de Avilés wants you to give him your magic powders."

The Portuguese smiled, and said: "They're not magic, because I'm not a necromancer, but a scholar and observer of Nature, as were Pliny and Aristotle. It's there and nowhere else that God has put the remedies to mankind's ills."

"Have it your way," I said. "But I ask myself: why are you taking those big books with your notes and sketches, since you'll never find the same things back in Portugal?"

"I'm a traveler; my eyes have witnessed many strange natural phenomena, and I've always written them down," he said to me, looking thoughtful. "You must realize, Don Pedro, that there is only one Nature, great and unitary, which, like a mother with her daughters, shelters everyone beneath her mantle. Perhaps we can reach the mother by uncovering her daughters."

"If you are referring to the whole and its parts," I said, given an opening, "you should realize that you'll never live long enough to obtain the sum that you're trying to calculate, and since man is God's greatest artifice and the measure of all things of this world and of the entire universe, the Creator could but have ill conceived him as an investigator of everything that jumps before him, in search of a design, but rather he's here to use what he finds to benefit himself and the Church."

"Like gold and silver," the Portuguese said wryly. "By my faith, you're skilled in arts and sciences beyond those for making war, *maestre*," he added. "Are you a doctor?"

"A bachelor," I replied modestly.

"I congratulate you. You've made a strong argument, and I'm almost ready to pronounce myself convinced, but I should like to reflect a bit before replying."

"As you prefer," I answered delicately. "You'll always find me well disposed to hear you."

"You said that the *Adelantado* was looking for me," he said, taking a black, slickery pouch from one of the trunks. "I wouldn't want to offend him, and my being delayed here might do that."

I agreed, and pointing the way to him with the greatest courtesy, while with my other hand I clutched my dagger's hilt beneath my cape, I cautioned him:

"Be sure the powder does its work."

As we walked through the corridor, the Portuguese said to me:

"Yes, yes, *maestre*, your reasoning seems very clear to me: you come to the New World and get the Indians to trade their gold for bells and bonnets; you take the surplus to buy favors in court, obtaining new concessions; you build a house of stone with servants and slaves; you pay toward the construction of a good church, then you dress yourself up in a silk robe as its patron saint; you buy indulgences, you tithe, and you give as many ducats as the bishop wants for alms; you endow your daughter with a dowry and you make your son your heir, you make the best possible marriage for both of them, and then it all starts over again," he said, in one burst, as though he had thought it out before. "What a deluded fool I am to study the strange Nature of these provinces! But now that I think of it, I see that what I said does not really apply to you, because there is no gold in Florida, and the Indians you get won't be able to extract any. What will you do then?"

"I'll use my sword to serve God and my king," I said, stung by the liberties that he was taking.

"By my faith, you're a noble, valiant knight," he said, smiling. "I, on the other hand, who carry neither sword nor dagger, must serve the Lord by preserving the health and energy of those who, like you and your brave father-in-law, have set your sights so high."

I would have answered him if I hadn't seen the *Adelantado* coming out to meet us.

"Has the *señor doctor* had his supper?" he asked the Portuguese, in a very jolly voice. "If not, come in and partake of some tender game that my captain of the guards, Castañeda, shot for me. The meat is quite tasty and well seasoned."

"I bring your excellency the vigor that he can't get from all the game in the world," said the Portuguese, following the *Adelantado* to the table. "When does my ship depart?" he added as he lay the black-skinned pouch on the tablecloth.

"At dawn," said the *Adelantado,* taking it up almost in midair.

Seeing this, I drew my dagger and went up on the Portuguese, cornering him.

"Are you going to kill me, *maestre?*"

"It's merely a precaution, learned doctor," the *Adelantado* answered for me, as he examined what looked like a pinch of salt in the palm of his hand. "If there were a bit more of this powder you'd have to try it first; I've seen it done that way at the king's supper, and there's nothing wrong with it. As for you," he said, directing himself to me, "if something should go wrong, do me the favor of cutting *señor* de Alentejo's throat, which I doubt will be necessary as he seems so calm and secure."

Very deliberately, the *Adelantado* poured the powder into his cup and, after kneeling before his chair and reciting the Act of Contrition, he drank it down with a steady hand. Immediately, he sat down, raised his head to rest it on the back of the chair, and closed his eyes.

"Go up to the table, slowly," I said to the Portuguese, without lowering my weapon, as there was not much light and I wanted to look closely into my father-in-law's face for any bad signs.

"It's not good to get too close," he said. "It can mar the effect."

"Come," I insisted, my blade pushing against his neck. I could see my father-in-law out of the corner of my eye as he sat there trembling and touching himself all over.

We approached the table together in lockstep, when the *Adelantado*, possessed by a sudden, obscure passion, let out a long burst of laughter. Hearing him laugh so, I thought him at least ten years younger. But it was the same man sitting in the chair. Certainly his eyes were animated, but his beard was still streaked with gray and the crow's feet clutched his cheeks as tightly as before.

"Ha ha ha ha ha, long live the *señor* doctor! I feel so happy! Pedrillo, my dear, tell Castañeda to bring in the musicians; ha ha ha ha ha, a miracle!; Sheathe that stupid thing, Don Pedrín of the Pedrines, and I'll have you dance some pretty *seguidillas;* ha ha ha ha ha, drink my wine, most learned doctor! Will you finally sheathe your weapon, you rascal?, ha ha ha, Castañeda, Castañeda! Where are you, you butcher?"

On hearing Castañeda's heavy footsteps, I hid the dagger and, with the edge of the tablecloth, covered the pouch as well as I could.

"What's happening to your excellency?" Castañeda interrupted, brandishing his red crossbow, his eyes jumping. "Is everything all right?"

"The musicians! Delightfulness! Let's have dancing in the plaza! Hurray for the chaconne! Hurray for the sarabande! Bring on the dancers! Let's hear the *castrati* singing! Hurray for the fandango!"

Castañeda looked at me reproachfully, made a furious bow, and strode out of the room. The Portuguese, seated beside the table with a jar of wine in his hand, watched the *Adelantado*'s face carefully.

"Come closer, *maestre;* the drug has started working deeply now," he said to me, his voice grave.

Incredulous, I seized a big candle from the candelabra, but before I could lean over the table Alentejo had thrown the jar at my feet; the wine spattered my boots, the glass scattered under the table, I saw a fat drop of wax fall and sizzle in the pool of the inkwell. "Notice how rejuvenated your father-in-law is," the Portuguese kept repeating to me, and his voice seemed to be coming from far off.

"Get a good look, Don Pedro," he said to me insistently. "Look at the change."

I looked up and held the candle to an enraptured face that danced around like a carnival mask, and I saw that it was the face of a strapping twenty-year-old.

"The bodily effect will last until dawn; the effect on his will and passion will be there until a dagger or a bullet knocks him down," said Alentejo, looking fixedly at me. "If I were you, I wouldn't let him see himself in a mirror, and I wouldn't let his captains look at him until tomorrow."

"Don Pedro! Don Pedro! You big panderer! Bring me an Indian girl and another one who's a Lutheran or I swear I'll burst!"

"Go ahead," the Portuguese advised. "It's best for everyone if you humor him."

"You're the one who does the Devil's tricks," I replied angrily, feeling myself free of his magic. "You go," I added, giving him his sword and leaving the room.

Provided with a safe-conduct from the *Adelantado*, Rodrigo de Alentejo sailed at dawn with the Lutherans. The ship went out with the tide and gained the horizon very quickly.

⟦ X X I ⟧

FOUR HUNDRED MEN went with Ojeda to take the gold from Cibao. But you, Antón Babtista, stayed back with the Admiral in Isabela, having no desire to wear out your hemp sandals on the southern crags.

They can take all the gold they'll find there and stick it in my fly, you thought, as the troop filed through the stockade's new gate, to be sprinkled there with a drop or two of holy water from Friar Buil's hyssop; only a few horses had survived, there was not much powder to waste in the salutes, and the infantry and cavalry had scarcely any flesh left on their bones. Do you remember, Antón Babtista, how the second march to Cibao was so different from the first? I'll bet a castellano that a quarter of them don't come back alive, you said. But no one took your bet, and everyone who heard you backed away and looked at you suspiciously. A bird of bitter omen, grumbled Roldán, a steward of the Admiral's, and it dawned on you that it was all the same whether a person went to Cibao or stayed behind, because disease and hunger would come equally to everyone in that godforsaken land. And so before a week had passed you were sorry that you hadn't gone, because the ration of cassava and fish soup in bowls could not revive the energy expended in the carpentry and stonework that the Admiral wanted done.

The sun's heat seemed to burst out like a whiplash, at least that was Chanca's first impression, though soon corrected. It was the spotted fever, with its usual hectic flush, except that the red blotches were a little late in appearing on the trunk. It had begun in the cabins that were cramped together in the lower quarter of the settlement, which soon had to be burnt, and another hospital was built to handle the sick. Then a detachment came back from Cibao, made up of men who'd gone out earlier with Ojeda; they had an Indian with them, whose ears had been lopped off because he stole a shirt, and also a chief with his consort—all in chains; Ojeda had sent them down to be made examples of, and the Admiral sentenced them to hang. Ojeda's men reported that not one mine had yet been found and that the only gold they'd seen was what the Indians brought to barter in exchange for trinkets, and with that news there was a new wave of discontent in Isabela; the hidalgos, furious, were the first to lay their hammers, saws, and barrows down, and soon no stones were quarried anymore; the houses stayed half-finished and the mahogany barely covered the church's nave and the hall of honor at the Admiral's palace. Do you remember your discouragement, Antón Babtista? There was nothing to be done but to attack the ships, bribe the pilots, and head back to Spain: that was the notion that you spread among the soldiers.

The Admiral must have sniffed out some conspiracy, because the crier called one morning for the whole group to assemble on the barren flat that never quite had managed to become the *plaza de armas*. The Admiral stood there on a platform, along with Friar Buil, Don Diego Colón, the captain Coronel, Sanchez de Carvajal, and Juan de Luján. The Admiral's face seemed longer than ever, yellower than ever, but his eyes were two live embers and his words, calm and persuasive, went on fabricating dreams that took flight like big auspicious birds. He had put together some reports: the Great Khan lived on a peninsula that the Indians knew as Cuba, which was none other than the province on Mangi that Marco Polo had described; the lavish island of Cipangu lay just southward, toward the setting sun, and the Earthly Paradise had been passed by because he hadn't known those seas, and it was the terra firma that the female captives of the Caribbees had spoken of, which extended like a tapestry of flowers, unicorns, and songbirds from a point that lay a few leagues past the island of Dominica; gold, silver, pearls, silk, ivory, pepper, clove, cinnamon, and dozens of spices never tasted yet awaited the arrival of the Castilian ships, and Prester John and the Great Khan were personages known to be both grand and generous.

When the Admiral sailed away in three caravels that he had readied with a fugitive's haste, you resolved to leave the village behind with its hunger and its fevers, and to set out again toward Cibao. Do you remember, Antón Babtista, your hesitation in deciding where to cast your lot? For you chose to throw in with Ojeda's troop rather than going with that evil-tempered Catalan, Margarit, and the way you judged Ojeda is curious, because on Monday you might have damned him for an hidalgo, overbearing, an evil blowhard, and then on Tuesday you would say he was the best captain you had ever had, his skill and bravery unequaled on the island; but as it happened, Ojeda was stuck in the old fort at Santo Tomás, where the humidity would mildew your breath, and *mosén* Pedro de Margarit, under the Admiral's express orders, began a tour of the Indian villages of the Vega Real, which were well stocked with food and women. Without really deciding on it, you took to the road with your quiver and crossbow; Guacanagarí's Indian, whom you were to call Miguelillo, carried your shield on his skinny back, and also your breastplate, your helmet, your worn-out pouch, and your string of little bells, stolen the night before, which in those parts were worth the ransom of the Twelve Peers of France; and as you approached the southern mountains you began to sing, treading on caterpillars on a rainwashed April day, the ballad of Granada's loss, *you killed the Bencerrajes / who were Granada's flower,* and Miguelillo laughed, Miguelillo whose name was not Miguelillo but rather Mayael, which to you sounded like Miguel; and Miguelillo, half crushed by his load, laughed and laughed, and you pointed to an indic almond tree and he said *jobo, jobo,* and you pointed to a stream and he said *toa, toa,* and you sang *you'll lose your self and all the kingdom / and Granada will be gone;* and so you went happily through the mountains, Antón Babtista, leaping through the springtime from one stone to another, following the trail of an *almiquí,* shooting an arrow at a flock of parrots, roasting a spitted *jutía* from head to tail while Miguelillo innocently chewed on butterflies; *Oh, woe, my fair Alhama!* you sang out, and Miguelillo laughed and tried to imitate your gestures and your discordant sounds; because for Miguelillo you and your kind still came directly from the sky, not merely from the sky but straight from heaven, that's right, you're a kind of god to him, or at least a man-saint, a human angel, you, a saint, Antón Babtista, who would have guessed? Who but Miguelillo could have hatched such arrant nonsense? That's what you were thinking when the Indian, as the stars came out, looked up at the grandeur of the night then being born and affirmed in a graceful, elegant pantomime your flesh's origin on high.

But your flesh was of this world, Antón Babtista, you knew that well enough, although you enjoyed your moments of feigned divinity, putting your hands together and nodding to create a spurious little miracle for Miguelillo; with the beard that you no longer trimmed, and the tabard of the Calatrava Order that you had found in a deserted cabin, and the raving idiot's face that you assumed, and the pompous visages and litanies gleaned in ignorance from prayers and chants, you seemed a sandaled apostle, a catechist of the madhouse, a lunatic saint who preached to the great nothingness, and nevertheless, Antón Babtista, it was only in those moments of awe and admiration that you felt as though you'd risen above your sins to live up to the Admiral's estimation of your worth, for you started to believe yourself committed to the saving of Miguelillo's little soul. But the Admiral had also said: if they kill, hang them; if they steal, cut off their noses and their ears, for it's only in this way that we can teach restraint. And unfortunately Miguelillo had tied a little bell to his prick, not knowing that the tinkling could be heard beneath his loincloth.

Do you recall the afternoon that you came on the Vega Real? Before you had walked a hundred steps through palm and calabash you ran into a detachment of Margarit's soldiers, what do you do here? well, it's a good land, we live off the Indians, we go from one village to another, we have the girls to ourselves, we eat all the corn and yucca, and then we leave the village, we find another one and we put up there, and that's how it is; what's

Ojeda up to? he's at the fort in Santo Tomás, preparing to fight Caonabó; well then I'm coming with you.

How many weeks did you spend roaming and idling your way through the Vega, Antón? Time passed differently there, and it wasn't that the days went by faster or more slowly; no, it wasn't that, it was that it seemed like Eden there, pleasure and abundance stretched out in a sequence of suns and moons not found on any calendar. On one of your vagaries you went into a hut that sent out, from its little square of earth, the aroma of smoked rabbits, of skinned game and fresh blood, of marinated birds; to judge from the vessels and the tidbits by the door, it was the dwelling of a *nitaíno,* a *taíno* elder, son or brother of a chief who had fled toward Marién or Jaraguá; in the darkness within, a cluster of shadows ran away and squeezed against the wall of palm leaves, and slowly you distinguished a small group of women who hid a bulky form that lay in one of the hammocks; you pulled down half the house to get a look, and in the light you saw a body laid out in the hammock: the sweat-covered and still bloody body, softly swaying, of a barely pubescent Indian girl who had died in childbirth. From curiosity, amid the old women's wailing, you pulled off the cotton tatters and came face to face with a vermillion ball of fuzz and pinkish, palpitating skin, and then thought back to the small girl with breasts like olive pits whom you had mounted back there by the river in the reeds, and so this was your child, and you picked it up out from its still-warm mother's unstrung arms; you went away confused, not knowing what to do, with the infant tucked beneath your arm like a loaf of bread; and then you had an idea of time, of the weeks and days and nights that you had spent on the Vega Real; when you got to the river you didn't dare drown the little kicking, squalling creature, for the notion of good and evil, lost in the Vega's verdant paradise, had come back to you; you bent down above the weeds along the riverbank, dipped your hand into the cool water, and bathed your son's head, murmuring, startled, contrite, feeling redeemed in the act I baptize you Miguel Babtista in the name of the Father, Son, and Holy Ghost, amen.

You left your son in the care of a strong, big-breasted Indian woman whose milk you tasted after prying away the stiffened lips of a two-year-old child still held in her arms. You had no memory of those fat, juicy nipples, Antón Babtista, or of the girl that you had forced to suckle you months before to cool the burning of a stew with chili peppers. But she remembered you, Antón Babtista, which was quite enough; to her, as to Miguelillo, you were an idol come down from the distant forests of heaven, a white angel molded from the sacred yucca's pulp, a demigod who must be appeased to keep some fabled tragedy like a hurricane from descending on the weak palm roofs or on the little furrows of corn and yams that had been dug out with the heel, piled up by hand, and sown with the tip of a wooden rod; and the woman, whom you named Doña Antonia, passed as the mother of your son, and her husband came to be something like Joseph; and so she started to receive small presents from the *behique* who cured fevers with leeches applied to neck or belly, and she even got gifts from the humble Indians who worked on the common lands; and when dawn came there appeared, at the lodge's door, upon the palm leaf mat, some lovingly placed offerings of plumes and branches, pretty stones, flowers, little vessels cut from gourds, all for the guamohaya, daughter of the *behique* Toabay, she who nursed the son of the living, breathing idol, the idol whose down was golden as the corn, the idol who appeared and disappeared from the village and who surely went back to some secret cavern where he visited his brothers Márohu and Boínayel, the propitiators of the rain. You began to think then that the place was yours, Antón Babtista, the Indians your servants, their poor structures the moats and towers of your castle. If only Ojeda saw me now, you sighed, stretched out in Doña Antonia's springy hammock, or laying your miracle-working demigod's hands upon some ache that neither tobacco smoke nor purges of *cañafístola* could dispel. The detachment of Margarit's that patrolled that side of the island soon came to call the town *La villa de Antón;* you went to great lengths every time the half-dozen gaudy soldiers paraded down the village's main street; you shouted orders and scolded the women, and you had ten guinea pigs taken from their cages, and you roasted an iguana with a seigneurial jowl, and filled the stewpot with little sweet fish and mustachioed langostinos from the river; later you applied yourself to the making of a guava brandy that would drive both Indians and Christians wild, if only Ojeda were to see me now, you sighed, as you lifted up your gourd to toast the Admiral's health and their Majesties' long lives, if Ojeda saw me now. . . . But he never was to see you, at least he never saw you as a feudal lord with pedigreed wife and first-born son. One afternoon, as you came home with two guinea pigs you'd shot with your crossbow, you found nothing left of your village, your castle, your servants, anything; a mounted party of hidalgos had set fire to the palm huts after disembowelling every Indian at hand; when you bent over to pick your string of bells from the ashes, Doña Antonia appeared on the path that led to the river; she squeezed against you, trembling and sobbing, holding little Miguel.

Do you remember those unhappy days, Antón Babtista? Doña Antonia wept unceasingly, even when you possessed her. You wandered through the Vega of villages deserted, sacked, and burned, and you found scarcely anything to chew on; Doña Antonia's milk dried up and the baby began shitting green. The last news you'd had of Ojeda was that he was under seige by the forces of Caonabó. And so you decided to return to Isabela. It wasn't easy for you, Antón Babtista, making that decision, remember? You were ashamed to enter the white settlement with an Indian concubine and, above all, with an almond-eyed son whose lips were thick and whose complexion every day became less pink, more parroty. You could already hear the gibes. But let's make the best of it now, you said, and once again you crossed the northern mountains, although you didn't see Isabela's stockade, not even from a distance. A partly fanned-out column marching beneath the Admiral's pennant and the Castilian flag surprised you on the plain with its colors and its melody of war. You took this as the path that destiny was showing you; you looked down at your wife and son, asleep beneath some bushes, and without any bad feelings you left the string of bells to be their fortune, then you picked up your crossbow, slung the quiver over your shoulder, and, holding your shield, set out running toward your own.

They had set you down as dead, though nobody rejoiced at seeing you alive; they felt the rolls of fat that you still carried from your months in paradise, and they held their peace in expectation of some sign of penitence from you, a tardy *mea culpa* and some breast beating. You learned in the ranks that Margarit and Friar Buil, with the men from Catalonia, had taken advantage of the Admiral's absence to throw off the authority of Diego Colón, and finally they had seized the caravels that had just brought Don Bartolomé, and told everyone that they were going to give their Majesties a full report of the tricks and outrages perpetrated by that evil band of Genoans. Then, as if a lightning bolt had cracked Isabela's bell, the news arrived that the Indians at Cibao had attacked the Spaniards left behind there, falling on them in a heap to split their skulls with wooden swords. The Admiral, recovered from the illness that he'd had on landing, suppressed the uprising; fifteen hundred Indians were herded into Isabela, among them the treacherous Guatiguaná, who was smeared with excrement to reduce his power of incitement; shoved into the plaza's clearing, they lived there many days, grazing on the grass that August's cloudbursts nurtured; clumped together and on all fours, drinking from the puddles, eating, shitting, pissing, and dying any way they could, they astonished the men, women, and children who came with Antonio de Torres's flotilla to populate the settlement; many of the new arrivals honestly believed this to be the Indians' natural state and, in their charity, threw them table scraps and called out here sooie sooie. When the ships were about to sail off, there being no gold to send to their Majesties, the Admiral ordered four hundred relatively healthy-looking males and females to be picked out and sent to Seville for auction; the rest were divided among Isabela's residents, and the ones too puny to suit anyone were driven from the settlement in a hail of stones and spit. Antón Babtista never learned that one of Torres's caravels carried the parents of the twelve-year-old girl who had borne his son Miguel. It is very possible that the pair did not survive the trip to Spain; Antonio de Torres took the wrong course and lost a month tacking around the environs of Dominica; luckily for him he steered northward and hit the strong March trade winds at the latitude of San Juan; on the journey's last leg, between Madeira and Cádiz, "some two hundred Indians died," wrote Michele de Cuneo, "from the unaccustomed air, I think, which was colder than theirs. The first land that we saw was Cape Espartel, and very soon thereafter we arrived in Cádiz, where we unloaded all the slaves, half of them sick. For your information: they are not a people given to work, and they greatly fear the cold, and do not live long." Don Juan Fonseca, armorer and provisioner to the Admiral by appointment of the Crown, put the survivors up for sale in Seville, saw them tremble in the cold and faint from hunger on the wharf; he saw them eating vermin and drinking their own urine, naked "just as they went about in their own land, just as they were born, with no more shame than animals have, and they fare very badly, for this land does not agree with them."

But you, Antón Babtista, never found this out, nor did you care to. You were no better and no worse than the other Juans and Antóns who went with you, gun or crossbow at their shoulders, pouches open for the dice and the deck and the furtive handful of gold. And you're going with the Admiral to teach another lesson; you're going out with your detested and admired Alonso de Ojeda, now the conqueror of Caonabó, you're going with two hundred infantrymen, twenty horsemen, twenty mastiffs, and an auxiliary troop of northern Indians; you're going out to riddle the lungs and guts of the little brown painted clownish naked men who wait for you, quivering with fear and rage, in the glorious forest of the Vega Real.

〚 XXII 〛

A S *SEÑOR DE AVILÉS LAY* recovering from some severe prostrations that overtook him after the Portuguese
had left, three Indians arrived at St. Augustine with the
news that a large band of Frenchmen was coming down the
coast. Tired and melancholy as he was, the promised vigor
having lasted but a few hours, and finding himself lacking the
energy to leave his bed, the *Adelantado* sent Diego Flores to take
some men and a boat to estimate the Lutherans' strength and
fighting temper, if any. A little while later, Gabrielillo awakened
me with a message from my father-in-law directing me to arm
myself and come to his bedroom immediately.

I found him armed from head to foot; he seemed dressed
more for a tourney than for crossing those sandy beaches.

"With discipline and prayer I have conquered that Portuguese magician's spells, and if I hadn't done it I would be as
black and wasted as that burnt-out candlewick, which is just
what the scoundrel intended for me, to keep me from conquer-
ing these lands for God and the king."

"You've grown thinner, *señor*," I said, seeing how loosely his
armor hung upon his body.

"That's true," he answered, steadying himself with a chain
hung from the ceiling, "and a dizziness has come over me like
none I ever felt at sea in any storm."

"It seems to me that you ought to stay back here and not go
out to meet the heretics, for no matter how strong your spirit
might be, your joints are still weak."

"If you weren't my daughter's husband," he answered in a

voice from beyond the grave, "I'd take your words as an affront. My God, how quickly the young forget the sacrifices of men like Orellana and Cabeza de Vaca!" he added, his glance darting toward the crucifix that hung above his bed.

"Forgive me, I wasn't trying to displease you, merely to spare you an ordeal that may be unnecessary," I replied. "Don't you think I'm brave enough to put down the Lutherans?"

"You're brave enough, Don Pedro, but you're squeamish," he said to me angrily, "and those two things don't go together here."

"Try me, señor, and you'll see my faults corrected."

He looked at me in silence. Then he called for Castañeda and told him to muster all the guardsmen on the dock.

"A few days ago you were wondering when a governor should be merciful to his enemies and when he shouldn't," he said to me gravely. "I gave you the best answer that I knew. Nevertheless, today I find I must obtain my captains' opinions, although I know better than to call them here in council on such an urgent matter."

"I follow you with all my heart, señor," I answered, sensing a delicate situation. "And since I take fidelity and frankness to be but two wheels on the same cart, I ask your permission, before I even know your question, to speak according to what my understanding tells me, and if that should turn out to be dim, it will at least be well intended."

"You hide yourself adroitly, Don Pedro, and I assure you that you'll rise quite high in the court if you set yourself to it," said the Adelantado, smiling. "But more to the point: I've called you here to learn what you, in my place, would do about the Frenchmen that the Indians have just brought to our attention."

"I would fight them."

"Your cousin, the admiral, got here an hour ago: the heretics are four leagues from St. Augustine, missing some two hundred men because their ship broke apart on the shoals, and they've lost their boats and provisions. Surely they know nothing about what's happened to the rest of their fleet and they've decided to follow the coast to our encampments and ask for help. Your cousin also informed me that their march is being held up by an inlet, since they have no energy to go into the forest to find a way around. Now then, *señor,* what would you do?"

"Are you sure they're not coming to take the fort from us?" I asked, somewhat disheartened.

"I'm sure," he said, lifting his heaviest buckler and preparing to leave the room. "Your cousin took one of them prisoner and I talked to him."

"Well, in that case I'd go out and capture them, and then I'd ship them to Spain in irons to humble themselves before King Philip and the Holy Inquisition, which will know quite well what should be done with them."

The *Adelantado,* struggling to come up with the right word or signal to answer my proposition, took down a visored helmet and strode quickly out of the room.

Castañeda was waiting for us on the dock, and we took the brig that we had seized from the Lutherans at Carlefor. Shortly after daybreak, we anchored in a bay surrounded by mangroves, near the inlet that had the Frenchmen on the other side. Making a path for ourselves on land, we marched single file for a good quarter of an hour. When we reached a little stand of palm trees, the *Adelantado* told Gabrielillo to climb the highest of them and let us know if he saw any Lutherans.

"They're on the other side of the water, facing us," Gabrielillo shouted. "I see many people and two flags."

Then, opening our way through the underbrush, we marched toward them until they could see us. Right away we saw one of them strip and then throw himself into the water to swim over to our side.

The man had scarcely set foot on land when the *Adelantado* asked him: "What kind of Frenchmen are you?"

"We are some two hundred," the soldier replied in Spanish. "Our general is Jean Ribault, who rules these lands in the name of the king of France."

"Are you Catholic or Lutheran?"

"We follow the new religion."

"Why did you swim over here?"

"Our captains would know who you are."

"Would you like to go back to your side?"

"Yes, but not before I know who you are."

"Tell *señor* Ribao that I am Pedro Menéndez de Avilés, governor of these provinces, come to populate and Christianize them in the name of the king of Spain."

"General Ribault is four leagues back," said the soldier, extending his arm toward the north. "I can only talk with the captains in council."

"Do so," said my father-in-law, getting up from the fallen tree trunk on which he'd found himself a seat. "You'll go in one of my boats. If your captain desires to talk to me, bring him back in it. His life will be respected. If he wishes to, he can come over with a few men, but not more than five."

Very soon the Frenchmen arrived. The *Adelantado* and I, along with eight guardsmen, received them. Castañeda and the rest of the soldiers stayed half-hidden in the trees, in a way that made it seem that they were the advance guard of a whole troop.

The captain of those heretics told us that, after their encounter with our ships, in which we had killed some of their men, a storm had hit them, spilling them on the coast. The men now on the bank were the survivors of one of the four galleons, who had decided to march south to seek the protection of our flag and to borrow a boat to take them to Carlefor.

"*Caballeros*," said my father-in-law very circumspectly, "your fort has been taken and all of its defenders are dead, but for the women and children and four soldiers who follow the true religion. I have brought two of them with me, and you may speak with them to verify what I've just told you. If that doesn't satisfy you, I'll show you some arms and armaments that my men kept for themselves, there being no other riches there."

The *Adelantado* had the Catholic Frenchmen sent for and had the things from Carlefor spread out on a canvas, after which we retired to eat while the Lutherans spoke freely with the soldiers.

After a while they came to us saying that their captain wished to make a proposition.

"Are you satisfied that Carlefor is gone?" the *Adelantado* asked.

The captain replied that he was, and he begged to be given ships and provisions for a return to France.

"I would willingly provide them, but you are not Catholics. Nor do I have the ships for such a voyage, since one went back with your women and children, another is heading to Spain with the news of our victory, and I have dispatched the last one to San Mateo, which is what the fort is called now, to reinforce it with more cannon."

The captain said in that case might they be allowed to live peaceably in St. Augustine until a ship arrived, there being no war between the kings of France and Spain.

"There is no war, it's true," the *Adelantado* said, "but Florida is a house forbidden to all who are not Spaniards. You are heretics as well, and thus the enemies of Spain. And I have to fight you as such, for my king has entrusted me to do it. Whether you choose or not to surrender your arms and flags unconditionally is entirely your affair. You are free to take one course or the other."

The captain replied that he understood well and asked that he be given two hours in which to make certain deliberations in council. After that time had passed, and if nothing had been heard from them, we would then do whatever our consciences told us to do.

The *Adelantado* agreed and the Frenchmen went away.

After thinking to himself for a while, my father-in-law took his helmet and walked alone among some dunes that could just be seen behind the thicket. Seeing him stop for a moment, I decided to follow him. I found him tracing a line across a little path that ran naturally between the dunes. I thought that he must be trying to calculate the time by the shadow of his lance, because the sun was partly out and Gabrielillo had carelessly broken the hourglass. But I soon became aware that he had another purpose as, without saying a word to me, but smiling vaguely, he clutched the lance and returned to the riverbank.

A little while later the Frenchmen, signaling from their side, asked for a boat to bring them over, and the *Adelantado* sent one.

When the heretics' captain reached us, he said that there were barons and counts among them who stood ready to ransom their lives for five thousand ducats.

"I have always been poor," my father-in-law replied, "and that money would suit me well. If you were Catholic I would accept it, perhaps, but you are Lutherans and I shall have to kill you."

"I see nothing wrong in your excellency's taking the ducats. It is the usual practice in war, although, as far as my information reaches, France and Spain are at peace."

"I shall fulfill the mission on which my king has sent me, and as surely as there is a bond between heaven and earth I will not change my view. When an hour has passed I'll cross the waters, to come upon your camp and put you to the sword."

The captain returned again to where his men were, and soon came back in the boat, which was now filled with arms and pennants. There were seventy harquebuses and twenty pistols, as well as many pikes, swords, and daggers.

"We implore your excellency to show mercy on us," said the captain, with a hopeful bow. Eight knights had come with him, and all, as soon as they stepped off the boat, bent over gravely to offer their respects to the *Adelantado;* when the latter asked how many others had agreed to their course of action, they replied that none had disagreed and that all awaited the boat's return so that they could surrender their swords. Then *señor* de Avilés told me to take twenty soldiers in the boat to bring back more Frenchmen, no more than ten on each trip, and he recommended that I see to it that no heretic was mistreated in the crossing.

But I was not the one who brought them, for at that moment my cousin Diego Flores appeared, to claim for himself the right to cross the Frenchmen, as he and not I was the admiral of the fleet. Over my opposition, the *Adelantado* granted his request. Once the boat had gone, he signaled me to come away from the bank and, gathering most of the soliders, he marched with eight captives toward some dunes that were a distance of two gunshots away, out of sight of the Frenchmen on the other side. When we got there, near the place where I had seen him mark the sand with his lance, the *Adelantado* said to the Lutheran captain:

"*Señor,* I have only a few soldiers, and none with any experience of war, for these are not the ones who fought at Carlefor. It seems to me that the safest thing for me would be to have you tied together for the march to St. Augustine, since it would be easy for you to avenge yourselves on us along the way."

The Frenchman replied that he was right, in fact, and that he might do the same if he were in the *Adelantado*'s position. So then all of them were tied to each other and their hands tied behind their backs with the straps of our harquebuses. The *Adelantado* turned to me and told me to go back and wait for the boat, and as soon as it landed to take the Frenchmen up to that spot.

I did so, without any objection from the Frenchmen, who were well-disposed and worthy men. On seeing them approach, the *Adelantado* went up to meet them and said the same things to them that he had said awhile before to the captain, and they too acceded willingly to being tied with the harquebus slings.

By nightfall, two hundred and eight Frenchmen had arrived at the spot behind the dunes, for the captain had spoken truly about their willingness to surrender their arms and emblems, and it seemed fine to all of them to march tied to St. Augustine, given that they were so many that they might otherwise have overcome us.

"Is there among you any Catholic who wants confession?" asked the *Adelantado.*

Eight of them said that they were Catholic, and at a signal from my father-in-law, Diego Flores took them back to the boat.

After receiving food and drink, for they were quite weak, the Frenchmen were formed into two files and the *Adelantado* gave the signal for them to walk along the path. When they reached the lance mark, Castaneda and the soliders of the vanguard fell upon them with swords and pistols. Seeing that, all of our men followed suit, including the *Adelantado*, who was with the rear guard and to the right of me. I then realized that, without my having noticed, everyone in the party had received previous orders from him. When my astonishment had passed, I drew my sword. But it was too late, none but our own men were standing on the path.

"How many Lutheran pigs have you killed, *maestre*," the *Adelantado* asked me mockingly.

⟦ XXIII ⟧

O N SEPTEMBER 23, 1588, the ruined remnants of the *felicísima armada* that Philip II had sent against England arrived in Santander. In the days that followed, an appreciable number of straggling ships entered the port, equally damaged by the English culverins and the adverse weather that had prevailed during that singular summer on the English Channel, the North Sea, and the vast stretch of the Atlantic west of Ireland, that is, along the entire retreat of that ailing flock of ships that was to be called later, and ironically, the *armada invencible.*

Of the one hundred and thirty vessels of various kinds that had left Lisbon on May 9 that year, barely half returned, most of them unserviceable; of the thirty thousand men who had sailed with the great fleet—twenty thousand soldiers, eight thousand sailors, and two thousand oarsmen—ten thousand came back alive, although many more would die in makeshift hospitals along the coast and in the stifling murk of their own ships' lower decks and holds, for Santander and its environs for weeks had no way of housing, feeding, tending to the many thousand sick and wounded men brought home by the Armada. Typhus, dysentery, scurvy, hunger, and, above all, weakness from the dehydration of the final days of the return were maladies spread all throughout the remnants of the fleet. It is known that one ship ran aground in Laredo only because her crew was too debilitated to lower her sails or drop anchor.

The disaster, then, was dire; its impact on the public mind, tremendous; its political and economic consequences, verging on the incalculable.

The great house of Fugger, from July until November 1588, shuddered on receiving, as if from broadside cannon blasts, report upon report that carried news of the Armada.

Throughout the previous century, the Fuggers had been bankers, always liberal creditors, to the Hapsburgs. Among their celebrated financial strokes were those of having won the Austrian crown for Charles V by lending more than a half million florins and of having borne the collapse of Spanish credit on their backs during the crisis of 1557. Count Felipe Eduardo Fugger, who, together with his brother Octaviano II, directed a prosperous branch of the family business, organized a private information service founded on three sources: dispatches sent by agents and correspondents throughout the world; *Neue Zeitungen,* newspapers sold in Austrian and German cities; and materials furnished by the agency of Crasser and Schiffle, of Augsburg, dealing with the most diverse aspects of mercantile, military, political, and religious activity chiefly in Western Europe.

The Armada, of course, drew the Fuggers' attention. Availing themselves of their couriers and informants, they followed, from Augsburg, every circumstance of the enormous operation, like astrologers who calculate the consequences and the course of an unsettling comet just appeared.

Cologne, December 24, 1587: It is assumed in Brussels that the ships now being outfitted in Antwerp and in other ports are destined for the war with England. Four regiments of German mercenaries are to go with them. It is thought that this coming spring will see strange happenings, for there also are reports that the Scottish king has publicized his enmity toward England and will ally with Spain.

Madrid, May 18, 1588: The late dispatches from Lisbon say that people there do not want to embark with the Armada, because there have been dire prophesies. It is said with confidence that English Catholics will help the Spanish troops to land, directed by several great lords who are still faithful to the true religion. There were women, many of them, with the fleet. The duke of Medina Sidonia, its commanding general, told each captain to submit a list of all the women on his ship within four days. It was found that more than seven hundred women were on board. Not only were they put ashore, but they were expelled from Lisbon. This was done when the soldiers had already come aboard, so everyone complained about the measure. They were comforted somewhat on being told that many thousand willing lasses lay awaiting them in England.

Hamburg, June 23, 1588: I must report that Captain Hans Limburger has just arrived from Cádiz. He penetrated the blockade to bring a shipment of salt, raisins, cinnamon, and a bit of sugar. He sailed on May 20, and reached the latitude of Lisbon four days later. He saw the Armada in the distance, aligned in battle formation, though on the following day he lost it because of a strong wind that blew him northward. Hans Limburger believes that the Armada must have left from Lisbon on May 23 (old calendar) or June 2 (new calendar). An English warship sighted and intercepted his hooker, which it took to Plymouth. He was very well received there by Drake, who rejoiced to learn that the Armada was at sea, and who ordered his ships readied. Captain Limburger was given a safe-conduct that saw him into Hamburg without incident. His opinion is that if there is to be fighting in the channel, the loss of life will be enormous. The moon has been stained the color of blood for two nights running. God alone knows what that sign means.

Rome, June 25, 1588: The pope has recently declared himself an ally of the Spanish king. He is considering a gift of one million ducats once the Armada's men have landed in England.

Antwerp, July 2, 1588: This afternoon we heard from Bruges. The duke of Parma has got word from Calais of the Armada's meeting with the English ships. The Armada has been routed. There are no details.

Salzburg, July 14, 1588: War between Spain and England is in the air, and there is no sign of peace. His Holiness, in the presence of our gracious highness the lord of Salzburg, has let it be known in the Vatican that he regards Elizabeth Tudor to be unfit to govern England or to claim its lands or subjects, and the latter have his dispensation to renounce their vows of obedience to the Crown. The pope withdrew as well all titles and honors he had given her, which now are transferred to the king of Spain, whom he considers to be chosen by God to sit upon the English throne, as protector of the Catholic faith in that country and in Ireland. His Holiness, then, has proclaimed His Majesty, Philip of Austria, to be the king of England, Spain, and Ireland, with the condition that His Majesty should pay tribute to the Holy Church of Rome, as is done in Naples. To help His Majesty defeat heresy more quickly, His Holiness has conceded him a million crowns, payable upon the Armada's capture of some English port.

Middleburg, July 22, 1588: Five ships from Lisbon docked at Calais carrying salt and spices. They have begun the rumor of the Armada's defeat. According to the crew's accounts, they met with Spanish ships twice during their trip, once with a group of twelve and once with sixteen, all extremely battered. When asked about the rest of the Armada, both groups had answered that they knew nothing, for a storm has separated them. Admiral Howard and Drake remain at sea, and no one knows for certain of their whereabouts.

Constantinople, July 26, 1588: The queen of England has instructed her ambassador to give the different viziers an idea of her wishes. Nonetheless, we may suppose that he remained until he heard definitive news of the Armada. We may wonder how the sultan intends to respond to the queen's offer of her friendship. Let us hope God wills that justice should prevail and that the queen's designs are met with the defeat that she deserves and that the projects of His Majesty succeed. Let us pray and trust in God. Yesterday the French ambassador sent his cousin running back to France. They say the duke of Guisa has become the virtual king of France, and that he's tossed King Henry from the throne.

Hamburg, August 3 and 4, 1588: Hans Buttber has arrived in port in a great ship. He comes from Sanlúcar and has sailed through the channel. He was with the English for five days last month and he says that they have had a victorious engagement with the Armada. According to him, the English ships acquitted themselves very well and, never ceasing their fire, maneuvered in such a way that the big galleys could neither reach nor board them. Drake captured Don Alonso de Valdés, the commander of fourteen ships, whom he brought to England together with ten Spanish noblemen. There he entertained them with a banquet, with excellent food and music. Valdés's galleon was one of the most powerful in the Armada, and it fell into Drake's hands intact with its sixty cannons and four hundred and fifty men. The galleon *Santa María del Rosario* was left behind at the channel's entrance by the *San Felipe*, the Armada's flagship. According to the account of Don Pedro de Valdés, his ship had lost her bowsprit in an accidental brush with another vessel; with the rigging thus unstrung, the foremast soon blew over in the wind. Valdés complains of the ignominious conduct of the duke of Medina Sidonia, whom he accuses of not having been able to control the actions of Don Diego Flores de Valdés, who from the *San Felipe* acts as the Armada's virtual chief. Don Pedro and Don Diego are cousins, but estranged by an old rivalry, to such an extent that the *San Felipe* passed right alongside the dismasted galleon without so much as throwing her a cable. Drake came upon the *Santa María del Rosario* with her sails furled in the middle of the night and, after making himself known, accepted Don Pedro's sword. They found a rich booty on board: one hundred barrels of gunpowder, a huge store of firearms, and fifty thousand ducats meant to underwrite the rising of the Irish Catholics. At noon today a ship arrived from Holland; it had been at Enkhuizen near the end of July. It brings word that eighteen Spanish ships are sunk and eight removed to England as prizes. The rest of the Armada, it is said, has fled to the coast of France.

Hamburg, August 5, 1588: It is now confirmed that the English have defeated the Spaniards, from whom they've captured twenty-two ships and sunk eighteen. Many ships have caught fire and burned. Some two hundred counts and dons, as they are called, have been taken as prisoners to England. Drake seems to have been badly wounded, although the English have not called off their pursuit. The duke of Parma could not get to Dunquerque, and as a consequence his forces were unable to help the Armada as was planned.

Middleburg, August 12, 1588: On the fifth day of the current month a pinnace came from England bearing orders for the hollanders and zealanders to take up arms, and above all and at all cost keep the duke of Parma and his ships from leaving Dunquerque. On the following day another English pinnace arrived with the same order, but this one brought the news that twenty-two Spanish ships were sunk and many others captured. It has been learned from the captives that the Armada was to reach a point in the channel between Dover and Calais, there to engage the English fleet while Parma landed seventy thousand men in England. On the eleventh came another English pinnace carrying orders to pin down the duke of Parma at the coast and keep his troops from crossing. The pinnace reported that the Spanish and the English ships had fought for eight hours running in the straits of Dover, and that at the end the English had given chase to ten of the Armada's ships. Of these, some ran aground upon the coast, the rest were led away to England, where prisoners were taken. On the tenth the English attacked again, this time with their entire force, and they sank or damaged almost all the Spanish ships. The English cannonades have stripped them of their sails, masts, rigging, and tackle, so that they are now ungovernable. On the eleventh, the Dutch sacked two such ships, one named the *San Felipe* and the other the *San Mateo,* both galleons of twelve hundred tons, one run aground at Blankenburghe, the other at a place near Dunquerque. The sea is washing up remains of many ships and many burned and broken bodies on the Flushing coast, all horrible to see. Within the town of Flushing there are dozens of imprisoned Spaniards who complain of having been betrayed by Parma, from whom they got no help despite his promises. They damn him with their hearts and souls, and it is likely that the Spanish king will soon take Flanders from him. The Dutch sailors wanted to kill the captured Spaniards, because it cost so much to get them to surrender. Their ships were tall as churches, but all razed and riddled by the fire of the English culverins. After they had all been sacked, there was a grand procession in which fifty Dutch sailors marched along all clothed in sumptuous dress of Spanish knights, in such a way that one of them looked Portuguese, another Basque, the next Italian, and so forth. A Scotsman has just come who is sure he saw the Armada in the North Sea. It has no more than eighty vessels left, and is chased by upwards of two hundred English ships. For two weeks past the Spaniards have had no rest by day or night. The Englishmen will press the fight, for they can count on five or six hundred armed and well-manned ships, which they may yet send out to Spain and Portugal, whose naval strength has been reduced severely by the Armada's losses. The Spaniards had among their forces several galleys, two of them Italian and of huge dimensions. The Dutch thought they might capture them, but they sank far out to sea. The English lost but three or four large ships; the largest of them, the *Elizabeth* took fire in the fighting. Many things must have occurred about which I still know nothing. May the will of God be done, but I fear the fighting will continue even after all of this.

Venice, August 23, 1588: The Spaniards in this city have got letters from Madrid. His Majesty has retired to the Escorial and is granting no more audiences, which is his custom when he has important matters to consider.

Staden, September 22, 1588: We recently reported that the Armada had invaded Scotland. This is not correct. There were certainly some landings there, but merely to take on fresh water for the passage back to Spain. A lack of powder and munitions has compelled the English ships to halt their chase, and they have all turned back. Were it not for this, they would have sunk the last ship in the Armada. The losses of each fleet cannot be listed yet. A few Jesuits and women found among the Spanish prisoners have been hanged in London, along with an Englishman accused of spying for the duke of Parma.

Antwerp, November 12, 1588: The queen of England has served notice to all ports of the Levant that they should not allow the sale to Spain or Portugal of any products that are used to outfit ships. Those who ignore this notice will suffer said materials to be confiscated upon falling into English hands.

Complete and final account of the Armada, originating in Hamburg and received in Augsburg on the nineteenth day of November 1588: King Philip of Spain's Armada sailed from Portugal with one hundred and thirty-five ships: four large Neopolitan galleys, four Portuguese galleons, ten hookers carrying provisions, fourteen Venetian ships, some galleons among them. The rest consisted of small, medium, and large warships, including galleons. The Armada arrived in La Coruña on the fifth of June, from whence it was to leave for Flanders, there to join the duke of Parma's forces for an invasion of England. The English fleet was stationed then at Plymouth.

Eight days out of La Coruña, the Armada reached the channel, where over the course of four or five days it carried on several skirmishes with the English fleet. In the first one, the English captured two ships, one of them commanded by Don Pedro de Valdés, and towed them off to England. After a storm that swept away four Portuguese galleons, grounded on the coast of France, the Armada continued on its course and put in at the port of Calais, it now being very dangerous to press on toward Dunquerque. The duke of Parma sent word that it would take his forces eight days at least to reach Calais, which made the duke of Medina Sidonia consider a return to Spain. That night Drake's squadron, making use of a strong wind from the sea, ignited several fire ships and sent them toward the Armada, whose ships lay grouped together. The Spaniards, frightened, cut their moorings, and each ship thus lost two anchors. Four galleys were shipwrecked in their flight, grounded on the Calais shoals. On the following day the two fleets fought a long engagement, bombarding one another for eight hours. The Spaniards lost four ships, of which two were Portuguese galleys and another a galleon from Biscay. All four of them went to the bottom. Three great Venetian ships were left behind at Flushing, very battered. The people of that city overpowered two of them and left the third to break up in the surf. The Sevillan guards' commander was on one of these ships; when he fell prisoner he estimated that more than four thousand men had been lost in the battle of Calais, among them the commander of the cavalry of Naples and Seville. The Spaniards were thought to have one hundred and twenty ships left, although some counted only one hundred and ten. During the battle no one saw the duke of Florence's great galleon.

From here, the English chased the Armada as far north as Scotland. When the Spaniards called the roll, they found that they had lost eight thousand men, most killed in battle or struck down by sickness. Then, without taking on provisions, they sailed on to Ireland. Soon the *San Sebastián* and the *San Matías* sank, with four hundred and fifty-six men. Because there was no water, mules and horses were thrown into the sea. The losses from then on were very great. As the Armada sailed away from Ireland, the duke of Medina Sidonia had his captains set a course for La Coruña or the first Spanish port they saw. After ten days, a storm cut off the duke and twenty-seven of his ships from the rest of the Armada, and nothing has been learned about their fate. At the last count, the ships totaled seventy-eight. There were no galleys left. Two galleons of the duke's squadron, which were foundering, headed toward the Irish coast, where only three or four of their men were saved. When taken prisoner, they declared that there were no casks of water left in the holds of the *San Felipe*, the duke's flagship, nor was there but a very little bread and a few barrels of wine, and that the masts had been so ruined that they could not support their halyards. On September 10 a five-hundred-ton ship ran aground on the coast. It carried Oquendo, the commander of part of the fleet, and the Prince Ascoli, bastard son of King Philip of Spain, twenty-eight years old. Also aboard were ten nobles, seven captains, and five hundred soldiers, all of whom were killed, except for a pilot who saved himself by clinging to a spar. The ship carried fifty cannon and twenty-five smaller guns, fifteen thousand ducats, and many silver *reals* and gold ingots. On the same day, two larger ships headed toward the coast, where they landed more than eight hundred men. All were killed by the English ground forces. On the twelfth, another great ship broke apart in the surf, and four hundred men, including thirteen nobles, were taken prisoner. Another ship came apart on the coast, and seven hundred bodies washed up on the beach. Later on another vessel ran aground, from whose wreckage there were saved a bishop, three nobles, and seventy-nine mercenaries, who were taken as prisoners. On the seventeenth of September two great galleons, the *San Joaquín* and the *San Martín,* went to the bottom. One of these ships was Recalde's, and eight hundred soldiers, sixty Portuguese, and forty Basque fishermen were with her. No one had eaten anything for four days. Finally another galleon, displacing almost five hundred tons, was thrown upon the rocks; Alonso de Leyva died there, he who was field commander of the Milanese cavalry, and so did an Italian margrave and the veteran garrisons of Naples and Seville. On the eighteenth of September the news came from Ireland that the waves had washed bodies by the hundreds up on the beach.

Even with all the information they received about the Armada, doubtless partial, imperfect, and late, but still essentially true, the Fuggers never quite managed to explain to themselves why the disaster had occurred. Nor was it ever understood by Philip II, who saw it as something beyond the scope of reason, like an act of God. In his first public pronouncement about the disaster, contained in a letter sent on October 13 to the Spanish bishops, he said: "We must praise God for that which He has willed." With these words, the principle of *designio divino* was held up as justifying the defeat.

Paradoxically, Elizabeth also held it up to justify her victory; she had this sentence etched on a commemorative medal: "God blew and they were scattered." Certainly it was a matter of life and death to the Protestant cause to have God on their side.

And so the Armada, through the years, slipped back behind a curtain daubed with storm clouds, sheeted rain, thunderbolts, and giant waves that made the galleons into toys of God.

But the Spaniards and the Englishmen who faced each other

in the channel knew that God would seldom condescend to mingle in their human struggles. They were professional mariners like Drake, Hawkins, Frobisher, Howard, Seymour, Martínez de Recalde, Moncada, Oquendo, Leyva, Bertendona; they were men who knew their business and they knew quite well what they were facing, though they may have been disposed to risk their necks for king and religion.

Shortly before the Armada was to sail, Pope Sixtus V, who had many qualms, dispatched an emissary to Lisbon to sound out the preparations. After a dockside conversation with an experienced squadron chief, perhaps Martínez de Recalde, the agent told Cardinal Montalvo what the Spanish officer had said about the Armada's chance of success:

"When you meet the English squadron in the channel, do you expect to win the battle?" inquired the envoy.

"Naturally," replied the captain.

"How can you be sure?"

"It's very simple. . . . It's known that we are fighting in God's cause. When we face the English, God will surely manage things so that we can board them, perhaps He'll cause some atmospheric phenomenon or, more probably, deprive the enemy of some possibilities. Hand to hand, our bravery and our Spanish steel, and the great number of soldiers that we carry, will insure our victory. But, should God not aid us with a miracle, the English, whose ships are faster and more maneuverable than ours, and have many more cannon with long ranges, and who know of these advantages as well as we do, will not get close, but rather keep their distance, to hit us with their culverins without receiving too much harm. And so," the Spaniard finished with a terrible smile, "we sail to fight the English trusting firmly in a miracle."

In one letter that the Fuggers received, there is a direct allusion to the tactic that the English used in fending off the Armada's power: " . . . the English ships performed very well and, without ceasing their fire, maneuvered so that the galleys could not board or even reach them."

It is a curious thing that the English should have adopted a style of engagement so like that practiced in the bullring. One may imagine the Spaniards' surprise when, on the night of July 30, they lost the wind at the channel's entrance, because the English ships were faster and could sail close to the wind. The toreador had tricked the bull, who with a contrary wind could do no more than snort and bleed beneath the wounding lances and the flaming banderillas.

On August second, upon reaching Portland Bill, there was a rather tragic, though instructive, encounter. The *San Martín*, proud galleon of the duke of Medina Sidonia, became separated from the half-moon formation that the Armada had tried to maintain. Admiral Howard's *Ark Royal*, leading her squadron at full sail, advanced to bar the Spaniard's path. Medina Sidonia rejoiced. Here was a fine occasion to show the English his men's skill and courage in hand-to-hand fighting. Up until this point, all naval engagements had developed in this way: flagship against flagship, commander against commander, boarding each other and fighting ruthlessly on decks that had been spread with sand and sawdust to keep the men from slipping on the blood. The duke ordered a trumpet call to battle stations, and had the mainsail furled; the *San Martín* cut into the *Ark Royal*'s path and awaited with drawn cutlasses the inevitable clash that would give luster to her arms. But instead of heaving out her grappling hooks, Howard's ship began to fire with her forechasers, turned at a right angle, and then, at close range, fired a blast from all her portside cannon as she passed. The duke had not got over his surprise when the next English ship in line performed the same maneuver, and after that one came another, and another, to the end. The *San Martín*'s dead hulk was now reduced to splinters, and the gaping breaches in her side let water fill her holds. A half-dozen men had fallen at the duke's side, and the scuppers ran with blood that came cascading from the poop. The *San Martín* would make her way back to Santander, but she was from this point forward more a coffin than a fighting ship.

It is known that Drake and Hawkins—"Draco y Achines"—had their squadrons reproduce this unprecedented mode of attack. It was clear that, for the English at any rate, the time of medieval tourneys had gone by.

John Hawkins, after his three famous sea journeys to the Caribbean, inherited his father-in-law's position as treasurer of the Admiralty. From this comfortable and prestigious seat, relying on his own experiences and on what the other sailors told him, he reshaped the English galleon's lines to make it faster, more maneuverable, and more heavily armed. The huge castles and poops, the wooden towers from whose parapets and portholes all the soldiers did their fighting, had their height reduced as much as possible, to produce less pitch and greater speed. There were no longer any soldiers on the English ships, but sailors who could fight as well as set the sails. This reduced the number of men aboard the ships, and it eased the food and storage problems that Hawkins, who was fussy, cared so much about. Replacing the stubby, wide-mouthed cannon with the stretched-out culverin allowed engagement at a greater distance from the enemy who, generally downwind, would sputter wrathfully at his own impotence to board or to return the fire. The object of a naval combat was no more to kill or to subdue the other crew, but rather to sink and cripple ships. The huge losses that the Armada suffered on the Scotch and Irish seas can be attributed to English broadsides, perforated planks, and splintered masts, not to the windy vicissitudes of storms.

Among the alarming letters coming to the Fuggers in that autumn, there is one dated October 6 that brought the following news: "Captain Cavendish, a nobleman who sailed twenty-five months ago with two ships and a pinnace, has returned to England. He sailed around the world along Magellan's route, and he sacked, burned, and sank nineteen ships in the Pacific. Ashore, he razed ten cities and inflicted grievous harm upon the Spaniards. Among his prizes was the great galleon that trafficked between China and Peru or Mexico. The ship was loaded with silk and other rich commodities whose value, according to the inventory, totaled three hundred thousand ducats. Cavendish transferred the most valuable goods to his own ship and set the galleon afire. After rounding the Cape of Good Hope, he returned a rich man. The two hundred who sailed with him were enriched as well. It is said that the duke of Cumberland will soon embark upon a similar expedition."

Drake had done all this and much more on his piratical circumnavigation of the globe aboard the *Golden Hind*. Exactly eight years before Cavendish, he had rounded Ram's Head and come ashore with a booty that returned forty-seven thousand percent to his investors after Drake skimmed off his share and the queen had gotten hers, which came to three hundred thousand pounds sterling. The Armada's failure, certainly, cannot be attributed exclusively to the abilities of men like Hawkins, Cavendish, and Drake, nor to Cecil's or Elizabeth's daring and foresight; they were, however, the relevant effigies stamped on a flood of coins and medals, the making of which gave work to thousands in the smelting, minting, and transporting; the raw materials, often stolen, weighed just as much as all the New World Indians' coagulated blood.

Perhaps, when Philip II read the duke of Medina Sidonia's desolating diary or Pedro de Valdés's angry letters written in England, he remembered bitterly the offer of marriage he had made Elizabeth thirty years before, in her first days as queen; perhaps he recalled those urgent messages that came and went across the waves between London and Brussels, whose arrival he would wait for with the quiet resignation that his father's death had left in him; in one sealed missive his faithful ambassador, the count of Feria, recounted a decisive interview with Elizabeth: "She said that she could not marry Your Majesty because she was a heretic. I was greatly astounded to hear these words from her, and begged for an explanation of the reason behind such a great change since the last time I had discussed the matter with her, but she made nothing clear to me. She repeated that she was a heretic, and therefore she could not be married to Your Majesty. I told her I did not consider her a heretic and I could not believe that she would sanction any of the bills that they debated then in Parliament. She answered that so much money left her country destined for the pope that she was thinking about limiting it, and she said that the bishops were all cowards and idlers." A few days later, she would declare herself the governess of the schismatic Church of England.

During the very week that Philip received Feria's letter, the mail arrived from Spain. The stack of letters, memoranda, petitions, denunciations, and documents of every other sort that his council and the Princess Juana thought deserving of his attention remained untouched for four days on the table in his office, as an attack of colic and diarrhea sent him to bed as soon as he had heard his envoy's spoken report. Who ever would have thought for a moment that the friar Bartolomé Carranza, the archbishop of Toledo no less, would stand accused of fostering Lutheran ideas? Was that same Carranza then a fraud, the man whom he himself had sent to Louvain and to England to remove heretical books, whom he himself had recommended as confessor to Queen Mary? But now here before him was a letter from the Inquisitor General, and though surely he was writing as an offended party, his arguments were impossible to refute. There was no doubt about it; Carranza was suspect, and though he may not have been guilty to the degree that the Inquisitor presumed, still anyone who had risen to the primacy of Spain should be completely spotless, and therefore he'd sign an order to incarcerate him and would give him to the Inquisition. The next folder that he picked up terrified him: heresy in Seville had spread from door to door, convent to convent, like a plague, and the man who'd been his father's favorite preacher, the sweet doctor Ponce, had been found living with two women and expounding Lutheran and Erasmian doctrines at nocturnal gatherings attended by knights, women, friars, my God, and the monasteries were centers of corruption and in San Isidro all the monks had fallen into heinous sin and read prohibited books, and in Valladolid the illustrious doctor Cazalla, his father's old chaplain, headed a licentious conspiration of *marranos,* and his brother Francisco, also a priest, was involved in it, and so were his two sisters, and Don Cristóbal de Ocampo, a knight belonging to the order of San Juan, and Cristóbal de Padilla, a knight from Zamora, and Judge Pérez Herrera, and the teacher Alfonso Pérez, and the bachelor Herrereuelo and three other women. . . . He would have to react rapidly and firmly, or Spain would lose herself within the labyrinth of dangerous ideas that Erasmus, Luther, and Calvin had set loose. Yes, every one of those unfortunates would have to wear the yellow penitential robe and then be led off to the stake. *To keep money from leaving the realm*, what could that be? a memorandum from a certain Luis Ortiz, an old man in gaiters who had charge of the accounting office, money is what we need, let's see, it's understood that from a bunch of wool weighing twenty-five pounds for which foreigners pay fifteen *reales*, these latter then make tapestries and other cloths outside of Spain and sell them back for fifteen ducats; and likewise, from a skein of crude silk costing them just two ducats for a pound, they manufacture satin in Florence, velvet in Genoa, drapery in Milan, from which they profit by more than twenty ducats; and as for iron and steel, from one ducat's worth they make hammers, pliers, bits, gun barrels, swords and daggers, and many other little things from which they take a profit of more than twenty ducats, and sometimes more than a hundred when they sell them back to us. And things have come to such a turn that even the iron ore is taken to France, and they have few foundries there, at just a short distance from us, which are injurious to our honor, for they treat us worse than if we were barbarians, and also to our economy, since they take away our money with these industries; and the same thing happens with the dyes and tinctures made in Spain or brought in from the Indies, and all this makes the foreigners deride our nation, for they treat us worse than Indians, whom we shower with trinkets in exchange for gold and silver, while we get, for ours, nothing but those foreigners' enrichment and their taking from us all the resources that they lack, taking our money with their industries without having, as we do, to extract it from the mines. *And the remedy to all this is to ban the export of all raw materials, and to prohibit the importing of all finished goods.* With this enactment, the foreign merchants will soon buy from us what they cannot get in their own lands, and as they now pay fifteen *reales* for an *arroba* of wool, they will pay fifteen ducats for the finished product. . . . It was so easy for Ortiz to set the world up right, he didn't realize that if Spain were to sell cloth instead of wool she would sink into the disorder that prevailed beyond her borders. . . . To start with, looms would multiply and the pasture lands would not produce enough to keep them busy, and the entire country would start raising sheep, and the land-owners would depopulate their holdings, even the villages, and this would throw up a rabble of moriscos, commoners, tenants, and laborers into the cities, and he had seen enough of the army of beggars in England, dying of cold and hunger along the highways, offering their miserable labors for a crust of bread, the children stealing and the women whoring, and that was not the worst of it, there would be counts, and even dukes, who coveted the monastery lands, and they would be so shameless as to take up heresy in order to obtain the Church's property, well, maybe this could never quite occur in Spain, but there were still the merchants, ah, the merchants, almost all of them *marranos,* they would sell their mothers just to fill a carrick and then spread out through the seas with bales of cloth, and they'd unite and pool their money, as they've done in England, and form companies like the Muscovy and Merchant Adventurers, and soon they'd take control of the Sevillan House of Trade, oh, Luis Ortiz, how little do you know about the world, let's see what other nonsense you have written, that we revoke the laws that hold in check the mechanical trades, and that we make and promulgate new laws to foster them, as they have done in Flanders and in other lands where there are ordered republics with these liberties. *It should be decreed that all subjects born in Spain within the previous ten years, and those born here in the future, shall learn to read and write, or be apprenticed to a trade, though they be sons of grandees and of noblemen and persons of all kinds and classes;* and those who reach the age of eighteen years without knowing or practicing a trade are to be regarded as foreigners in the realm and suffer other dire penalties: and this decree should not be applied to the peasantry and those who now work with their hands in digging, plowing, and cultivating the land, and keep-ing herds, and performing other labors and things that are needed in the countryside, nor to the carters who transport animals, supplies, and merchandise from one place to another, for these are to be given the same freedoms that we'll give the tradesmen, so we do not lose the labor of the countryside. And the decree is to be enforced four years after it is issued, so that in that time the subjects may learn trades and other tradesmen may come from outside, and from then on no one shall wear cloth or silk or linen made in other lands, but only those that have been made in Spain, from which great benefits will follow, and there will be skilled workers to perform whatever is needed for the realm and for the Indies; so that the hidalgos shall have to work with their hands, I swear that this man has gone out further on a limb than anyone yet, I doubt that he is even sane, what difference will there be then between a craftsman and a laborer and a knight? he even says grandees, is this blockhead going to have me learn a trade? *The principal source of the world's money is Spain,* for what is born within her and for what comes from the Indies, and if the gold and silver in these realms were to be husbanded, there could be no other outcome than that our most powerful king and lord, with this money, should subject the greater part of the universe, which is made up of infidels, and should make the other Christian princes, with no means of waging war, conclude perpetual peace, and when there are skilled workers and persons busy at their trades, there will no longer be the lawsuits and petitions raised by the many attorneys that there now are, the which, along with notaries and solicitors, stir up the parties to these actions, and today the decline of Spain has so progressed that any person of whatever state or condition knows no other trade or business than that of going to Salamanca or to war in Italy or the Indies; and at the same time there are a great many hidalgos, clerics, and other unanswerable persons, and all this is paid for by the peasants, most of whom are very poor and unfortunate; *as a remedy for this it can be ordered that all skilled tradesmen shall be free from having to donate their ordinary and extraordinary services, and likewise the carters and the peasants, and others who live by the work of their hands. . . .* This man has gone insane. He'll have to be replaced. But maybe he's not a madman, but a heretic, and look at how carelessly he underlines his points. I'll send him up before the Inquisition. Had he already done so? It was strange that he didn't remember. What had become of that Luis Ortiz? Forty years, how the time passes, forty years since my father's death, since poor Mary's death, forty years now of Elizabeth Tudor's reign, forty years since my vows in the Royal Chapel in Brussels, forty years of my apostolate, my martyrdom, my holding of the burning reins of state to keep a steady course, so that not a thing should change, but everything remain in order, tranquil, silent, inalterable forever like a holy relic venerated for the glory of the Lord. Yes, Elizabeth had laughed at him, but in the end she was defeated, rejected, held at bay outside his empire. Someone had brought to his attention, perhaps in consolation at the loss of Armada, that the sun could never set upon his provinces. Then, after reflecting on that truth, he had thought he understood what God expected of him, it certainly was not the sending of armadas and armies and crusaders against other kingdoms, whether they be composed of heretics or infidels, but rather that he should preserve the far-flung dominions that had been put into his care, that he should clean them of the sores that might spring up from deep within them, that he'd defend them from the piracies and the contaminations coming from without. That was the destiny of Spain, yes, to perfect herself like a nun in her convent cell while, beyond the walls, the world could change and lose itself in vices and confusions and could worship Baal. Elizabeth had sneered at him, that was true, she had taunted him and mortified him with her mocking gibes, but, as the common people said, he had had the last laugh and the better one, since her sea dogs had burned their snouts in their incursions on the Spanish coast, and Drake and Hawkins had just died in the Sea of the Antilles after suffering great failures. The Spanish empire was impregnable; he had called on the Italians to fortify it up and down, to garrison it with men and cannon, with militias and with trenches, with schooners and with galleons; if by chance the enemy should set his foot upon some desolate landing, he would not survive there long, he would end up like those Huguenots who dared to settle in Florida. He had devoted many hours toward defending the New World, for this was his empire's weakest flank, being so far off from his hands, having populators who had mixed with Negroes and with Indians, with so many riches there to lay before them. But by tightening here and relaxing there, to make it certain that nobody got too rich, and above all seeing to it that no one born there in those savage lands would ever hold a high position, from which they might help others to start running contraband, he had managed, from an ocean's distance, to construct a kind of axis that revolved entirely around Spain, like clockwork. Yes, he could depart in peace, unlike his father. The kingdom now worked like a huge and parsimonious machine, which any child could run. Spain prevailed because of that intricate mechanism of laws, certificates, decrees, councils, statutes, trials, bankruptcies, executions, orders, *autos-da-fé*, all institutions he had strung together with his fingertips, had screwed in and adjusted with a jeweler's delicacy. Soon Elizabeth would go to hell, and England's throne would then hold Mary Stuart's peaceful son; Henry of France and he had made their peace at Vervins; the hollanders, on the whole, would accept his daughter's rule, and the legions bled no more in Flanders. Everything was going well. Everything was in order. He only wished, as a reward for all his vigils and his pains, that God would offer him the revelation which that morning he had asked for.

‖ XXIV ‖

BECAUSE AS FAR AS you're concerned, the only bad
thing that you've done in your life, Antón Babtista, was
killing that swineherd in Isabela who stood, his arms
spread out like a Christ, between you and the half-ton sow that
you went to the pens to steal in the confusion of Roldán's revolt.
Of course, it was rumored of him that he'd had intimate commerce with the beast, and that he wouldn't have traded it for the
most elegant captive Indian girl, but still he was a Christian, and
he cursed you as he died stitched by your arrows in the pigsty
before his pawing, snorting mistress.

Remember those days of war and hunger, Antón? After the
business with the Admiral, everything was upside down and
smelled of blood. Every three months the Indians were supposed to present as tribute a Flemish bell filled with gold dust.
To tell who had paid and who hadn't, brass medallions were
given out, and any Indian caught without one dangling on his
chest could be taken as a slave and shipped off to Spain.

It was soon clear to you that this method would never produce
the gold that the Admiral was trying desperately to gather and
send back to Ferdinand and Isabella. The Indians were sim-
pletons, they lacked any ability to move the earth or open mines,
and they had none of the tools that were needed; they spent
their days squatting in the streams, patiently washing the sand,
staring and picking at it from dawn to dusk, never managing to
amass the tribute, not half of it. That enterprise was headed
toward failure. It was then that you began associating with the
malcontents around Roldán. Among them there was a man

named Rodríguez, who knew about mining and whom the Admiral had removed from the payroll after hearing him say that there was no Great Khan residing in these Indies. Rodríguez never tired of asserting that if the Admiral would only allow it he could find plenty of gold in the island's plains and rivers, even in the cordillera; he would be inclined to give a portion of what he found to their Majesties, and some castellanos to the Admiral, but he would keep the greater part, because the discovery and the extraction of the metal would be owing mainly to his own devices. One day, encouraged by Roldán, Rodríguez revealed his system:

Whenever a gold mine or vein is discovered, it is because someone has paid close attention to the places that experts in gold extraction such as I think it most likely to be found; and when it is in the plains, they first clear off everything above the ground and dig a pit some eight feet or so long and about as wide, whatever the miner thinks right, and about four to eight feet deep; without going any deeper, they then wash out the entire bed of earth found within that space; if they find a vein of gold, they follow it, and if not they dig down another four feet and wash it out, and if they find nothing there as well they keep on digging and washing until they've reached the bedrock; and if they don't find gold by then, they make no effort to go on looking in that place, but go somewhere else; when they actually find it, though, they don't dig any deeper, but work it entirely at that depth, and where the finder's mine ends, the next man stakes his claim, and in this way every man will have his mine, and from it he will give something to the Crown and to the Admiral, but not to the Governor or to anyone else. The mines on the level lands must always be sought near a river or a pond or spring, where there is water to work the gold, and Indians provided by the Crown will be used for excavation; and they'll put the earth on big trays, which other Indians will then transport to where the water is, and there it will be worked; but the ones who carry the trays will not wash out the earth, but rather they'll go back for more, and what they've brought will be transferred to smaller pans held in the hands of the washers, who will be Indian women and old people and children, not too small, for this task entails less work than that of digging and carrying; and the washers will be seated at the riverbank, their feet in the water up to their knees, more or less, depending on where they're sitting, and they'll hold the pan in their hands and move it around a bit and introduce a little water by putting it into the river's current, but skillfully, and with the same dexterity expelling it, little by little, until the gold has sunk down to the bottom of the pan, which will have to be concave and about the size of a barber's basin, and almost as deep; and when all the earth is emptied the gold will stay at home in the bottom of the pan, and it will be taken out and set aside, and more of the earth that the carriers have brought will be taken up, and so forth. In this way, with each worker at his job, each day's yield will be as great as God allows in favoring the business with the use of the Indians, for without Indians given or lent by the Admiral, or perhaps by Ferdinand and Isabella, which would be even better, no gold will ever be taken out, for no Spaniard will go about carrying trays and digging, digging; and as I understand mining, which I do, and well, for each pair of Indians who do the washing, another two will be needed to dig and to load the trays that are to be carried to the washers; and other Indians will have to be on hand, to make bread and to do other things for the working Indians, because the work is very hard; and a hut will be needed as well, so they can rest at night beside their women and their children, and to do what I've just outlined, one tray will ordinarily be carried by five Indians at once. Mines in rivers or streams will be worked in a different way, by diverting water from the bed, and then when the bed is dry the gold will be sought among the rocks and cavities and pools; I'm certain that when one of these riverbeds turns out to be a good one there will be much gold to be found, for I see that the Indians find nuggets in the beds of rivers that have dried up or changed their course; I'm certain as well that the gold is born in the mountain peaks, and that the rain water brings it down to the rivers and streams that flow from the sierras, and in the floods they spread it over the plains and the forests and wherever else the water spills, but in smaller quantities than those found in the rivers and streams.

After listening to Rodríguez, you said that you'd run right away to the Admiral's palace to tell him how easy it would be to mine the gold; everyone would get rich if the Indians could only be parceled out at the rate of fifty or sixty a head. But Roldán and the others burst out laughing, how little you know about their Majesties, Antón Babtista, the Indians are to be their vassals and nobody else's, and the Admiral knows this well enough: if he should find a lot of gold and put it on the ships, their Majesties will surely underwrite his discoveries, and they will make a rich and noble man of him; but if he finds few riches they will chain him to an oar, and that is how he'll pay them for his trips out to the Indies, and from the Admiral of the Ocean Sea he'll be reduced to oarsman of the royal galleys.

All of a sudden, and surely in concert, the Indians abandoned the villages and disappeared into the mountains, and they had to be pulled out of caves with biting dogs and cannon fire. The Admiral reduced their tribute by half, but he couldn't be convinced of the futility of that business with the bells of gold, the punishments and brass medallions. If they would just divide the Indians among us, you thought, as you saw them trembling behind their imploring chieftans, clutching in their hands the bell they owed, while those accused of laziness or of mixing copper with the gold dust were dismembered right in front of them. The poor devils are being finished off, Roldán observed under his breath, and who is going to maintain us? If their Majesties would only give us land, and Indians, and the right to open mines, everything would be all right. Otherwise, we'll have to go back to Spain.

Then, unexpectedly, after ruining their cultivations and everything that might be edible, even the still greening fruits that hung in the trees, the Indians began to kill themselves. Do you remember, Antón, that village in the Vega where you thought you'd find a smoked *jutía* or a little stuffed rabbit? You were returning from the south with a search party, marveling at the fresh water in the reservoirs, walking through the valleys that descended stepwise toward the vast savannah, and in the village all the Indians were dead. At first you thought that a hungry detachment, come from the fort at Concepción, had passed through there. But the Indians were lying in their hammocks, bellies swollen from drinking yucca juice; the planted fields had disappeared, and among the uprooted crops you came upon twenty or so children who had been crushed beneath a rockpile.

Hunger, in Isabela as much as in the mountains, squeezed in the belts and made the bones dance beneath the armor plates. The Admiral, disheartened by the many tribulations and the scarcity of gold, ordered the building of two caravels, left the government in the hands of Don Bartolomé, and went to answer, before Ferdinand and Isabella, the accusations certain to be made against him by Friar Buil and *mosén* Pedro de Margarit.

Don Bartolomé had little in common with his brother the Admiral; he was more energetic, more resolute, and he never spoke of the Earthly Paradise or of Cathay. As scarcely any Indians were left on the Vega Real, much less in the environs of Isabela, it was necessary to find another site on which to establish the main town. Once again, Antón, you witnessed the parade of hidalgos, soldiers, workmen, but no longer was there any visible difference among them. The troop that marched southward to build *La Nueva Isabela* at the mouth of the Ozama was a band of skinny, ragged men, almost barefoot, their shields broken, their flags torn, their breastplates dented and consumed with rust.

Isabela was scarcely more than a cemetery, and one night you bought a half sack of rubbery cassava from Rodríguez and then left before the dawn. Doña Antonia was a niece of the chief of Jaraguá, and you went out into the sunset, then headed south, your memory filled with the happy days of *La Villa de Antón,* the caged iguanas, the bowls of fish, the guayabo nectar, the guanábanas, the annonas, the mameyes, Doña Antonia's fleshy breasts, wouldn't little Miguel be something like a prince now? And you stepped happily through the rugged northern sierra, adorned with the red flowers of the cacao bush, and you thought that no place on the island could be better than Jaraguá to burst your belly's seams and give pleasure to your prick, for you took it for granted that there wasn't any gold there, and that neither the Admiral nor his brother the Governor, with their capricious orders, would disturb the long summers of rest and solace that your body asked for. When winter came, you would think about things to do.

And it turned out that Doña Antonia was in Jaraguá, as you had surmised; you found her at the door of the great lodge of the chief Behechio, who received you with smiles and openness, like the sun. To your surprise, everyone there was expecting you, and they called out your name as they waved their palm fronds at you. In an exquisite hammock, over which they had hung your old chain of bells, sat little Miguel with his green, almond-shaped eyes, and he responded to your tickling finger with a burst of laughter showing little teeth as white and crystalline as the newly grated yucca. What satisfaction you felt, Antón Babtista, what contentment swelled your heart, how well your hopes were met. The weeks passed brimming with celebrations: one day Behechio organized a dance, on the next a mock combat, and then a fishing party on the lake three leagues from the village, and a very graceful ball game, a hunt in the forests of *palo brasil* beyond the green savannah, a parade of damsels ending with the appearance of Anacaona, Behechio's sister, widow of the feared Caonabó, whose languid nakedness was covered by two boas of sewn flowers. You fattened like a pig on fodder, Antón; you grew rolls of flesh and sprouted patriarchal flanks that you would sway in the happy sty of your hammock, Antón, you suckling pig, you potbelly, you oozed lard up to your nose. But, who would have guessed it?—one morning someone ruptured your idyllic dream with two hard slaps. You opened your eyes and there before you stood Don Bartolomé, red with anger, who pummeled you and accused you of desertion in his booming governor's voice. He condemned you then and there to hang, but then he took pity on you and reduced the sentence to fifty public cudgelings which if they didn't kill you, undermined your privileged status in Jaraguá.

Contrite and desolate, not daring to go into the lodge that

Behechio had given you, you got permission to accompany a Franciscan who was traveling to Isabela, and Isabela was the same as ever: half-built stone houses, dry fields that were ignored, filth, temporary huts. The populace could hardly wait for the completion of the new village on the Ozama; there, on working a stone slab, they had found a vein of gold within it, and they talked about great hidden nuggets, of the freshness of the air, of the good disposition of the Haina Indians, of the excellence of the port, of the wide, straight streets, of the plazas, churches, towers, and palaces that were being designed and raised to be the envy of Burgos, of Valladolid, of Barcelona. But the construction went slowly, hunger was seldom deceived by the same tasteless cassava, and, finally, the rumor gained acceptance that the Admiral would never again return to the Indies, since he now considered them a discovery of ill omen. The Governor, for his part, showed himself to be more arbitrary every day, sterner, more inclined to have offenders hanged than beaten, and complaints about his governance were being scribbled in hundreds of documents, all rotting as they waited for some ship to make a call on those forgotten shores and then return to Spain. The Governor had a large caravel that he used to collect the tribute of hemp, cotton, rare birds, and *palo brasil* acquired on his trip to Jaraguá; the first offering given by the obsequious Behechio had already been put into safekeeping behind the heavy door of their Majesties' storehouse, and the ship swayed in sight of everyone, unmanned and arrogant, like a temptation of the devil. It was Roldán who lit the fuse, why not take that idle hulk and sail to Spain? what reason could there be to keep the sick and discontented here? do you think their Majesties would permit so many abuses if they knew of them? who were these Genoans to offend against Castilian liberties? and, after all, Antón Babtista, your friend Roldán was not just any cat skinner, he was the mayor, a position that the Admiral gave to him before he left, and he was regarded as an honorable man who had risen through legitimate merits and achievements. But the Governor responded by banishing Roldán from the settlement and scuttling the ship, and with it plainly visible there, broken on the rocks, a deep resentment made almost everybody's life turn bitter.

On the night that Roldán marched against Isabela, you were on guard at the corrals, Antón Babtista. You didn't know what to do right away, but Roldán shouted long live their Majesties, and that made you decide for him. The pine torches ran flaming and hissing through the streets, leaving in their wake a whirlwind of sparks, gunshots, and threats hurled against the Governor. Someone found the storehouse key, and the vats of wine were poured, and the cheese and bacon went from hand to hand, and men put their bare feet into boots of cordovan leather. Someone lifted up a stack of cotton blankets destined for their Majesties, and someone tried a shirt on, and another threw a bundle of lances out into the street. Then, Antón, a sudden urge to raise a hunk of meat up to your chops, something other than the worm-eaten jerky that you ate on Sundays, came upon you and took you to the pigpen and there the swineherd stood with his arms crossed, and there he stayed, bleeding to death and cursing you as you carried off the sow as best you could, the half-ton animal that stomped and bellowed even after your arrow stuck it ear to ear. It was a good thing that Ojeda was not around, you commented to Rodríguez, on the road to Jaraguá, stuffed with fried pork and holding the bridle of some hidalgo's skinny mount, which seemed more like a pack animal with the sacks and wineskins that it bore. Long live the king! you shouted every now and then so that Roldán could hear you, down with the tributes! give us the land! give us the Indians! let us start mines! and Rodríguez said again that everyone could really get rich now, forgetting that in Jaraguá the rivers bore no gold.

⟦ X X V ⟧

THE FOLLOWING DAY, as we departed for St. Augustine, the Indians reported more Frenchmen coming toward the river. The *Adelantado* judged correctly that these men must be under the command of Juan Ribao, the general of land and sea brought by the Lutherans, and he sent fifty men ahead to face them, to follow later himself with his guards and knights. We had been forced to make our camp at the site of the killing, though staying there was a bad thing owing to the stench of the two hundred Frenchmen who had been cut down the day before, and the sky was black with scavenging birds. After the night had passed and the morning breezes came, my father-in-law set up some lookout posts, and so it was that as the day wore on there started to appear, at a distance of two gunshots away, some four hundred Lutherans with a big canoe that they had made to cross the river and come down upon us. We could also see the standard of the king of France and other insignia, and we heard the brilliant music of their drums and bagpipes. They quickly formed themselves in battle order, but the *Adelantado* told us to be quiet and to hold our fire, just as if we had never seen that they were offering to fight us, as their only purpose was to frighten us.

At mid-morning the enemy hoisted a white canvas as a sign of peace, and the *Adelantado* sent Diego Flores to them with a boat, for their canoe was weak and badly suited to a river crossing.

In less than an hour Juan Ribao himself had landed on our side, and with him several knights, all armed and gaily dressed. My father-in-law received them with courtesy and magnanimity, inviting them to eat with him, which the Frenchmen declined to do, because the strong odor took their appetites away. When Juan Ribao inquired about its source, the *Adelantado* replied:

"Those are two hundred of your excellency's men whom we killed yesterday, and as they were heretics we did not bury them."

Juan Ribao was very shaken by this, for he had thought the dead ones Spaniards. But when he recovered, he told the *Adelantado* that if he were in his place he would provide ships and provisions for a return to France, now that Carlefor belonged to Spain, and many of his people would go with him, and would even pay a hundred thousand ducats for their deliverance.

"Your excellency may say whatever you wish, but I must kill all the heretics that you have with you," the *Adelantado* answered, "for such are the orders given me by His Majesty the king of Spain."

Juan Ribao then said that the kings of Spain and France were friends, and that his party had come to Florida as men of peace belonging to the new religion.

"All heretics must die; that is their only fate," the *Adelantado* answered. "In the dominions of King Philip no heretics shall thrive."

Juan Ribao was very saddened now, and he asked the *Adelantado* if he could return to his camp to speak to the captains and soldiers waiting there to hear what he had learned.

By mid-afternoon Juan Ribao had come to our shore a second time, and after greeting the *Adelantado* he said that the knights, soldiers, and artisans in his command held two opinions, some wanting to surrender themselves to the mercy of the Spaniards and others preferring to go into the wilderness to deal with the Indians.

The *Adelantado* replied that it was all the same to him, since before night fell he would cross the river and fall upon all those who declared themselves heretics, sparing none of their lives, and if they fled he would hunt them down like rabbits in the brush.

Juan Ribao then offered two hundred ducats for the favor of keeping them in St. Augustine, but my father-in-law replied:

"It pains me greatly to hear those words, for as God is my witness, so many ducats would fit my task of fighting and settling, as a ring would fit around my finger. But I promised to my king that I would baptize all the Indians I found here and kill all heretics from France who chose not to embrace Christ's one true faith."

Juan Ribao begged him not to cross the river until morning, for he would convince all of his men to pay a ransom, and if that were done Spain would receive many hundreds of thousands of ducats, for there were very rich men among them who had everything that was to be had in France.

The *Adelantado* acceded to Ribao's plea, but said that he would give him no more time beyond that, and if they did not return by midday he would come across the river to fall upon them like the Exterminating Angel.

Juan Ribao kept his word, for at ten in the morning he arrived on our side for the third time, and he brought the standards of the king of France as well as those of Admiral Gaspar, also the seal that they had given him to stamp the edicts and the titles that he promulgated there in Florida, and his sword and his arms, which were quite lustrous and inlaid with gold and jewels. He told the *Adelantado* that almost all of his men were ready to place themselves at his mercy, and he trusted that they would not be maltreated, since no war had been declared, and they would pay a fortune for their lives.

The *Adelantado* proceeded to deal with these heretics exactly as he had done with the ones who were already rotting on the dunes. Diego Flores brought them over ten by ten and then they were tied with their hands behind their backs and also to each other, so that they couldn't run away without tripping and falling down.

When Juan Ribao saw that he was about to be killed with all his men, he kneeled on the sand and began to sing a very fine hymn that the Lutherans have, called *Domine memento mei*. And then many beautiful and harmonious voices sounded on the beach, with the music from the bagpipes, and everything in counterpoint, so that it was as if a Mass were being sung. Then the *Adelantado,* seeing us grown docile and enraptured, gave the signal and we fell with blade and pike upon the ones who sang most fervently, and never without asking first if they would cast away their false belief.

My father-in-law had pushed me over toward the kneeling Juan Ribao, who said to me:

"Dust we are and unto dust we shall return. I might have lived another twenty years. But what are twenty years of life if I am lost for all eternity? Kill me then; I die entire in my faith."

After saying these words, Juan Ribao put his hands together, looked up to the heavens, and began to sing again. Seeing him like that, meek as a lamb, I started trembling and my sword fell from my hand. But as I remembered that the *Adelantado* would not forgive my weakness this time, I picked it up quickly and ran it through Juan Ribao's breast. I was so agitated that I missed his heart, and he stood up on the sand, very pale, and began singing yet again, though quietly, choking in the blood that ran out of his mouth and nose. I drew my dagger and felled him with one blow, thus giving him a better end.

When I pulled myself together, there was no more singing on the beach. Castañeda and the *Adelantado* came up to me, all smiles and contentment.

Castañeda congratulated me: "A good dagger-blow, *maestre.*"

"In good time, Don Pedro," said my father-in-law, pressing me in his arms. "Now I can die in peace, for in you these lands shall have a good protector."

[XXVI]

WHEN ANTÓN BABTISTA reached Jaraguá with Roldán's rebels, he did not find Doña Antonia there. In
Behechio's lodge he learned that she, accompanied by
her legitimate husband, had set out two moons earlier toward
Isabela to deliver the young Miguel to him, since the elders
thought that the boy's permanent separation from his father
would bring great evil upon Jaraguá, as had happened already
when the Governor imposed his tributes. Antón shrugged his
shoulders and took in compensation another of Behechio's
nieces, whom he named Doña Antonia as well.

During the two years and some months of Roldán's rebellion,
Antón Babtista had little occasion to complain. Following his
leader's advice, cohabiting with a daughter of Anacaona, em-
bedded in Behechio's family like a gluttonous, burgeoning chig-
ger, he settled into a place on the other side of the lake, at
the foothills of the sierra, where the new Doña Antonia lived.
There, through the ceremony of the *guatiao*, he became blood
brother to his father-in-law, whom he helped in governing the
straitened village, which in a matter of weeks saw itself one step
from destitution, as Antón in one sitting devoured enough to
feed a family for a week. At this point he got an idea: to replace
the arrows that he hunted with, he conceived a dart made of the
resin from which the Indians made balls, so that when he shot
his crossbow at a *jutía* or an *almiquí* the creature was not always
killed, but stunned and ready to be put into a cage; the small
rabbits that the Indians called *curic* were the quickest to procre-
ate, although their fraility made it difficult not to kill them with

the first shot; what's certain is that Antón, with this and other devices, made a bestiary where he bred, with some success, various species of birds, fish, reptiles, amphibians, and mammals, whose bones and entrails he left for the villagers. One afternoon, as they celebrated the first lustrum of Granada's reconquest, the new Doña Antonia's father, mixing some potent concoctions, murmured his unhappiness at the manner of food distribution; Antón sat pensive, as though taking extraordinary note of his father-in-law's meaning, but he suddenly drew his sword, clove Doña Antonia of one of her ears, and held it out to the old man in a bowl. The village elders and its ablest youths went to Jaraguá, sworn to scatter his brains, but Behechio and Anacaona persuaded them to go home quietly, as anything was better than seeing Jaraguá fleeced through paying the Governor's tributes, and what's more it was useless to do battle with those men with yucca-colored skin: Anacaona had lost her husband Caonabó, the bravest and strongest warrior ever seen, and powerful chiefs like Guatiguaná, Guarionex, and Mayobanex had succumbed with all their people after horrendous butcheries and numberless afflictions; nevertheless Behechio agreed to present a delicate protest to Roldán, who immediately got Antón to promise, under the threat of losing more than his ears, that he would stop those abuses, which threatened the army's easy life in the always green province.

The news that Rodríguez had found a mine flowed through the savannah to wash up, days later, on Antón's upland possessions. Until then nobody had bothered to look for gold in Jaraguá, for it was patent that the riverbeds and streams were dry of metals. Rodríguez, nevertheless, after exploring the environs of his adopted village, had set *his* Indians, as he put it, to digging, in a terrain that seemed promising to him. It was a middling discovery: after much effort he was able to amass only a fistful of gold pebbles. But it was *his* gold, not Ferdinand and Isabella's, and that was enough to make every one of Roldán's men demand immediate distribution of the lands as compensation for wages not paid and tribulations and privations undergone in those years, not to mention the risk of having risen against the

Governor. Roldán, who had sown those ideas to be able to reap arms to back him up, faced the alternatives of acquiescing or dying pinned by arrows to the trunk of a ceiba somewhere. A bit frightened at his presumption, certain that Ferdinand and Isabella would never pardon such excesses, he met the demands and saw to his surprise how he was slowly becoming the regent of Jaraguá, surrounded by the palmy castles of his unlikely counts and liegemen.

Antón, with his Indians for above ground and below and following Rodríguez's recommendations to the letter on how to go about getting the gold, soon took on a style that he considered proper to a grandee and, after the construction of a litter came to naught, had himself carried about in a hammock. He found some gold now and again, but only at the cost of breaking the backs of the Indians who dug and carried for him. If anyone had asked him whether he wanted to return to Spain in the Governor's big caravel, he would have answered that he'd rather wait a year or two, as he was happy in the independence he had achieved in Jaraguá, with nobody telling him do this and not that, with nothing to worry about but looking for mines, hunting, making offspring, and widening the tillage of the farmland. Certainly his health had begun to decline, but by now he was getting used to distemper and vertigo, rashes that reddened his skin, pustules on his calf that got better or worse but never healed, clusters of aching knots that swelled in his groin, which Rodríguez called *mal de bubas.* During one vomitous, diarrhoeal night he caught the new Doña Antonia behind the house, fondling with one of her cousins; in a rage he drew his sword to behead her, but something that he couldn't then define held him back, and he stood there like a terrible moonlit statue in the sweet grasses of the mountainside; in the hammock he thought through the motive for his brusque clemency: that woman was his only link to the chief, and if he cut it the Indians would not accept his rule, for he knew they tolerated him not because of the privileges he had extracted from Roldán, but for his kinship with the old man in red and white paint whose daughter he had taken as his wife. The next day, resorting to his prerogative as an aggrieved husband, he cut off the seducer's ears, nose, and lips, condemning him further to walk in train as bearer of shield, cuirass, and helmet.

Behechio listened sadly to his vassals' murmuring complaints. He thought of sending a protest to the Governor, sorely put as he was to decide the easier course for his people, whether to pay tribute or to cohabit with this insatiable plague of white men who knawed Jaraguá like a bone. Only the arrival of some fugitives from the north inclined him to accept Roldán's presence: the Governor had wrought such destruction on the ciguayos that scarcely three or four dozen remained on their feet. The fugitives brought, along with their grim tales, a piece of news that Behechio weighed with some consternation: the Admiral had landed and had quickly set upon Roldán, who at that time was up against a pack of hidalgos united behind the royal standard on the road to Isabela. Behechio thought that he could see, floating on the waters of his own lake, those huge huts that launched murderous thunder and lightning from their flanks. Weeks and weeks passed, however, and the Admiral's vengeance did not in the end make itself felt.

When Antón learned that Behechio was approaching his village, he got into his hammock, picked up a tobacco pipe, and again feigned the mysterious illness with which he had received Roldán on the afternoon when he had come to recruit him for his campaign. He found the chief grown old, taciturn, and wary as a big mountain bird. On recalling the celebration that would have met his arrival three years before, the old man began to pout and moan. Ah, those happy days would never return; Jaraguá was lost; the Admiral would surely destroy it, because it had taken in Roldán and paid no tributes. A shiver of unease climbed Antón's fat spine, for he had always believed that the Admiral would never come back to Hispaniola. He couldn't sleep that night, and at dawn he had himself carried along the eastbound trail. He would grovel at the Admiral's feet, he would beg forgiveness for his transgressions, he would be his servant for life, he would surrender his Indians, his village, everything he owned.

None of that was necessary.

On the second day of his trip to Santo Domingo, Antón saw, in the distance, a man who seemed to be sick, carried in the arms of two Indian women. A little while later, when they passed, he discovered that it was Rodríguez, and without leaving his hammock he awoke his friend, who was drowsing. Rodríguez half-opened his eyes and flashed a moribund smile: after many days of bluster and intimidation the Admiral had reconciled with Roldán, recognized him as Alcalde Mayor, and come to an agreement so generous as to meet all his demands: anyone who wished might return to Spain with an Indian slave; overdue wages would be paid as if there had been no rebellion; ownership of the allotted lands would be recognized, along with the rights to sell, give, trade, lease, mortgage, and dispose of them however one pleased as something held in lawful title.

"What about the Indians?" Antón asked, happy at the good news and worried by the omission. "Who else is going to work my land?"

"Indians?" Rodríguez asked, his voice a thread.

"Yes, these right here," said Antón, sitting up and extending his arms out from the hammock in a gesture that took in his jaded retinue.

A stinking, yellowish froth welled up, bubbling, at the corner of Rodríguez' lips.

"Do you hear me?" Antón asked, and he shook his friend's wasted shoulders.

"The Admiral wrote to Ferdinand and Isabella," Rodríguez stammered, his face taking on an ominous pallor. "He asked them to give them to us . . . one or two years."

"Can we start mining?"

"One third of the gold . . . to Ferdinand and Isabella," Rodríguez moaned, his eyes gone blank.

"There aren't any good mines in Jaraguá," said Antón in disgust, as he fell back into the hammock. "I'm squandering my Indians for nothing; I'm not finding any mines. They say you've hit on a good one."

"I'm dying," Rodríguez sighed.

Antón leaped from the hammock and ordered the Indians to lay his friend out on the ground.

"Leave your mine to me."

"Confession."

"Give me your mine," Antón demanded, shaking his friend's bloodless head.

"I have sinned, . . ." Rodríguez mumbled in his froth; he tried to sit up, opened his mouth for air, and after two or three jerks and shivers, let go of his life in a whistling rattle.

"He went off in a fart," Antón snorted indignantly. Then he made the Indian women dig a hasty grave and returned to his dominions.

As the months went by, Antón's character became embittered; he never resigned himself to Jaraguá's having no gold, and he went all over with his tools and buckets, ceaselessly, restlessly, setting up here today and there tomorrow, in a frenzy of sunstroke and intransigence; what pained him most was that in lands ceded elsewhere a mine now and again appeared, so that it was rumored that the Admiral would realize four million maravedís for Ferdinand and Isabella, a sum that well exceeded those accumulated in tribute when they had filled the Flemish bells with gold. One torrid night, as he lay spread out and fanning on the couch grass by the sugarhouse, Antón saw, up above the treetops, a spurt of fireflies all in line; the insects flew over the settlement like an unexpected river of stars, and instead of flying straight they drew a wide arc above the camp and turned toward the palm roofs, over which they dispersed in spirals and ogives that held for an instant and then dissolved in a stream of green sparks. Antón, in open-mouthed surprise, stood looking at the mysterious dance of the fireflies when a gibble-gabble of plaints and cries made him stand up in alarm and run to his father-in-law's lodge to seek an explanation; he found the old man in the middle of the enclosure, bathed in the fireflies' gleam as they threw a murmurous crown of light around his head; he was seated at his beautiful bench, immobile, very erect, his face painted black, his pupils fixed on a clay vessel broken in two, spilling out shark's teeth, shells of wasps, spiraled seashells, and human bones. Antón learned quickly that the chief was no longer alive and it was useless to direct a word to him, but a cold, metallic fear, unknown to him until then, nailed him to the spot and froze his bowels in pain. . . . When he escaped from the hut it was almost daylight and the fireflies had disappeared; the village seemed suspended in the silent gray air, still colorless, and he remembered the faraway dawn when from the deck of the *Mariagalante* he had observed the islands' awakening. But now he did not see those birds in their plumage, or the fruits whose skins were bursting and gay as streamers, but rather the bodies of hanging Indians, inert, leaden, their tongues protruding in the early light.

Of all the village's inhabitants, only Doña Antonia and her eight maidens, all pregnant by Antón, resolved not to take their lives; had they heeded the call of the spirits of their people— none of the women spoke of fireflies—they would have given birth *there* to Spanish children, and these would force their maternal relations to dig for gold until the end of time; Antón, without energy or will to bury so many strung-up corpses, set out toward Behechio's village to find some Indian servants; there he found everything in a tumult, guns fired in the air, jousting contests, flowing wine, *vivas* for their Majesties and even for a certain Don Francisco of whom he had never heard; he learned from one of Roldán's servants that the Admiral and his brothers had just left for Spain in chains, charged with a thousand offenses; Don Francisco de Bobadilla, the prosecuting judge who had condemned them, was now the one who made and unmade men in Hispaniola, a just and good-natured man who had immediately emptied the jail, distributed the Genoans' wealth, and lowered to ten percent the royal tax on gold extraction: "take it while it lasts," Don Francisco had said in Santo Domingo, and the phrase, flying over mountains and rivers, over laughter and joy, had come to Jaraguá to be repeated without rhyme or reason as the motto of the local enterprise, since it was clear that neither the gold nor the Indians were going to last forever. The celebrations at the Admiral's imprisonment came to an end the following day: every Spaniard in

Jaraguá, feeling that the entire island was his and answering the call to take it while it lasts, took up his arms, tools, and Indians and marched away toward the mountains of Bahoruco looking for likely streams and gorges; at the last minute, Antón decided to head with his squadron of hirelings to the central region, as he remembered having seen many waterfalls in his comings and goings through those places. Halfway there, jolted out of his siesta by a bad dream, he saw that Doña Antonia and the other women were chewing on some evil-looking leaves; no matter how he hit and kicked them to prevent their swallowing even a mouthful, at dusk they started moaning, and at dawn gave birth one after another to nine dead children; fearing that his concubines would soon follow, Antón convinced them that if they killed themselves he would do the same, since he could not live without the pleasure of their bodies, and he would possess them all the same in his hammock beyond the grave.

After weeks of searching in the Maguana mountains, Antón hit upon a small but productive mine. When the rainy season came, he broke camp and went back to Jaraguá with gold nuggets worth five thousand castellanos, of which he tendered none to the coffers of Ferdinand and Isabella, although he had to tip one of Bobadilla's lieutenants with just under a half pound of gold plus the gift, by now a bit shopworn, of two of Doña Antonia's maidens, inveterate suicides whom he'd had to cut down repeatedly from the noose. Tired of Behechio's sighs and tears, of Anacaona's pitiful dirges, and the beggars' outstretched palms, he decided to sell his lands and set himself up in Santo Domingo. There, swelled by the attention he got when he showed his gold, he put on airs and began to dress presumptuously; anyone walking by his door could see him crammed into a vesture of loud brocade, sweating heavy droplets, smiling and nodding right and left. A month after taking up residence, when he still lacked provisions, he bought a country house with a ranch for three thousand castellanos; the place was an even mile from town, but it had the virtue of fronting the Ozama's bank, and the trip downriver by boat could be made in under an hour; he could be seen very early on Mondays at the marina, sitting on a bell, awaiting his boat of cassava, potatoes, and cornbread, products that he could sell for gold dust right away. In time he arranged it so that the cleverest of Doña Antonia's maidens handled those duties, which he thought beneath the dignity of a man of his stature, and with nothing better to do, he spent every day in a tavern run by some of the Admiral's old crewmen, where gradually, over pickled fish and cheap wine, he glimpsed the contours of the New World that the Admiral had delivered to be probed now by his followers; drunk with wine and cosmography, after declaiming with passionate insufficiency on the last voyage of Ojeda—whom he judged a better navigator than Niño, Bastides, and Pinzón—Antón came home like a driving wind, had his supper served him on the patio, and pressed the somber Doña Antonia at table with the minutiae of some new discovery, you ought to know, my dear Doña Antonia, that below Hispaniola and toward the left of the island of Xamaica, and yet below that, many leagues beyond, there is a big mainland of swift rivers flowing to a fresh-water sea, and above that, on the right flank, is the island of Trinidad, named by the Admiral, who saw it to the south, and this before he penetrated the Gulf of la Ballena, which is also called Paria, through the terrible Serpent's Mouth, and left it through the Dragon's Mouths, and I have called them by these names because they are the very doors of the Earthly Paradise, and at the Indians' throats there are strings of pearls, and these grow whenever a drop of dew falls on an oyster opened for the night, because that's when they breathe, and at dawn they close their shells and jump into the sea and sink to the bottom, and the pearls congeal inside and harden so they don't break no matter how hard they're bitten, and when you leave the fresh-water sea there's the Isle of Belaforma on the right and on the left, where the sun sets, Margarita, an island two weeks' sail from Santo Domingo bearing north northwest, which must be done carefully or else you have to tack windward for many days, because you're leeward in a line of subtle and perfumed isles called the Queen's Gardens, and it's not easy to leave.

When Brother Nicolás de Ovando moored his thirty ships in

the Ozama estuary, and came ashore at the head of twenty-five hundred ambitious hidalgos and royal functionaries, he found the riches of Hispaniola in the hands of scoundrels like Antón Babtista, who had been elevated through Roldán's insolence, the Admiral's irresolution, and the "take it while it lasts" of Don Francisco de Bobadilla. To purge the venality of his fellow travelers he let the gold rush begin at once, and soon the newcomers, crazed by an idea of the island as one enormous mine, could be seen trading everything they had brought with them for Indians and mining tools, and then dispersing in ant columns through the plains and sierras, cicatrizing the earth around the clock. In a few weeks, more than a thousand reckless fools had died of hunger, sunstroke, and disease, and it was then that Ovando, with the chastened survivors, set out to clean up Hispaniola. His first steps were meant to sweep the place clean of everything he had found there, and so he put to the sword the Indians of Saona, Higuey, and Jaraguá, who had never been conquered properly, and after dispatching Roldán and Bobadilla on a providentially disastrous voyage, he got busy constructing a new Santo Domingo on the other bank of the Ozama, as a punishing hurricane, well suited to his purposes, had uprooted all of the foundations laid by Bartolomé Colón. After hanging Cotubanama, Higueymota, and Anacaona, who had succeeded Behechio in the chieftancy of Jaraguá, he felt secure in his flank and began to consider the second act.

One afternoon, as Antón sat running through, for Doña Antonia, the details of Ojeda's hazardous second voyage to the Costa de las Perlas and the island of Coquibacoa, a royal official under Ovando's command called at the door of his new stone house: it seemed that the resident Antón Babtista was living flagrantly in a state of sin with an Indian lady, and such conduct set an extremely bad example to the new settlers, and Ferdinand and Isabella were seriously engaged in stopping the lewd actions by which Hispaniola was being corrupted, and the pope was as well, and it seemed that the Franciscans would begin issuing excommunications, and there would be incarceration and Holy Inquisition in Hispaniola, and as a result Antón Babtista married Doña Antonia in a quick and tumultuous ceremonial. Once the three hundred soldiers, plebeians, and ruffians—Ovando's words for them—who had jumped onto Hispaniola in its riotous years, were married off to Indian women, a decree was posted to the effect that anyone guilty of undermining Castilian dignity through the contraction of marriage with an Indian or a pagan was to lose forthwith his lands and holdings and ranches and houses and huts and fiefs and chiefs and *nitaínos* and *naborías* and everything held in whatever way under whomever's license.

As soon as Antón Babtista heard the announcement, he hurried home, found Doña Antonia, and strangled her forthwith by the cotton strip that she wore as a tiara. He called the notary and six witnesses immediately to update his civil status, but the sagacious Brother Nicolás had foreseen that evasion and, even as the notary sealed the document, a decree divesting the widowers of Indian women was announced in the plaza.

Folliwng his ruin, Antón took on sundry occupations in the bureaucratic machine put together by Ovando, none more elevated than that of *portero,* the municipal factotum for running errands; when Ferdinand and Isabella set up the encomienda system, he dared to ask for ten Indians, and was instead caned ten times and fired from his job, as ownership of lands and encomiendas was reserved for hidalgos and people of quality; hungry and beaten down, he enlisted in one of the marine expeditions sent out to hunt *lucayos* for the slave market, but a fierce nor'easter blew the big caravels off course, and he ran aground at Dominica where he fought Caribs for a week; anxious and emaciated from this unlucky adventure, lame from an arrow wound that kept him from following Velázquez to Cuba, he resolved to leave the city and gain employ as a foreman in King Ferdinand's mines, which were worked by strong-armed Guinea blacks. Voyages and conquests—even Ojeda's failure in New Andalusia—scarcely whetted Antón's curiosity, since he and his fellow workers and the soldiers who kept watch had eyes only for the carelessness of the administrator, an hidalgo from

Murcia, from whom he was able to steal a moderate amount of gold from time to time; his dream was to put together a hundred castellanos, buy a handful of *lucayos,* and head for the Maguana mountains to explore the environs of his old mine; but he gambled heavily at cards every night in the crackling torchlight, and as he lost more than he won, his thefts gradually became more frequent and riskier; one morning, the hidalgo caught him with his hand in a tray that two Negresses were balancing; stripped of his savings, with shackles screwed on tight, he was set digging in the underbrush for four weeks, at the end of which he was demoted to common soldier; after that he was never the same, and when the encampment shifted to Bahoruco he cut a very sorry figure on the road, his ailing leg dragging, his aspect cheerless, his voice broken and short of wind as he sang, weapon on shoulder, the ballad of *The Conquest of Alhama* in unison with the troop. When a patrol broke away with the hounds to hunt down seven blacks who had run off, Antón was left lagging in the depths of an overgrown hollow; thirsty, puffing and snorting, groping through the reeds and thickets, he reached a clearing with a spring and stretched out on the ground to drink; it was a beautiful spot, with bluebells and red mother-of-cacao flowers that lent a graceful, murmuring air, lilting and iridescent; when he lifted his head he saw himself surrounded by a band of Indians, whose leader seemed to be a green-eyed youth with a face painted in the *nitaíno* manner; Antón reached for his crossbow with one hand, his shield with the other, but it was too late: he felt the arrows' burning laceration dig into his back and pin his lungs into the ground, leaving him with just enough breath to ask God's pardon and to damn Ferdinand, Isabella, the Admiral and the hidalgo from Barcelona who had lured him many years before as he walked in youthful expectation through the Generalife garden.

> *It serves you right, my peerless king,*
> *good king, it is deserved.*
> *You murdered the Abencerrage,*
> *who were Granada's flower.*

You hanged the Christian renegades
of Cordova the renowned.
Now for these things you'll get, my king,
a sorrow doubly served:
you'll lose yourself and all your realms,
Granada will be gone.

〚 XXVII 〛

F OR ALMOST TWO MONTHS, as his flesh kept on dying, he had ceaselessly prepared his soul. ("I love my soul," he once said to Brother Diego of Yepes.) As zealous always as he had sworn to be in his Brussels days, he now reviewed his long reign with the tenacity that he would show when squeezing the beads of his rosary, again and again, to begin and to end at the holy cross. But his sweaty fingers slid down the laquered riddle without ever evoking a tremor, or a holy signal to foretell some revelation's luminous assault. When the doctors' knives, probes, and cauteries had poked around in his wormy leg, when they'd had to drill right through his mattress and set a basin underneath to collect his feces and his humors with a black humiliating noise, he had believed that this insult to his majesty, along with the quiet sacrifice of all the days of his existence, ought to allow him a special state of grace from which he might divine an answer to his only real and true question. Unlike his father at Yuste, he was not aching to know how many centuries lay between himself and God; he had given the problem of his salvation to Brother Diego and the learned prelates. After purging his rankest sins, they had absolved him entirely of guilt, assuring him that his zeal in keeping Islam, heresy, and pagan idolatry at bay had gained him the gates of heaven many times again. Nor did he want now to know what his son would do in taking up the scepter; the boy was a dolt whom one or another court voluptuary would lead by the nose. A few days back, when the Council of State had asked him whether the prince might then take on the affairs of the realm, he had answered with a sharp negative; he would rather that the government of all the Spains should slumber than that he should bear the shame of living as the subject, even for a night, of the strutting simpleton who bore his name. He was troubled no longer (he was sure of this) by wondering if he'd ever had the power to deal heresy a fatal blow. Even if he hadn't interceded with Mary for Elizabeth Tudor's life, and she had died on the scaffold, he could never have hoped to repress the vast conspiracy first stirred up by Erasmus, then Luther, later Calvin, that had rotted half of Europe's heart. His wretched son Carlos had not escaped this plague. Oh, and as if all that were nothing, there were the Jews, the *marranos*. These counterfeit converts lay behind everything. It was the ancient hatred of the scribes and Pharisees who had shouted "Jesus of Nazareth, come down from the cross and we will believe in thee." There was that Joseph Mendes, who would corner the spice trade and earn himself the name of *Nasi*, as in Annas; there was Miguel del Hospital, the hypocrite who had talked Queen Catherine into trying to govern over two religions, as if it were possible; there was that fiendish Teodoro Beza, who went from one city to another leaving behind a trail of fires, sackings, and assassinations; there was Tremelius, who had united the sects and hurled them like a bundle of snakes against the Roman Church. There were the judaizing converts, who threw stones and then hid their heads within his realm itself, like Pedro de Ponte, who had taught the English pirates Spain's trade routes to the Indies. There were so many! But little by little he had defeated them. He had gone bankrupt three times, and he had borne the shame of having to import bread from across the sea in Poland when he hadn't wheat enough to kill the hunger in Castile. He had survived, though, and had never let the evil winds compel a deviation from his charted course. The treasures of Africa, India, the Moluccas, Mexico, and Peru still came, to splash throughout Europe on the galleons' arrival, and his royal fifth would barely pay the interest on his debts. But he had stood firm, not needing dukes and counts, not puffing up the burghers, economizing here and there, giving to this and taking from that, doing justice where he could, keeping the true faith's chalice undefiled.

None of those things worried him anymore. Those were not the doubts that his dignity had heretofore kept covered and simmering, only to set him thinking now as he stares in nervous interrogation at the pleated hangings and foggy profiles that spin around his bed. One happy day, during his victorious French campaign, a weird hunchback had come along the Paris road to present himself before the royal tent as bearer of a horoscope from the great necromancer Nostradamus; he had received the man with every courtesy he knew, squelching a cold shiver that had come over him when he learned the prediction's extraordinary compass, which extended far beyond his death. After he had accepted the disquieting parchment and had paid the magician's servant, he'd sat down to think about the decision he would have to make; that night, securely, with a firm hand, he had tossed the horoscope into the fire without ever having cut the waxen seal: to have read it would have compromised his free will throughout his earthly voyage and bumped him from salvation's road in his passage through the heavens. Today he might have paid ten million ducats for the document. But what was God thinking, to let him fall into such temptations? Why didn't He listen to his entreaties and respond to them? Would he have to invoke his father's soul?

A sudden chorus of sweet silvery voices bathes the bedchamber. Repenting his despair, enraptured with consolement, he hears the still distant song of hosannas and alleluias. It must be the sign! It must be God's answer! He tries in vain to open his eyelids for the merest glimpse of the glorious enveloping band of angels and cherubim. But this frustration, of no more than a mundane curiosity, was unimportant. God must have known what his modesty had kept him from imploring in his daily prayers. Yes, the Lord had listened and now He was announcing: You will be a saint! You will be Saint Philip of Spain!

His image would be venerated on the altars. Pilgrims across the ages would clamor for his miracles and favors; virgins would strew tears and roses on his sanctuary; true believers would try to follow the example of his prudence, his asceticism, his diligence, his confronting all the world's filth without a grumble, his answering of fools and madmen with amiable circumspection. And so the Lord would reward him for his vast sacrifice of sleeplessness and colic, his effort to bring mankind to its senses; so the Lord would thank him for having tried to return to the Church its forgotten percept of poverty and temperance as the rule of life, so the Lord would bless his patient apostolate of rubrics and ordeals, of dossiers and summonses, of the Holy Inquisition, the Holy Office, the Holy Brotherhood, the Holy Crusade. . . .

"He'll die before the Mass is done," someone murmurs above the canticles.

"Tell the prince," sighs another.

He makes a final effort, manages to open his right eye: frozen flames surround the bed; floating above, like live coals and embers, are the blackened faces of the dead; from one side, through the secret door, the Latin singsong of the morning Mass comes in.

There is no chorus of angels and cherubim.

There is no heavenly sign.

There is no answer to his question.

There is no Saint Philip of Spain.

The fly leaves the canopy to perch upon his greenish-white eyeball, now fixed, congealed, opaque, hardened like a frozen drop of wax.

Outside, in the gallery, the man with the halberd hails the new king's clumsy tread.

〚 XXVIII 〛

THE AFTERNOON THAT Pedro de Ponte and John Hawkins sealed their partnership was like the one on which Don Cristóbal had tacked around Punta de Teno and down the eastern coast; bitter, sandy gusts from the southeast wailed in the stairwell's chimney, burst into the tower's upper floor, and before leaving through a roof hatch to the battlements, extinguished in succession one or another of the seven candles—relighted by a prompt Inés—on the great candelabra that illumined, on the stone table, a corner of Guillaume le Testu's latest map. Unblinking, his brow arched tightly in amazement, Don Pedro slid his finger right to left across the quiet stretch of ocean that separated the Guinea coasts from what the cosmographer on his chart was calling *La Mer de Lentille,* yes, my dear John, but these are lentils such as Puerto Rico, Hispaniola, Cuba, la Xamaica, and here below, La Margarita, lentils of gold, silver, pearls, hides, scents and tastes, and colors unsurpassed. And Hawkins, reserved, absorbed, wary, leaned over the puzzle of tropics and meridians, thinking more than he spoke in a Castilian that lurched and cambered: that's true, Don Pedro, but no Englishman has ever sailed among those lentils, my father only went from there to there. Inés: yes, Juan, you'll go, you'll see, you'll conquer.

He would not forget that dark and wind-whipped evening at Adeje; Don Pedro's magisterial play of enthusiasm and astuteness and feigned innocence in pushing his design sank into Hawkins's memory like a brazen nail; the image of that old man floating in his outlandish black silk tunic, as he traced out daring courses on Guillaume le Testu's chart and cupped his hand as if to hold an invisible bag of gold or a pearl the size of a hen's egg, who swung his head from side to side, now winking at Inés to pour more wine, now to have her intervene on his behalf with a gay mimicry of Caesar's phrase, the gestures and nuances of his voice, his amiable dignity, his delicate rejoicing, all were stitched into the hem of Hawkins's cape, to sketch a model for his own behavior in the aggravated dealings and negotiations that would fill his life henceforth. More than anything he would recall the awe he felt for the tenacious millionaire when dropping some trumped-up obstacle or pretext in feeble Spanish over the outlines of islands, capes, gulfs, and peninsulas that trembled there beneath the candelabra's seven lights; he loved to hear the subtle fencing of this old man who had once been the *man with the dark brown beard* to him and who was now, behind a beard grown thin and coiled and faded, his teacher in the diplomatic arts; and so he stayed until midnight, and only after he had caught a weary wrinkle in Inés's stretched-out smile did he affect a sigh of acquiescence and declare himself convinced, knowing in fact that *he* had conquered, that the Pontes' plan fit into his own dreams like his sword fit its scabbard.

Nor was Hawkins to forget the nights that led up to the signing of the contract; he was to take them out on all his voyages, retasting them like some forbidden wine, caressing them between his fingerpads, projecting them in chiaroscuro upon the swelling canvas through the quiet rain, seeing them beckon in the bank of fog that hid the bowsprit; remembering those nights he washed away the doldrums' blistering tedium, the trials by colic, flux, and fever, the rotten water, and the wormy meat; only amid some towering storms, with masts illumined in Saint Elmo's fire, would he reprove himself for what he wanted to relive, and a wall of spume and driving wind, too great, would bring him down kneeling to the deck in a stammering and insecure repentance; he wondered, in his prayers and supplications, whether with his modest rubric under Ponte's broad, uneven writing he had hazarded the loss of something more eternal than his seven nights of pleasure at Adeje.

The celebrations would begin as soon as he arrived, when Pedro de Ponte had held out the sleeves of his tunic like huge batwings and had drawn him to his bony chest. Then (how well he recollected it) Inés had clapped three times and gone up to the table to blow out the candelabra's seven lights. Or had it been the maid? A din of flutes and tambourines would erupt at the tower's base; gradually it would spiral up the staircase and explode into the room; Niculoso in the semidarkness, dressed as a bishop, pillows underneath his robe and donkey ears swinging from his mitre, would lead the uncanny carnival of masks that was to spin around the big stone table, goofy and grinning, beating with handskneeselbowsbuttockstitsheads on the taut drumheads and tinkling rims, shaking timbrels and rattles, snorting and puffing without a break on sackbuts, fifes, reeds, and Pan pipes, plucking untuned strings, shouting, wailing, enveloping, flattering the fancy of that young severely muffled Englishman who stood openmouthed and white with inhibition, to be dragged startled into the wild farrago of faces, pushed out toward the doorwell, lifted and suspended over pinches and forbidden touches, pulled down dizzily to navigate in great distress the undertow of noise and wriggle that grabbed him at his ankles and undid his figure, caressing and casting him down into a corkscrew fall to bring him back reeling, astonished, coughing for air, into the jumbled garden he had just traversed, an intemperate space with compass for the dawn, the violet air, the flapping of his sundered cape and then Inés's voice, rather distant at his back, John, John my dear, I waited for you, I waited for you, and when he turned around, trembling, there she would be, as night approached, reclining at the trunk of an enormous flowering *draco,* and she would draw a humid cluster of grapes out from her corselet, fat as plums, which they would nibble. Niculoso and Alonso, elegantly dressed, with thick, shining chains of gold around their necks, would come out from among the rosebushes, now scarcely visible; their hands at their breasts as they would bow a circumspect salute and then take up the instruments, guitar and lute, which their servants would be holding out to them, and the melancholy air would start to penetrate the silence as the low strings slid like tears into the night. . . . *What do I want with their gifts of water, milk, and bread, if Agarfa will not look on me,* Inés would sing in a soft, lamenting voice, and the elegy would sit in Hawkins's ear like a bird with an injured wing, fluttering frightened and in pain within that tower's walls, damaging its beak against the unyielding solitude of one day and the next, come with me, Inés, I've always loved you, he would say, enraptured. A row of torchlights would burst then from the house, and a half-dozen Negroes, rapidly transporting Pedro de Ponte in his litter, would approach the *draco,* come to table, it's time, the night revives, come, follow me. A supper of Spanish stew, liver, fried fish, and goat cheese would be served to them in silver plates and marmites, and eaten with restrained dispatch, as in a game of sleight-of-hand, in the candelabra's blurry light; Inés's seven sisters, whose long ringlets identified them as the naughtiest of the masqueraders, would leave the table curtsying, then disappear in a lick of taffeta and smothered laughter; Niculoso and Alonso, seated, with their stiff-backed wives, at each side of Don Pedro, would still be guzzling, amid fleeting whispers and vague gestures, cup after cup of malvesie wine; after rinsing his mouth and spitting the water into a basin held out by a veiled Moorish girl, Don Pedro would stand and ceremoniously, pompously, toast the lucky star that oversaw the dealings of the Pontes and the Hawkinses, whose interrupted association will continue, I hope, with business of the greatest benefit and least risk imaginable, when you're rich will you take me to England? Inés would ask him as she rubbed him with her bare foot beneath the table, why not tomorrow? my father would kill me, a deal to garner fifty times the amount invested, well don't tell him and come with me, religion forbids me to deceive my father and he would condemn me, then I'll come to your bed, first you have to marry me, a virgin enterprise which we will be the first to enjoy, let's get married tomorrow, only when you're a man, I am a man, you're not rich, a deal worth thousands of ducats, will you wait for me? I've always waited for you.

And that week in Adeje would run with his blood, would

warm his temples as the *Peter,* pitching toward the east, departed Tenerife by wave and cloud.

Hawkins debouched at Plymouth's dock and gave the hooker to his brother Will, as if to leave a ramping horse in a good groom's hands. Five days later he was in London, in the office of Sir Lionel Ducket, a friend of his father's; the old man had prosperous cheeks; he heard Hawkins's proposition without remark, and then, after a frowning silence, looked him straight in the eye, his elbows on the table, carefully squeezing and cracking his gouty fingers; there were books and ship models on the shelves, and flasks of blood-tinged oil holding open-mouthed lizards and snakes, monstrous spiders and scorpions, a monkey's fierce head, a man's blackened, tattooed hand; there were bows and crude flint-tipped arrows spread in panoplies on the walls, shields made of tree bark and hardened animal skins, worn, disheveled tiger, zebra, leopard hides; all right, Sir Lionel grunted, I'll get the ships, Ponte, Ponte, I used to know one Giacomo de Ponte, he married his daughter to Sir Walter Raleigh of Fardell, in any case we will trust him to show us the way to the West Indies, you've always got to trust someone, well, John, come to supper tomorrow, the wars have made you dull.

Inside a pair of ample trousers, with slash-sleeved blue doublet underneath a cape that dangled from his shoulder, Hawkins called at Sir Lionel's door, his hand wrapped round the pommel of his sword; there he saw Sir Thomas Lodge, William Winter, and, most of all, Benjamin Gonson, of the Guinea Club, the Royal Navy's treasurer, whose mediation had convinced the queen to lease to them the *Minion* and the *Primrose,* two excellent ships, for the voyage of John Lok; Winter joked amiably about Hickman and Castlyn, the superstitious partners who, after the *Primrose* collided with a pinnace near Dover and the *Minion* suffered a strange epidemic as soon as she unfurled her sails, chose to withdraw their money from the venture; of course they were not the only ones to be unsettled by those signals; John Lok himself had wanted to delay departure for a year, poor old Johnny, as if his heart had held a premonition of disaster, but what were we to do? at that stage you've got to be hard, cold as a statue, money cannot remain idle, and further-more, said Benjamin Gonson, the queen was involved and she is as impatient as her father was, blessed good Hal, and she was going to demand her one-sixth right away, sailors don't under-stand these things, lamented Sir Thomas Lodge, what can you do in such a case? you've got to act, Sir Lionel, act, so we made it plain to Johnny, God forgive his sins, that his attitude was im-possible, and just between us, Sir Lionel, I want you to know that Johnny cried, he cried like a child whose parents have rebuked him, of course he was no longer the John Lok that he had once been, he had gotten rich and had begun to mumble about retiring and becoming a warehouseman, he was shameless, he'd gotten much fatter, Sir Lionel, all those trips to Africa had stuffed him with grease and gold coins, you've got to keep an eye on sailors, a close eye, they get rich and they want to run out on you, I wish that they would take a lesson from this young cap-tain's father, Sir Lionel said, you needn't start swelling up, mas-ter John, but William Hawkins truly was what they call a good sailor, he died with rheumy bones and he never left any man behind who'd risked his merchandise in one of his ships' holds, but Johnny Lok got soft, William Winter interjected, he got soft as a biscuit, and he's lucky, added Gonson, that he lost nothing but his ship en route to Guinea.

While returning to the inn, his cape wrapped tight and his step quickened by a sudden snowfall, John Hawkins replayed the glorious scene; his project had been adopted and approved by the merchants of the Guinea Club, and with their sterling he would recondition the *Salomon,* the Hawkins family's faithful *Salomon,* and he could further acquire the *Swallow,* one hundred tons of the finest oak, which he would put under Tommy Hamp-ton, there was none better suited to take charge of her, and soon Tommy would help him pick the crew, and finally there was Katherine Gonson, the treasurer's daughter, who had done nothing at the meeting but circle the table and gape at him with her big sheep's eyes, her tongue pouting from her puss as though he were a field of wet green pasture, and the next night, in the fire's warmth, the chess game having ended, he found her in his guest room; at first she had been a kind of ghost come out from behind the curtains, but her white clothes fell quickly to the floor with the whisper of snow shaken down from a tree; step by step, her head rigid and her eyes fixed in the Ponte stare, she advanced through the bedroom until wholly within the circle of candlelight, and there, beside his bed, she stopped to provoke his wonder and desire, he held out his arm but Inés fell back to the shadow's edge, to keep him in her game of look don't touch; he ogled her from within the sheets: a thick, bushy down between her plump thighs shone in the candleflame, narrowing and curling to reach the jumbled skein that seemed suspended from her navel. . . . Three sharp knocks, like three handclaps, came out of nowhere, and he jumped to the floor, pushed the door ajar and almost hit the Moorish slave girl's veiled face, señor, Don Pedro wants you, he dressed quickly, left Inés in a corner, followed the whizzing flutter of tulles and slippers to the tower, the stairs, the tall granite table, the seven-armed candelabra, ah dear John, you must forgive me, I'm so happy you've come that I can't sleep, let's play another game, I offer you the white.

When he returned to his bedroom, the cocks announced the sunrise at Adeje; Inés was gone.

Katherine Gonson, as it turned out, was a much more energetic and less silly woman than Hawkins had supposed. One morning, as he left the treasurer's office, she hung on his arm to complain how tedious it was that a girl of her age should have the habit of awaking early, since in London everything happens after five in the afternoon and none of my friends would get out of bed before noon, even if they were nuns, are you Popish? I'm so glad, my father was afraid you were, many are in Devonshire, hang them all I say, how much will you earn by selling Negroes? damn it, that's a fortune, and the trip will make you famous too, are you married? good, though I was sure you weren't, you like to please and you're rather presumptuous, that's what they say, there must be more than one girl in Plymouth who's mad for you, my father says you have what it takes to snatch success by the throat, snatching things by their throats is everything to him, I think he's right, don't you agree? times have changed, Bess is a great queen, did you know she sent away the Spanish king? you may call me Kate, Katherine is too long and dignified for me, it always makes me think of one of old Hal's wives, why don't you move your business to London? when the priests and nuns are sent off you'll find room enough inside the walls, though the beggars are there yet, we have a real plague of them. In Plymouth too? my father says it's good, he has more than a hundred fellows working for him for nothing, a plate of watery soup, a crust of bread, but they smell awfully and their looks are fell, the lords threw them off the land to make room for sheep and now they're starving, papa's got the children carding wool, he says it's a game for them, but the women go about weeping and it's a nuisance, just a real nuisance, and thank God Bess is going to put an end to them, they say she'll sell them into slavery or something, or she'll brand the ones who go traipsing about and begging, robberies have increased outrageously, did I tell you that I might put thirty pounds into your voyage? of course I will, I've done it before several times, it's a much bigger thrill than betting on dogfights, though the last one I saw was sensational, they tore each other to pieces and it was just sensational, they put bears up against dogs too but they aren't so much fun, do you like minstrels? I just adore them, and the masquers, too, I have a plan, let's walk a bit along the river and pretend we're in Venice, you can't imagine how I'd like to go to Italy, in the plays everything happens in Italy, have you been to Italy? no matter, you will someday, well I said we'd stroll along the river, then we'll eat at Cross Keys and we'll stay there, someone told me there was a good acting company there now, the earl of something or other's, you flatterer, you tickle me, I know I'm not quite what they call a pretty girl, but I know I'm not bad either, like my dowry, tongue hanging out? I always stick out my tongue when I see something I like and want to have, my mouth starts watering, I've done it since I was a little girl and I don't know what to do about it, well, I've asked you to take me to Cross Keys, now ask me for something, isn't there anything you want?

Within a few weeks they were married.

Gonson, Ducket, Lodge, and Winter put up enough money for the *Salomon,* the *Swallow,* and also the *Jonas,* which was scarcely more than a pinnace, to be sure, and unable to cross the ocean twice, but good enough to sail to Guinea and return to Plymouth with some ivory; it had not been easy to enroll the crew, because Tommy Hampton kept finicking and he found some fault in ten of every twelve of the enlisted; still, when October came there were a hundred on hand, and although someone else might have wanted to ship out with twice that number, Hawkins sent the crier through street and tavern with the news that the ships would soon depart; Tommy Hampton would have had him set things back a week, in order to complete the *Swallow*'s crew by his own reckoning, but *he* had figured the advantage in having fewer hands on board; water and food would last longer, and what's more he had observed that sickness struck more often on a crowded ship; Tommy Hampton clenched his jaw and went along.

That Sunday morning, lost in thought as he left the holy service of Saint Andrew's, Plymouth's mother church, Hawkins felt Kate's tug at the sleeve of his gray doublet, the very one that he had worn when he was married; he stopped there in the middle of the square and turned his head to follow his wife's look: the cock on the weathervane had changed its bearing and the wind was breezing out now from the land; it wasn't the custom to raise anchor on a Sunday, but by morning's end he had decided, and in an hour the chanteys beat out time for sailors as they marched along the pebbled streets that led to Sutton Pool, from whence they waited for the longboats that would take them to the ships, which had been completely ready for a week, anchored in the sound; Hawkins embraced his brother Will, kissed Katherine on the mouth, and jumped down from the dock to fall in among his men; the send-offs, tears, and hurried admonitions rained down long upon them; from the boats they started slowly to perceive some details of the *Salomon* and *Swallow:* wood escutcheons in a line along the bow, a Tudor dragon, long gonfalons that flapped like ribbons from the top-masts, tapestries that hung above the crow's nests, pennons, streamers, the mainmast's royal standard, the foremast's silks emblazoned with Saint George's great red cross, the shining mouths of brass that poked outward from the gunports, and then, beyond, the *Jonas,* framed in gulls, small and sprightly like a toy; now the crowd of women pressed together on the Hoe, for although the distance was too great for them to recognize a brother, son, or husband, it was still a comfort to the heart to be there when the ships sailed off, and some thought that it might yet bring a bit of luck; the sailors, now in their working clothes, barefoot, hooded, climbed slowly up the ratlines to gather at the crosstrees and the yardarms like gray migratory birds just stopped there for a breath before continuing a flight to some antipodean shore; a muted trumpet call was followed by the raising of the anchors, and then suddenly the canvases began to plunge down from the spars, one by one, the wide mainsail and the topsails of the mainmast, the enormous spanker set out on the gaff, the jibs upon the bowsprit; the sails began to fill and then the ships took on the shapes of lilies having huge globed petals, fattening and spreading out; a distant clamor blew in from the rocks beside the Hoe, frightening the seagulls, while the ships' prows, jubilant and winged, slid through the sound.

The autumn days, with their busy gray skies and their mist-crowned waves, would propel the ships toward Tenerife; Hawkins, from the *Salomon*'s bridge, would recall Inés and begin desiring her again; he'd know that from then on she would be his mistress on the highways of the sea, of the abysses, just as Kate would rule his every step upon the tiles and squares and gardens of the shore; no, he couldn't tell Inés about his marriage, or his little house in Kinterbury, or the child who was expected, or his solid, quotidian, equilibrated happiness; nor would Kate make any sense of his romancing with Inés, the giving of oneself in earnest, dark and secret as a crime; he'd recall their first encounter deep in the forest, the legendary cave of Zebensui, the old black stones that smelled of smoke and goats, her bodice loosening beneath his kisses, her breasts appearing, heavy, ripe, the nipples taut, the downy dark brown precinct, taste of cinnamon, what is this? what are you doing, my God, you'll leave Adeje and never will come back, what happens to me then? who'd have me for a wife when I'm dishonored? don't you know my brothers would behead me and my father die of shame? my God, what can I do? can't you see my soul is bursting and I'm running over like a pot of oil? would you like to take me in this way? would I please you? wouldn't I be your wife then? wouldn't it be just the same?

With every moan that issued from the *Salomon*'s lines, its boom, its ribs, its planks, Inés would reappear to him, face down, rump thrust up like a fat mushroom, livid, fleecy, swollen, grieving, pummeling and kicking out between his knees to send him flying, cast off, dizzy, reeling from the world, to fall while sea and land both vanished like a coin hurled down a well, with bitter frozen terror in his throat, his hair on end and his stare fixed on the blank eyes of the void; every precipice of spume, every sink of lightning in the night, every eddy in the seaswell, every irrecoverable reach of stars or bubbles would strand him in turbid, painful liquids, make him sink in agony into Inés like an oar that had been stuck into the mire, crusted with scum, tangled in rotten seaweed, dead crabs, lacerating jellyfish polyps. How could he explain all that to Kate?

But Inés wasn't in Adeje. No, she wasn't there.

Don Pedro begged forgiveness for his vagaries, I'm getting old, I get distracted, I can't remember if Inés went to La Laguna or to Santa Cruz, they all went, they have an aunt in Grand Canary, Inés gave me something for you, I don't know what it was, could it have been a message? excuse me, sometimes I feel as though my mind is gone, but this man is Martínez, a pilot from Cádiz, he'll take you to Guinea and the Indies, here's a list of everyone who should buy Negroes, don't let one get away for less than eighty ducats, if you do you'll let yourself be robbed, take gold before silver, lots of pearls, don't shun leather, it sells better every day, I've done my part, your ships should be provisioned yet, but that's for tonight, there's nothing left for me to tell you, *bon voyage*, my son, and God go with you, I hope I'm here when you return, what's that? no, I can't remember what Inés's message was.

When they heard the boatswain's whistle, the crew jumped down from the rigging and emerged from holds and hatches to the runway of the forecastle; the patter of their bare feet on the planks grew sharper on the foredeck, then went silent; all hands looked upward to the bridge, where Hawkins faced them in his battle dress, his aspect grave, his breastplate martially expanded, I salute you, men of Devon, I shall speak but little and yet clear, to keep secrets from you now would render me unsuited to command you, for you men are brave and strong, and you have left your wives and mothers to embark with me, and I would have you understand why I was forced to hide from you till now our mission's true intent, we'll see perforce the coasts of Africa quite soon on our port and there too we are most sure to land, all this you know by now and I congratulate you for embarking on a journey of such moment, but you are Her Majesty's good subjects, brave and strong, and I would not keep you from knowing that we are out for commerce in the Indies, why so far away? you must be thinking, why not turn the prow around toward England when we've boarded all the spices and the ivory? that, if you should wish it, we shall do so, you need but holler master Hawkins, we renounce our riches, we renounce the fame of having been the first from Albion to look on El Dorado's bath of gold, the golden walls of Cíbola, we renounce the casting out of wrinkles, rheums, and sores at the Font of Youth, but you men are strong and brave and I know that few of you would choose that course, to face unending ridicule from those who journeyed homeward with a fortune at their belts, but well I know you, men of Devon, as my father did before; I have no fear of this, and I shall tell you not what you might lose but rather what you stand to gain, and there is much to gain, now then, as subjects of Her Majesty, the good queen Bess, you will have noticed her maltreatment by the popes, those ravening leeches who have split the world just like an apple between Portugal and Spain, who is the pope of Rome that he dare think himself the sole inheritor of our first father Adam? are we English then the devil's children? why should the Negro be a chattel to the Portuguese alone and all the Indies' riches go to Spain? shall we sit calmly and accept this outrage? are we less worthy than a Spaniard or a Portuguese? that question, men of Devon, is one the queen herself asked me in London, Mister Hawkins, tell my subjects please, she said, that I, a woman, nay a girl, would willingly go with you in your ships to smite those popish popinjays, and know you how I answered? why kneeling and with hand on heart I said, my queen, your place is here upon the throne, from whence you may keep watch upon all matters of the realm, and mine and that of the brave men who follow me is out upon God's seas, the seas of all good Christians, the seas the Lord created so that Noah's sons might trade among themselves, and I was weeping when I told her this, but I'll not wear you out with speeches, for it's time to eat and soon the distance will disclose the level shore of Africa, and we shall have to be prepared for anything that may arise, and that was all I wished to say, good men of Devon, but I remember now that I had also meant to tell what we shall do with the Negroes, you may be unaware that in the Indies they will bring, each one, a hundred golden coins, well then, we shall leap ashore and seize them by their necks and thrust them bound into our hold, where there is room enough, and if they run in terror from our hackbuts and are hard to catch, we'll come down like Saint George's sword on some big-bellied Portuguese ship that's transporting them to the Lisbon market, by the devil's beard we'll do it, and now eat hearty, dear and valiant sons of Devon, and find someone to read the Articles aloud, it's there you'll find the essence of true faith and hope enough to counter all obstruction on the road to your enrichment, God bless you, let us pray, amen.

Many details of John Hawkins's first voyage to the Indies have been lost; Hakluyt, from whom we need not accept every word, relates that Hawkins sailed before a favorable wind to Cape

Verde and continued on from there to Guinea, where on landing in an unattested region known as *Tagarin*, which his father had explored some thirty years before, he captured nearly three hundred blacks by force of arms; other sources say that he attacked en route the Portuguese flotilla that sailed regularly, too complacently no doubt, along the coast of Africa, and the first to fall to him was no less than Captain Veiga, whom he dispossessed by force of arms, near Caces, of over three hundred Negro slaves, and merchandise worth fifteen thousand ducats; at the mouth of the Mitombi his squadron grew by one upon his seizure of a carrick holding half a thousand blacks; he sent the *Jonas* home well stuffed with goods from Africa, then threw all the sick slaves overboard and veered to westward in what seems to have been a very happy crossing.

Perhaps, at the moment of the lookout's certain sighting of the New World's lands, Juan Martínez came to Hawkins with a letter in his hand, from the *señora Marquesa,* the pilot might have said, from behind an arcane smile, what *marquesa?* the *marquesa de Lanzarote,* I know no person by that name, yes, you know Dona Inés de Ponte, then she's married to the lord of Lanzarote? I myself was at the wedding, Inés married? I assure you that she has been for some years, perhaps Hawkins, with a wry grin, grabbed the paper from Martínez's hand, I'll not forget you, John, we had bliss together for a week, and now I'm going home, I've read your fortune in the stars, you'll cross the ocean three times, but don't ever try a fourth, respect my father and your business will go well, good-bye John, we shall never meet again.

Hawkins may have smiled, just to himself, in irritation; after a regretful sigh, he surely must have understood that Inés had been a harpoon of Don Pedro's, thrown to draw him into his design; his pride may have been burned in disappointment and regret, but the icy smile was slowly to take on another cast, another course, and Juan Martínez, curious, would see it cheerfully directed toward the setting sun, where clouds spread out like sails in a huge, opulent flotilla; then Hawkins may have thought, with rampant, cynical greed to befit a member of the

Guinea Club, that after all he hadn't been the only one to be deceived, and how could it really matter who had been the mocker or the mocked, for he would keep Inés's memory forever, and what was more he had a route map to unlock a door that opened on the Sea of Lentils, into whose refulgent waters his two ships had now begun to probe.